## A delicate situation . . .

"Scandalous!"

*Dear Lord!* It was Mrs. Drummond-Burrell, the most disapproving of the Almack's patronesses. Landy Horseley and Princess Esterhazy crowded behind her. Each was appropriately robed as a Fury.

Mortification burned his face. . . .

He glanced at Joanna and cringed. His arm remained around her shoulders. Her domino gaped, exposing her gown's bodice. Her hair tumbled widly about her shoulders—his flush deepened as he recognized the allure of that curtain of hair. Even if he were not responsible for her dishevelment, the appearance of impropriety was enough to condemn her.

But his guilt was clear. His hands had opened her clothing and unpinned her hair. His cap sat beside her spectacles on the table. His arm still absorbed her heat.

There was but one redress. Rage dimmed his vision, but he set his face into a fatuous smile.

"Hardly scandalous," he drawled, "though I am as clumsy as the greenest cub this evening. I actually knocked Joanna into the wall as I spirited her from the ballroom. But you may wish us happy, for despite my stammers and blunders, she has done me the honor of accepting my hand. . . ."

# Birds of a Feather

## Allison Lane

A SIGNET BOOK

SIGNET
Published by New American Library, a division of
Penguin Putnam Inc., 375 Hudson Street,
New York, New York 10014, U.S.A.
Penguin Books Ltd, 27 Wrights Lane,
London W8 5TZ, England
Penguin Books Australia Ltd, Ringwood,
Victoria, Australia
Penguin Books Canada Ltd, 10 Alcorn Avenue,
Toronto, Ontario, Canada M4V 3B2
Penguin Books (N.Z.) Ltd, 182–190 Wairau Road,
Auckland 10, New Zealand

Penguin Books Ltd, Registered Offices:
Harmondsworth, Middlesex, England

First published by Signet, an imprint of New American Library,
a division of Penguin Putnam Inc.

First Printing, July 1999
10  9  8  7  6  5  4  3  2  1

# Chapter One

~

"I saw them with my own eyes!"

"Shockingly scandalous!"

"Her reputation will never recover."

Stepping around the knot of gossips, Joanna Patterson entered Berkeley Square, where shrieks of laughter from two lads playing in the central garden revived her homesickness. She missed her brothers, especially young Jeremy. But it was time to build a life of her own. This job was the first step.

Another shout from the boys drew a censorious stare from a passing dowager and attracted a ratty-looking dog, to the dismay of their nurse.

Joanna forced her mind back to business. Her half-boots beat a quickening tattoo on the cobbles, for she had dawdled too long over this errand, entranced by the sights and sounds of London. If she didn't return soon, Lady Wicksfield's fretting would plunge Harriet into tears—a terrible fate, for the girl recovered slowly from any upset. Tonight's ball was vital to her come-out. An emotional scene before they left the house would reduce her chances of finding a good match—not that either mother or daughter would understand. Lady Wicksfield was as hen-witted as Harriet, and her stubbornness had ultimately led to today's errand.

The arguments over Harriet's wardrobe had started even before last week's arrival in London. A limited budget meant patronizing a less-fashionable modiste. But Madame Francine was so eager to please an aristocratic patron that she meekly accommodated every demand, even when she knew the countess was wrong. Joanna had protested, but not until two hours ago had her reasoning finally carried the day.

"The neckline on Harriet's ball gown is too low," she had said again, ignoring the cloying scent of potpourri and heavy perfumes in Lady Wicksfield's sitting room. Changing the countess's mind was too important to be distracted by an inability to breathe.

"Further discussion is pointless," the countess had snapped, flushing with irritation. "Wicksfield's folly has already squandered half the Season, leaving Harriet barely eight weeks to find a husband. She must attract attention."

"Attracting the wrong attention will prove fatal," Joanna had countered. "Surely you saw the disapproving stares at last night's rout! There wasn't a dowager in the room who looked on her kindly. Harriet's beauty will draw sufficient notice, and you know how gentlemen respond to her sweetness. But she is barely seventeen. Low-cut gowns make her appear desperate, forward, or both—not the image we wish to cultivate." Harriet also sang like an angel and seemed so fragile that men rushed to protect her—an irresistible combination if they kept the image pure.

"Miss Cathcart wears even lower gowns."

"Miss Cathcart is in her third Season without an offer. Is that what you wish for Harriet?" A gesture cut off the response. "And I know that the Silverton twins have lower necklines, but even gentlemen consider them shockingly encroaching. If Harriet were older, she would have more leeway, but at her age, flaunting her bosom can only court derision."

"How can you know? We have attended two routs and one small ball—hardly typical entertainments."

"Exactly. And none were top-drawer, but that does not mean we can ignore the disapproval. The guests may lack the breeding of more exalted families, but they aspire to the same manners. Tonight's ball will include society's most glittering figures. Even the Regent was invited, though no one expects him to appear. If Harriet makes a poor impression, she will be ruined; the Season is too advanced for her to recover. Tonight she will meet the very gentlemen she must attract."

Lady Wicksfield had shrugged. "We cannot afford a new gown, so this discussion is pointless. She will have to act demure." It was the closest she had ever come to admitting fault.

Joanna had silently accepted her capitulation. "Madame Francine can modify the rest of the order. For tonight, I will add a double row of lace like Miss Cunningham wore last evening."

"Not lace." She glared. "It is far too sophisticated. Surely ribbon or a fichu would be better."

Lady Wicksfield's objection had more to do with money than sophistication. Every shilling spent on Harriet was one shilling less she could spend on herself. She had already declined to make morning calls twice, pleading a headache, but Joanna knew she had slipped away for some surreptitious shopping. She could only pray the debts would not prove exorbitant.

The lies, like the arguments about Harriet's come-out, were born of resentment over Joanna's position in the household, for she was more than Harriet's companion and chaperon. Though she deferred to Lady Wicksfield in public, in truth, she was in charge. Thus their relationship was awkward and frequently hostile.

On this occasion, she had merely repeated, "Lace," then gratefully escaped the drugging perfume. But the confrontation had revived other fears. So much could go wrong.

She was unsure whether a fichu was even accepted as eveningwear in town—it wasn't near her home—but she had opposed it because the excitement of the moment often drove society's rules from Harriet's mind. High spirits prompted broad gestures and loud tones. Humorous tales released unrestrained laughter. An unkind word sent tears rolling down her cheeks. The girl might easily remove a fichu if she felt overheated—which would be inevitable if the Regent actually did attend the ball. His fear of drafts was notorious.

Joanna stifled her rising trepidation. Imagining poten-

tial disasters served no purpose, so she returned her
mind to London.

As always, Berkeley Square brimmed with activity.
Servants, vendors, and delivery boys scurried in all direc-
tions. Ladies strolled about, taking the air. Others
alighted from vehicles to make the first formal calls of
the day.

Deftly sidestepping a footman carrying a tray of ices
from Gunter's, she threaded a cluster of carriages before
cutting through the grove of plane trees that shaded the
garden. The nurse was gathering up her charges. Abandoning hope of a game, the dog turned on a cat nearly
twice his size, happily chasing it toward Mount Street.
A horseman swerved around the pair, his reckless speed
drawing a glare through a gentleman's quizzing glass and
a snort from a scowling lady.

Her eyes scanned the rows of elegant Georgian
houses, finding their clean, classical lines more pleasing
than the facades of the great houses near her father's
vicarage, most of which were centuries old.

*You are dawdling again.*

Tearing her eyes from the view, she briskly followed
the dog. Woolgathering served no purpose and would
likely draw a stinging rebuke from Lady Wicksfield. A
well-deserved rebuke, added her conscience as she
stepped over a pile of dung. She was not being paid to
enjoy the sights. The countess pounced on every mistake, in part to avenge her demotion.

She sighed.

Perhaps she would be less entranced if she had expected this visit. But barely a fortnight had elapsed between Wicksfield's summons and her arrival in the
largest city in the world. Was it any wonder that she
tried to see everything at once?

Yet London was more than impressive houses, elegant
wardrobes, or even a stunning variety of entertainments.
It was more than bustling crowds, high-stepping horses,
and the vast array of shop goods.

She frowned at two dandies mincing toward Gunter's,
their enormous buttons and nosegays nearly obscuring

wasp-waisted coats that stretched across improbably broad shoulders.

London was a state of mind that combined excitement, awe, and longing, though that didn't describe it exactly. She wasn't sure just how to describe it. Even her current position on the fringes of society so far surpassed her dreams that she found it overwhelming. Perhaps she needed more than a week's residence to understand. But the memories would stay with her forever. And the experience would make it easier to prepare her future charges for their own come-outs. A governess post awaited her once Harriet was settled.

"Watch where yer goin'!" shouted a coachman, jerking his team sharply aside. The horses screamed their own insults as a dray cut the corner too sharply, locking rear wheels with the carriage.

"Watch out yerself! Wearing fancy livery don't mean you can drive."

The coachman cursed, trading increasingly strident accusations with the draysman across the combined lengths of their vehicles. Within moments, they had drawn a vociferous crowd. Even those who hadn't seen the actual accident hurled advice and blame.

Joanna cringed, though much of the language was incomprehensible. New arguments were breaking out among the bystanders over which driver was at fault. She gingerly detoured around the mob, hoping to reach Mount Street unscathed.

The drivers leaped down to exchange blows. Within moments, half a dozen others had joined the fray, pushing and shoving as their own tempers shattered. Shouts of "A mill!" brought men running from all over the square.

Joanna ducked into Mount Street, grateful to escape. The men were exerting less control over their tempers than her youngest brother usually managed. How could they shed their gentlemanly facades so easily—and for so little reason? Shivering, she hurried toward home.

But despite the unexpected brush with danger, London still enthralled her. Afternoon sunlight glinted off myriad windows, once more drawing her eyes. Never

again would London be the same, for a governess would
not attend fashionable gatherings and would never be
charged with running the household. Should she rejoice
or weep over Lord Wicksfield's demand for assistance?

The earl had fallen into folly, losing nearly everything
through bad investments. His best hope of recovering
was through agricultural reform and expansion of the
cottage industries already existing on his estate. But that
would cost more than he had left, and loans were not
forthcoming. His recent lack of judgment left the bank-
ers skeptical. So he hoped Harriet could find a husband
who would help.

But Harriet needed a chaperon, so he had asked the
advice of his cousin, Joanna's mother.

Joanna sighed. Her mother had recommended her,
and Wicksfield had accepted. Their brief interview had
seemed to cover all her duties. Only later had she realized that he'd allowed no questions, extracting a commit-
ment even before introducing her charge.

Her head shook. She should have demanded more information, but she had believed that she could handle
any crisis. Fool. Despite eight-and-twenty years spent addressing all manner of village problems, she was only
now realizing how naïve she remained and how many
details he had withheld.

"Harriet is young," he had acknowledged, his blue
eyes guileless. "She will need someone with her at all
times, lest an inadvertent word or deed spoil her
chances. Without frequent reminders, she might blurt
out our circumstances. But Lady Wicksfield will wish to
renew old acquaintances. Your mother swears that you
unwaveringly fulfill every duty, so I can count on you to
avert any scandal. You must also screen Harriet's suitors, sending only the most qualified to seek my
approval."

"If you wish—"

"Excellent." He had interrupted before she could explain that she knew nothing about London gentlemen.
"I understand that your judgment is impeccable. Keep
records of any expenditures. I cannot provide the allowance I would like, but you will know how best to utilize

the funds in your care. I can no longer trust Cophelm,"
he added, naming the man of business whose advice had
precipitated his problems.

He had continued for nearly half an hour, larding his
orders with praise and preventing any protest. But some
of the blame was her own. She had allowed him to ride
roughshod over her good sense, stifling every warning
her conscience had tried to raise.

Only now did she understand his reasoning. They
were sufficiently related that he could retaliate against
her family if she let him down. Since her life would be
spent in servitude, she would do nothing to jeopardize
her reputation. And the fiction of assisting his wife covered the fact that Lady Wicksfield was incapable of
bringing Harriet out on her own. An interesting *on-dit*
was enough to drive all thought of duty from the lady's
mind, and her instincts were extravagant. Since the earl
was remaining at Wicksfield Manor, he had needed a
keeper for his family.

She had reconciled herself to her odd position. In public, she was an unobtrusive chaperon who deferred to
Lady Wicksfield. In private, she ran the household, controlled the purse strings, decided which invitations to
accept, and screened all suitors.

Unfortunately, Wicksfield had ignored the ramifica-
tions of placing her above his wife. The countess resented
this reversal, indulging in countless petty arguments to relieve her pique.

As if that wasn't enough, Wicksfield had omitted a
great number of facts. Harriet's lack of intelligence had
been the first shock. Sweet, yes. The girl could also be
caring and giving. But her age and disposition worked
against making a successful entry into London's demanding *haut ton*. She was naïve, high-spirited, shockingly frank, and probably had other faults Joanna had
not yet discovered. None of these were bad in themselves, but Harriet's behavior was a long way from the
controlled ennui that was currently the mode.

Lady Wicksfield's lack of sense had provided the second jolt. But not until they'd arrived in town had Joanna
faced a more basic problem: Her only knowledge of

London society arose from tales her mother had heard
from her cousins during childhood and from comments
made by her upper-class neighbors. Even Lady Wicksfield had not visited town since her marriage twenty
years ago. She doubted that Wicksfield had understood
what a handicap that posed, for despite attending most
sessions of Parliament, he avoided the social Season. She
lacked the intimate knowledge of noble families that
would allow her to appraise any suitors. And knowing
society's rules did not adequately prepare her for min-
gling with the *ton*.

Every day she discovered additional problems. Lady
Wicksfield's goals were baser than the earl's. Only his
direct orders had kept the countess in the country all
these years. Now that she was back in London, she was
determined to return regularly, an impossibility if Wicksfield rebuilt his finances slowly through loans and hard
work . . . But she could handle Lady Wicksfield.

Her conscience was another matter. Her vow to hide
Wicksfield's financial reverses fought daily duels with her
innate honesty. She had already faced one determined
fortune hunter who believed the earl remained wealthy.
And how could she find Harriet a caring husband who
was willing to help Wicksfield obtain the loan he needed
when she could explain none of the circumstances? After
only a week in town, the guilt gnawed at her. She lacked
the most basic skills necessary to judge anyone they met,
so how was she to manage? Could she even control
Harriet?

The girl needed a firm hand on the reins. She already
basked in the attention of her growing court of sprigs,
blind to anyone's background or intentions. Unless Joanna steered her toward the most eligible suitors, she
would likely form a *tendre* for an impoverished lad or a
flattering rogue. Or Lady Wicksfield might maneuver her
into the arms of someone who would make her miserable. The woman was already making lists of the wealthiest lords.

Whatever the outcome, they had little time. The Season was near its midpoint. Their late arrival meant that

many eligible gentlemen were already courting girls in earnest, so—

A yelp of pain jerked her head around. Pushing her spectacles up her nose, she gasped.

The predator had become prey. The cat was gone, but two boys had cornered the dog and were now tormenting it.

"Stop that!" she ordered, fury blinding her as she raced to the rescue. Helping others had been drummed into her since birth.

Only after a shouted warning penetrated her anger did she realize that a carriage was rapidly bearing down on her.

"Admit it, Randolph." Lord Sedgewick Wylie grinned at the Earl of Symington, his closest friend. "You not only survived a month in town, you actually enjoyed it."

Randolph laughed. "Thanks to Elizabeth. Her pleasure casts society in a different light, and our betrothal removed me from the sights of the matchmakers."

"Deflecting their attention to the rest of us," Sedge moaned in theatrical agony before turning his quizzing glass toward Randolph's wife of four hours. "Congratulations, my dear."

"Will you put that down," Elizabeth begged, flapping her hand at his glass. "You know how I hate being quizzed."

"Very well, but only for you." He made a dramatic production of dropping the glass. "Now may I congratulate you?"

"Thank you, dear Sedge. Your welcome has made the past two months bearable."

"And your presence has made the Season memorable. London won't be the same without your company."

"I never expected such fustian from you." She shook her head mockingly. "With all of society prostrate at your feet, will you even notice my absence?"

"How could I not? Impressing you is impossible, for you delight in pricking my pretensions."

"An admirable sport," said Randolph with a chuckle.

Elizabeth turned to her husband. "He only welcomed

my company because planning our wedding kept his mother occupied." She had spent recent months with Sedge's family, being estranged from her own.

"Alas! My secret is revealed."

"Doing it too brown, Sedge," admonished Randolph. His laugh hid an instinctive grimace. "Not at all. Mother is sure to concentrate on me now that you are wed."

Elizabeth sobered. "Too true. She has regaled me with complaints about your intransigence, and she vows to succeed this Season. So be warned. She may resort to dishonor. Her determination troubles me, for you know how I abhor force."

"As do I."

"Is she really that bad?" asked Randolph.

"Worse." He sighed, wishing their banter had not turned serious. "I appreciate your concern, Elizabeth, but Mother's insistence is hardly new. She was obsessed with the succession even before Father's latest spell. My one hope is that she will concentrate on Reggie." Reggie was his older brother and heir to the marquessate.

"I doubt she means to ignore either of you," said Elizabeth.

"And she has enough candidates to keep you both busy," added Randolph. "But count your blessings. Her antics may occasionally make Bedlam seem inviting, but at least she cares for you."

The reminder dampened everyone's spirits.

Why had Elizabeth raised the subject of families at her wedding breakfast? It was a depressing topic all around. Poor health had kept Randolph's family in the country, though they had insisted that he follow tradition by marrying in London. Elizabeth's father hated her, and her mother wasn't much better. They had ignored her nuptials, despite Elizabeth's hope that the occasion might lead to an eventual rapprochement. Her sister had also stayed away, which cut far more deeply. Cecilia had wed Sir Lewis two months ago, but they had promised to be here.

"Pardon, my lord. A letter forwarded from Glendale

House." The butler's silver tray held a missive directed to Elizabeth.

Sedge exchanged a puzzled glance with Randolph. Her luggage had been transferred that morning, but late-arriving mail did not warrant interrupting a celebration.

"It's from Cecilia." Elizabeth scanned the contents and gasped. "He's—" She swayed as all color drained from her face.

"Has something happened to Lewis?" demanded Randolph, easing her into a chair.

She handed him the letter.

"Good God!" Randolph gestured for wine.

"What is wrong?" Sedge kept his voice low. Elizabeth was clearly in shock.

"Fosdale is dead."

"Her father?" The news raised intense satisfaction. He had never actively hated anyone before meeting Fosdale, but the man had cruelly turned Elizabeth out into a raging storm, nearly killing her. Then when Cecilia accepted a baronet of modest means instead of forcing Sedge to the altar, Fosdale had tossed her out as well.

"You needn't whisper," said Elizabeth. She had regained most of her color. "I was merely surprised." She shook her head. "But how typical of him. And how appropriate. Refusing to repair the dairy after that last storm killed him."

"What happened?"

Randolph finished reading. "He was dismissing the dairymaid, blaming her for a decline in cheese production—not that she was at fault, of course; those spring floods decimated the herd." Disgust filled his voice. "A gust of wind collapsed the building, crushing him. The maid escaped with only a few bruises."

Poetic justice. Or perhaps divine retribution. Fosdale had been a thorough scoundrel, though Sedge kept the sentiment to himself. Despite the estrangement, the man had been Elizabeth's father. Shocked eyes belied her composed face. But comforting her was now Randolph's problem. At least the letter had not arrived before the wedding.

Bidding his friends farewell, he watched Randolph es-

cort Elizabeth upstairs, then encouraged the few remaining guests to leave. The newlyweds would retire to
the country in the morning.

Randolph had found a wife who suited him perfectly,
Sedge admitted as he headed for his chambers at Albany. He had dismissed his coach on arrival, expecting
to remain through dinner, but he liked walking.

In society's eyes, Randolph was his oddest friend, for
they seemed to have nothing in common beyond growing up on neighboring estates. Randolph was a re-
nowned expert on medieval manuscripts, who cared little
for appearance and less for society. Sedge had replaced
Brummell as the quintessential dandy, reveling in gossip
and the London Season. Few knew he cared for anything
beyond manners and the cut of his coats. Green cubs
slavishly copied his style, and even the older bucks
looked to him for sartorial leadership.

Yet the bond he shared with Randolph extended beyond a childhood friendship to a plethora of similar interests. Both cared deeply for people, working to better
the lives of others. Both kept a close eye on business
and estate matters, unwilling to blindly place their fortunes in other hands. And both possessed adventure-
some spirits, though expressing them had taken different
paths in recent years.

But Sedge kept his serious interests out of the public
eye, for society was suspicious of anyone it could not
easily understand. One-word labels were comfortable,
imparting the order and structure that made thinking
unnecessary. Lady Beatrice was a gossip, feared because
she knew everything. Lady Warburton was a hostess, her
balls the highlight of any Season. Lord Devereaux was
a rake, unprincipled enough that parents kept daughters
out of his path. Lord Shelford was a Corinthian, determined to best his own numerous speed records. Lord
Sedgewick was a dandy, caring only for clothes and
*on-dits*.

He derived considerable amusement from society's
antics, much of it rooted in this willful blindness. Few
people acknowledged that Lady Warburton was as obsessed with gossip as Lady Beatrice. No one admitted

that Devereaux knew as much about horses as Shelford did. And as for himself, not only did people ignore his intelligence, the pleasure he derived from helping others, and even his love of history and literature, but disclosing these interests would actually reduce his credit.

Not everyone adored him, of course. Some even held him in contempt. Like Lord Peter Barnhard, whose vast wealth had failed to dispossess Sedge of the most lavish suite in Albany or of London's most desirable courtesan. Or young Lord Braxton, who craved wealth and the power to ostracize those he didn't like. Or any number of sprigs who dreamed of leading fashion rather than following it.

Did any of these aspiring arbiters understand the responsibility attached to the position? Bestowing his favor on the wrong person could expose society to predation. Yet withholding his favor could harm innocents. Every day he had to assess others, often with little information at his disposal. Questioning his judgment kept him awake more nights than he cared to count.

Perhaps that was why his assumed ennui had become all too real. The shallow concerns of a jaded society now seemed trite rather than diverting. Even wielding his enormous credit to deter greenlings from trouble no longer brought satisfaction.

"Stop that!"

The command cut through the usual street sounds, pulling him from his reverie. A woman dashed in front of a carriage, oblivious to its approach.

"Look out!" he shouted, sprinting forward. *Stupid wench!* Didn't anyone think before acting these days? Only two months ago, Randolph and Elizabeth had each courted death by refusing to consider the consequences of their actions.

*As did you,* reminded his conscience.

"Move out of the street!" She had frozen at his first warning and now stiffened, turning his way rather than toward the carriage. He lunged, jerking her to safety and slamming her against his chest hard enough to drive the air from their lungs.

*Nice body,* noted his mind even as his eyes took in

her appearance. Well-worn half-boots. A threadbare cloak over a serviceable gown. Spectacles perched on the tip of a pert nose. Plain bonnet hugging her head. Obviously a servant, for she lacked an escort. But her features were refined, so she was probably a governess or companion.

"Not at all the thing to walk about in a fog," he drawled once he managed to inhale. His heart pounded from the aftermath of fear. Pain stabbed his left arm, which remained weak from a break suffered during his own recent lapse in judgment.

"Tha . . . dog . . . boys . . . I don't—"

He'd overestimated her position. Her voice was cultured, but shock had reduced her to incoherence. Such a woman would make a poor governess. Too bad. Lackwits had never attracted him.

Nor would they now, he decided, setting her firmly aside. The unflattering garments hid a wealth of curves that were stirring interest in his nether regions.

"Are you blind or merely stupid?" he snapped to cover his reaction.

"What—"

"Pay attention! You could have been killed."

"D-dog." A finger directed his attention across the street.

Two boys shifted their eyes from the departing carriage to the woman who had nearly died. Discerning their sport was easy. Hands pinned a whimpering dog to the ground.

Raising his quizzing glass, he adopted his most disapproving frown. "Well, well, if it isn't Tom Pratchard. Up to no good again?" This son of a Jermyn Street tobacconist had a penchant for mischief. He must speak to Pratchard himself this time. The lad's mother had done nothing to curb his tendencies. He didn't recognize Tom's redheaded companion, though learning the boy's identity would not be difficult. But that was for later. The moment he stepped off the curb, they fled. He turned his gaze to the dog.

"And Maximillian. I might have known you would be here. What have you done now?" Squatting at the ani-

mal's side, he checked him for injuries. Max licked
weakly at his gloves. But aside from one shallow cut, he
seemed intact.

By following him, the woman had successfully tra-
versed the street. She crouched in the gutter, making
incoherent noises. Either she was more addled than he'd
thought or fright had affected her wits.

Max took in her concern, wiggling with pleasure when
she scratched his ears. He always groveled to females,
treating them to none of the questionable temper he
inflicted on males. Thus they all adored him.

"Sweet little dog," she crooned, finding her voice
under the influence of Max's charm. "You are having a
miserable day, aren't you. That nasty nurse tried to beat
you with her umbrella. And a horse nearly stepped on
you. You really must be more careful, you know. If that
cat had been less of a coward, it would be dining on you
at this very minute. And how did you run afoul of those
horrid boys? Wicked monsters! Are you all right?"

Max squirmed with pleasure, licking her fingers.

"He will be fine," Sedge assured her, adopting a stern
tone to hide his relief.

She ignored him, prattling as inanely as his aunt and
her dotty friends, her focus wholly on the dog, who was
now pressed close to her side. She seemed unaware of
his own presence, which made his fight to regain control
of an unruly body even more irritating.

"He will be fine," he repeated sharply, furious at
being ignored. "But I can hardly say the same for you.
What sort of idiot steps into the street without checking
for traffic?"

That gained her attention. "I didn't . . . that's not . . ."
She inhaled deeply several times, lowering her gaze to
his cravat. "Are you sure he is all right?"

"Of course." How dare she question his judgment?
The woman was more addled than he'd thought. "He
merely escaped Lady Barkley's garden again. As for you,
this is London, not a country village. If you wish to survive, think before you act—or stay at home."

"Of all the presumptuous—"

"Thus speaks the woman who threw herself in front

of a carriage," he scoffed, interrupting. "Hen-witted fool. Are you even aware that I just saved your miserable life?" Giving her no chance to respond, he batted her hand aside and scooped Max into his arms. "Come along, Maximillian. Your taste in friends grows worse each day."

Max growled, snapping at his chin.

He tightened his grip, glaring at the scruffy animal.

"I can carry him," the woman offered. "He seems to like me."

"Which proves his lack of intelligence. Why would I trust an animal to someone incapable of crossing a street unescorted?" he demanded, stifling an urge to wring her neck. He hardly expected instant adulation, but couldn't she at least thank him for risking his life?

He nearly grimaced as his body recalled her curves. Even his facade was slipping out of his control. Never had he met anyone who elicited such a debilitating range of emotions.

Ignoring her reversion to stammered gibberish, he collected his walking stick, noting the chipped head where it had hit the cobbles. Turning his back on the woman, he headed for Barkley House, even more annoyed than before. This was not how he wanted to pass the afternoon.

"Don't turn that innocent look on me," he grumbled at the dog. "Your mistress may fall for that trick, but I know you better. That was a nauseating performance just now. How can you lower yourself to grovel? And to a brainless idiot."

Now that he had no female to wheedle, Maximillian squirmed around to lay a paw on Sedge's chest.

"No, I won't forgive you, you beastly little rat. It is bad enough that you've ruined my walking stick, my coat, and my newest pantaloons. Must you also destroy my waistcoat and shirt? Turrett will weep," he added, naming his valet. "He truly loved this outfit."

Maximillian yelped in delight.

"Proud of yourself, aren't you. Stupid dog. This escapade was not one of your brighter ideas. Adventures are all very well in the country, but sneaking about in London will be the death of you. I cannot be forever available to rescue you from these antics."

Maximillian hung his head.

"As well you should. I must now summon my coach, for I dare not resume my walk. Appearing on the street in so disheveled a state would destroy my reputation."

It was true. Even if none of Maximillian's blood smeared his coat, dusty paw prints would never escape notice. Every eye turned his way whenever he ventured out. And though he was noted for poking fun at current *on-dits*, how could he describe this encounter without appearing ridiculous? Not only had the woman ignored him, but his own reactions did him no credit.

"But summoning my carriage will not be the worst penalty I must pay," he continued. A commotion in the square was attracting attention, so if he reached Barkley House unseen, he could avoid any questions. "Your mistress is undoubtedly at home."

He cursed, then cursed again when he reached his destination, for his fears proved prescient. His aunt insisted on serving tea, then demanded to know when he planned to wed. She'd been his mother's bosom bow since childhood, and the two remained close. He wasn't sure which of them was more adamant about setting up his nursery. Why wouldn't they leave him alone? He would eventually wed, but in his own time and for his own pleasure.

By the time his carriage finally arrived, he felt like striking something.

# Chapter Two

❧

Joanna swore under her breath as her rescuer left, carrying the dog. Mortification heated her cheeks. After only a week in town, she had already made a cake of herself. Would she never learn to think before acting?

Heedlessness had been her bane for years. When something caught her attention, she forgot all else. Her penchant for walking into trouble was well-known around Cavuscul Hill, her frequent trances spawning countless jokes. So far she had injured only herself— a broken arm at age fifteen, cracked ribs at eighteen, concussion at twenty-four—but eventually she would harm someone else.

She shivered.

*The concussion wasn't heedlessness,* insisted a voice in her head. *Don't be so critical.*

True. That incident had been deliberate. She had known the bull was there, but leaving the Watkins boy sprawled in the pasture had been impossible. Cuts, scrapes, and a concussion were a small price to pay for a child's life.

Yet today's incident could have cost her much more, and this time there was no excuse for her carelessness. Waiting for the carriage to pass would have made no difference, but she hadn't even noticed it. Thank heaven her anonymous rescuer had come along. She could have been badly hurt—or worse.

His scold was well deserved. Even minor injuries could have consigned her to bed, ruining Harriet's Season and leaving Wicksfield in the lurch. She should have

mentioned her problem during that interview, but she
had been sure that her concentration would remain on
Harriet, who would thus benefit from her single-
mindedness.

Her cheeks heated. Wicksfield had asked if she could
handle the job, and she had said yes. Despite knowing
her history, she had agreed. The bitter truth was that
she had wanted to visit London so badly that she had
lied by omission. If she had told him, he would have
hired someone else.

Guilt gnawed at her conscience. She had set the stage
for disaster with her lie. What if she fell into an abstraction when she was with Harriet? What if she approved
the wrong suitor because she had missed evidence that
he had a venal nature? What if she walked into a wall
or knocked over a punch bowl, drawing ridicule onto
Wicksfield's family. It wasn't an idle fear. She had already been guilty of those offenses and more. Her clumsiness attracted as much ridicule as her heedlessness.

So far, she had managed well. Except for treading on
a dowager's foot last night . . . and jostling the butler's
arm so he spilled soup in her lap . . . and that little
problem at the inn last week . . . but that had been the
maid's fault; people carrying loaded trays should not
rush blindly around corners.

*Are you blind or merely stupid?*

She was not managing well at all, now that she considered it. Her cheeks heated. Her rescuer was undoubtedly
one of the gentlemen Harriet would meet over the next
few days. Would this encounter hurt the girl's chances?

Grimacing, she headed home, grateful that everyone
she met was hurrying toward the escalating battle in the
square. The foolishness of an impoverished chaperon
could never compare to such drama, thank God. She
was embarrassed enough as it was.

Her gentleman had actually been quite chivalrous, she
admitted as she passed the house into which he had disappeared. Most men would have ignored her in their
rush to watch the fight. And even those who might have
pulled her out of harm's way would never have seen
after the dog.

In fact, rescuing her had been more than remarkable. She was wearing an ancient cloak over one of her older gowns, for she donned her new clothes only when escorting Harriet. He must have known that she was a person of no consequence, yet he had risked his life to drag her out of danger, jerking her with such force that her spectacles had slid down to cling precariously to the tip of her nose.

She frowned.

The longer she thought about it, the more incongruous his actions appeared. He'd made no pretense of approving her and had actually sneered at her appearance. His own had been very elegant, his clothing unusually formal for afternoon wear. Which made his behavior incomprehensible.

None of the gentlemen she had met this past week would deign to touch a filthy, bleeding dog. Especially a scraggly mop of indeterminate breeding. Yet he had not only examined the animal, but had actually picked it up, holding it comfortably against his coat despite its objections. Even knowing the animal did not explain such disregard for his clothing. So he must be an unusual man.

New heat rushed to her face. Her own behavior had been appalling. The stupidity of rushing in front of a carriage was bad enough, but mortification had kept her from acknowledging his presence. Then she had compounded her sins by babbling so incoherently that he could not have understood a word.

That was another of her curses: Embarrassment tied both tongue and brain in knots, turning words into a mishmash of incomprehensible gibberish and mortifying truths—like the time she had addressed Lord Lipping by the village girls' nickname of Lord Liplock, derived from his penchant for kissing the maids.

She had been forgiven that one. Not so the incident of the squire's steward. In her embarrassment over stumbling into a private discussion while in a trance, she had wondered aloud if the steward really *was* skimming the profits. The squire hadn't suspected. The steward lost his job and threatened revenge. Both had been furious with a mere girl for meddling in men's affairs. No one cared that the information had been true.

She shook her head. At least she had only prattled to the dog this time instead of blurting out something horrid—like admiration for his broad shoulders, powerful arms, and unexpectedly muscular chest.

Goose bumps tickled her neck, for he was very well set-up. The encounter had made her too aware of his assets. No padding enhanced that physique, and his strength had astonished her. She was not a frail, petite miss like Harriet. She was as tall as many men, and no one would ever describe her as slender. Yet he had picked her up as though she weighed nothing, crushing her to him from shoulder to thigh, and proving that her head fit perfectly . . .

*Forget his assets!*

She repeated the admonition as she climbed the steps to Wicksfield House. He had dismissed her as the insignificant servant she was. Nothing but pain could come from mooning over his splendid form. Her duty lay with Harriet, who would need all her attention. Distractions would lead to disaster, betraying Lord Wicksfield's trust.

The carriage crept closer to Ormsport House through streets jammed with the cream of society.

"Pay attention, Harriet," snapped Lady Wicksfield, her nerves overset by the lengthy delay. The other gatherings they had attended had not been squeezes. "You will meet all the best gentlemen tonight, so you must remember which ones to encourage." She sniffed. "Why did Symington have to wed? As heir to a duchy that controls a legendary fortune, he would have been perfect."

"Which is irrelevant," pointed out Joanna. "He was betrothed well before the Season began. In fact, his betrothal predates your decision to launch Harriet." The wedding had been discussed often during morning calls, but descriptions of Symington made him sound far too intelligent to have any interest in Harriet. "You could as profitably mourn the loss of any gentleman who wed before meeting her—including the Regent. After all, if he had only waited another three-and-twenty Seasons, he might have chosen Harriet, and we would not now be mourning the loss of the only heir to the throne."

Apparently the sarcasm worked. Lady Wicksfield squared her shoulders, addressing her daughter. "Lord Almont is an excellent possibility. He seemed quite taken with you last night, and Lady Thurston claims he is seeking a wife. Mr. Parkington was equally smitten. He lacks a title, but his connections are good, and his fortune is excellent. But you must discourage Mr. Singleton."

"It is early days to be narrowing her choices." Joanna interrupted before Lady Wicksfield's admonitions overset Harriet. The girl had a soft heart that made it impossible to refuse any request—another reason Joanna's job included screening all suitors. "Mr. Singleton is too young to consider marriage, but he comes from a good family and is well liked, so his attentions are beneficial."

"Very astute," agreed Lady Wicksfield. "Amassing a large court will attract notice."

"Let us not dwell on individual suitors," she begged. "For now, I am more concerned with manners. This is the first top-drawer gathering we've attended, so making a good impression is crucial."

"I know that," said Harriet.

"But we will review it again, because most of the Almack's patronesses will be here tonight. You must remain at my side whenever you are not dancing."

"Of course," murmured Harriet, but her mind was clearly elsewhere.

"What did I just say?"

"Don't go outside?"

She sighed. "You should not go outside without my permission, but I was talking about watching your manners inside as well. The patronesses will be here this evening."

"The Almack's ladies? What if I do something wrong?" She had Harriet's attention, but fear now blazed from the girl's eyes.

"You won't, if you are careful. Smile. And always think before you speak."

"About what?"

"About the words you want to say and whether they will draw censure."

"Oh."

"I will keep track of your dance partners. But do not accept any invitations without asking me first."

Harriet shivered.

"Relax," she advised. "Eveiyone else knows the rules, so there should be no trouble. The important thing is to think before you speak." She had nearly reminded her to keep Wicksfield's dilemma a secret, but they were pulling up to the door. Harriet was likely to blurt out the last thing she had heard.

The ballroom was impressive, more than making up for the long delay in the receiving line. Lady Ormsport had draped pale pink muslin in great swags to lead the eye toward masses of flowers that rivaled the most luxuriant gardens. The ostentatious decorations increased Harriet's excitement. Joanna shuddered, foreseeing disaster unless she settled the girl down.

"Keep your expression calm," she murmured as they plunged into the crowd. "Try to look as elegant as this room. Walk slowly and keep your hands close to your body."

Harriet stopped a moment, then moved on at a more sedate pace. Most of the guests were too engrossed in gossip to note their passing.

"Fosdale had been dead a fortnight, but they didn't receive notice until after the ceremony," a gentlemen was saying as they passed.

His companion snorted. "I'll wager ten pounds that Lady Glendale held up the letter so the wedding could proceed. She wanted the chit off her hands so she could concentrate on finding wives for her sons."

"Ten pounds it is. She would never have opened a letter addressed to another."

Ignoring Fosdale's death, Joanna followed Lady Wicksfield toward a less crowded corner across the ballroom. She had already heard the tale from Harriet's maid. But the other information was new. Who was Lady Glendale? Would her sons be acceptable suitors for Harriet's hand? She again rued her ignorance of noble families. With no information beyond the woman's title, she had no idea of her place in society. Her husband could be anything from a knight to a marquess.

"Why are they frowning?" whispered Harriet.

"They are discussing a death. Their smiles will emerge in a moment. Always match your expression to the topic under discussion. Just remember that smiles should never widen into grins. Restraint is important, for the prevailing fashion is boredom. By controlling your expression, you can also control your impulses, thus presenting a proper image to the world."

If only she had remembered that earlier. By controlling her impulses, she could have avoided the embarrassment of dashing in front of a carriage.

She let Harriet chat with Lady Thurston's daughter while she scanned the crowd. A few girls wore revealing gowns such as the countess had wanted for Harriet, but they were accompanied by avid mothers who were actively shunned by the most elegant gentlemen—a reaction that increased Joanna's determination to hide any hint of desperation. Harriet's fragile beauty must stand on its own.

At least Lady Wicksfield spent most of her time with Lady Thurston and other old friends. The countess could easily become one of the matchmaking mamas that eligible men avoided.

Her own tactics seemed to be working. Within minutes, Harriet was surrounded by gentlemen they had met at earlier gatherings. Some introduced friends. As the crowd grew, other gentlemen stopped to see who was raising such interest. Most of the newcomers were barely out of school, but some were older, raising hope for finding a good match despite their late arrival.

Yet the very size of Harriet's growing court made Joanna nervous. She knew nothing about these gentlemen except that they were accepted by society. But mere acceptance was insufficient. Harriet needed a husband who cared for her.

Lady Wicksfield was no help. She rarely looked beyond the title and fortune she used to judge worth. Lady

Thurston was little better, and her determination to
snare the wealthiest lord for her own daughter made
her assessments suspect. At least one gentleman she had
recommended had a reputation for lechery and gaming.

By the time Harriet joined the first set, Joanna was
brooding in earnest. How was she to discover the truth
about any suitors when all of society hid behind social
masks? She chatted with some of the other chaperons,
eliciting comments on Almont, Parkington, and a dozen
others. Three sets later, she was more confused than
ever. No two opinions matched. Everyone had different
criteria for accepting or rejecting suitors.

"Mr. Wethersby wishes to drive me in Hyde Park on
Wednesday," said Harriet when that gentleman escorted
her back to Joanna's side at the conclusion of a reel.
Lady Wicksfield had long since abandoned them.

"She would be delighted to drive with you, sir." Joanna smiled to remove any sting from her next words.
"But she is already engaged to drive out that day."

"Perhaps Thursday?" he asked.

"That is agreeable." At least Harriet had remembered
to ask—or Wethersby had reminded her. The man was
too young to be a serious suitor, but Harriet's appeal
was working. She relaxed slightly.

Wethersby left to find his next partner. Half a dozen
eager sprigs converged, hoping to claim a spot on Harriet's dance card. But only waltzes remained, which made
her card effectively full. Harriet had not yet received
permission to perform that step.

Mr. Singleton had just left to procure lemonade when
a ripple of laughter drew her eyes to a nearby cluster of
gentlemen. In its center, her rescuer gestured with a
quizzing glass, his face reflecting weary boredom.

"Shockingly shatter-brained," he pronounced with a
sigh. "Though not as blind as I first thought. She uttered
the word *dog* while pointing to a member of that species.
Such a pity she hadn't learned the word *horse*. They are
so much easier to spot."

Another laugh rippled through the crowd.

Joanna froze. Odious man! He was deriding her, turning her into a laughingstock. She had thought him chival-

rous, but this was downright cruel. What would happen
if he recognized her?

His eyes wandered lazily around the ballroom as he
waited for the laughter to subside. Her first inclination
was to duck, but sudden movement would draw his attention. She could only hope that he hadn't looked
closely at her—gentlemen rarely noticed servants unless
they had improper designs on them. It was a fact she
must remember now that she had embarked on a life of
servitude. But her looks were so average, she should not
be in danger. Unless he had noted her height. A quick
glance around the ballroom brought relief. There were
half a dozen ladies as tall as she.

His gaze paused assessingly on Harriet, then slid on
with no flicker of recognition, allowing her to breathe
again. She was one of the few people who wore spectacles in public, needing them if she was to adequately
watch Harriet, but he had not connected her to the
woman he was holding up for sport.

" 'Twas Lady Barkley's Maximillian—again," he said
on another long-suffering sigh. "That makes twice this
week I've had to return the creature."

"As have I," remarked a man whose shirt points
nearly reached his eyes. Billowing Cossack trousers obscured his legs.

"And I," chimed in a sprig.

"As has each of us, I expect," added Lord Almont.
"If anyone is shatter-brained, it is Lady Barkley. Maximillian spends more time on the town than most
gentlemen."

"He ruined a most refreshing toddle by rumpling my
favorite coat," intoned Joanna's rescuer. "I had to summon a carriage."

Joanna turned her back, determined to concentrate on
Harriet. But she remained uncomfortably aware of him.
If she had thought him elegant this afternoon, his appearance tonight was breathtaking. His cravat was an
artistic masterpiece arranged in a style she had seen nowhere else. His dark blue coat clung so tightly that it
must have required several assistants to ease him into it,
yet it did not seem to hamper his movement. Every

muscle of very shapely legs was on display under ice-blue pantaloons that exactly matched his eyes. Silver embroidery on his white waistcoat glistened with every gesture. Despite moderate shirt points and a single fob, he immediately cast every other gentleman into the shadows. Only his quizzing glass hinted at ostentation, its handle encrusted with blue gemstones.

"Why does everyone hang on his words?" asked Harriet, nodding toward the speaker.

"That is Lord Sedgewick Wylie," Mr. Craven informed them, appearing surprised that anyone must ask. "He is the most powerful man in London."

"Like the Regent?" Harriet sounded breathless with awe.

"Socially, he is more powerful than the Regent," he said, smiling. "He can elevate a nobody or ostracize an Incomparable. He wields more authority than even Brummell did, for there is nothing about him that one can criticize. He does not drink or game to excess and has never been rakish. His knowledge of fashion and style is unmatched, as are his manners and breeding. And he possesses one of the larger fortunes."

"He sounds quite frightening." Harriet batted her lashes.

Mr. Craven stepped closer in protection. "You needn't fear him, my dear Lady Harriet. No one could ever find fault with you."

Joanna frowned, so he retreated to a more seemly distance.

"Are you sure?" Harriet asked.

"Even Lord Sedgewick would adore you," Mr. Craven assured her. "Though that is typical of his power," he added, nodding toward the gentlemen, who were now debating who had rescued Maximillian more often. "There is not a man in London who cares a whit for that plagued dog. It looks like a mangy rat and has a hideous disposition. But it belongs to Lord Sedgewick's dotty aunt, so we all trip over our feet to keep it from harm. A perilous undertaking. It escapes a dozen times a day and has bitten more than one captor. It nipped a hole in my favorite coat only last week."

"How awful!"

Mr. Singleton returned, bearing lemonade.

Joanna sighed. Harriet had captured another heart, though Mr. Craven was too young for marriage. As was Mr. Singleton, who also gazed rapturously into her eyes. Yet she now wondered if they were as acceptable as she had thought. Maximillian was sweet and gentle, so what had Mr. Craven done to incite attack?

Keeping an ear on their discourse, she turned her eyes back to Lord Sedgewick. She had heard of him, of course. His name arose in nearly every conversation. The premier dandy of London. The ultimate arbiter of fashion. The man who could make or break Harriet's Season.

She shivered.

If she had known his identity, she would have fainted dead away. Why did it have to be Lord Sedgewick who had witnessed her lapse? Would he blame Harriet for her chaperon's idiocy?

Nothing underscored the gulf that separated her from the polite world more clearly than admitting yet another misunderstanding. After listening to the awe that accompanied every mention of his name, she had imagined him cloaked in brilliant colors, bedecked in jewels, and strutting about with his nose in the air whenever he left off preening before mirrors. Only now did she realize her error.

If Lord Sedgewick was the ultimate dandy, then his following must encompass those who stressed understated elegance and absolute cleanliness. An important point, she realized as Lord Wiversham strode past, reeking of musk that failed to hide the fact that he never bathed.

But despite Lord Sedgewick's reputation, her opinion of him had sunk. A true paragon would not hold her up to public ridicule, no matter what her station. It called his supposedly exquisite manners into question.

As he paraded about the ballroom, she wondered what other mistaken impressions she had formed. Lord Sedgewick was not the only one displaying manners inferior to those she had observed at less exclusive gatherings. Ladies, especially marriageable girls, fawned on him, flirting outrageously and boldly stepping out to block his path. Since he wielded so much power, why did he not chastise such unseemly antics?

Yet she could understand their desperation. The Season was advancing. Girls without suitors feared failure, so they cast aside their demure facades. And not just with gentlemen. More than one glare had been directed at Harriet for attracting a court despite her late arrival. Those whose admirers had defected made little attempt to hide their irritation.

But Lord Sedgewick could keep them in line if he chose to exercise his power. Few would dare to cross him. Recipients of his nods and bows nearly swooned in delight.

A crowd of sprigs trailed in his wake, copying his gestures. If he raised a quizzing glass, they followed suit. If he smiled, so did they. A mild compliment could bury its recipient under a wealth of gushing praise from the sycophants—all meaningless.

His posture reflected the condescending arrogance she had sensed that afternoon. His chest protruded, the effect enhanced by an elevated chin and a discreet ruffle cascading down his shirtfront. When added to his stiff carriage and unsmiling face, it gave him all the hauteur of her father's prize goose.

She stifled a giggle, for he led a gaggle of equally officious goslings.

Sedge smoothed his expression into the ennui that would hide his irritation. For years, he had derived amusement from watching society's antics. Human nature intrigued him, and London provided an excellent laboratory for observing it closely.

But this Season was not providing the usual entertainment. The ever-present flock of sprigs dangling from his coattails annoyed him. The importuning chits more closely resembled grasping harpies than innocent maidens hoping to catch his eye. Even gossip no longer appealed. Who cared whether Lady Alderleigh's affair with Devereaux was nearing its conclusion, or that Blackthorn had converted the very conservative Harlow to the cause of reform, or that Mr. Lastmark was hopelessly enamored with the already-betrothed Miss Lutterworth?

Yet each of these stories would have amused him just two months ago.

Perhaps his dissatisfaction arose from spending those months with Randolph and Elizabeth. After enjoying so many intellectual discussions, society chatter seemed flat. And having to ignore their simmering passion had left him feeling lonely. Resuming his fatuous London facade had been more difficult than ever before.

It did not help that he knew his mother was right. At one-and-thirty, it was time to set up his nursery. Yet finding a congenial wife loomed as an impossible quest. He wanted what Randolph had found—the peace, the passion, the personal completeness that Elizabeth brought to his friend's life. Yet how could he find such a wife? Seeking help was impossible. His mother would redouble her pressure if she knew of his capitulation. Just having Elizabeth around had increased her determination.

"I s-say," stammered young Cathcart. "What do you think of that new hell on Jermyn?"

He paused to quiz the lad from head to toe. "Admirable waistcoat, Cathcart. An improvement on last week's. Commend your tailor." He paused so the youngster could stutter out his gratitude. "You were asking about Beckworth's?"

He nodded.

"It's not a place I would patronize. Gull-gropers and sharps crowd the tables."

"B-but LaRouche recommended it highly."

"Did he?" He let his lips form a slight smile. "I rest my case."

Gasps from his tail proved that more than one lad had accepted LaRouche's word about the new hell. La-Rouche was probably backing the place, which itself should warn the wise to stay far away. The man had long been suspected of sharping cards, though no one had ever caught him.

But he had no interest in gaming hells tonight.

Could he find a match this Season? The girls making their bows looked younger than ever. He wanted a wife he could love the way Randolph loved Elizabeth. A wife of passion. Of courage. Someone who saw beyond his public face and could accept him in his entirety. Someone with whom he could truly relax.

It was an odd thought, but important. Despite knowing that his parents cared for him, he could never relax at Glendale Close. They constantly sought to improve him, to mold him into their own image. They condemned his interests and derided any characteristic they did not share. But he needed more than such qualified support.

He had always envied Randolph his parents, and even more so now. They had welcomed Elizabeth, lavishing her with warmth and affection. But his own parents would never be like that. So if he truly needed a loving family, he must build his own.

*Devil take it!*

He hid a grimace as the Silverton twins practically leaped in front of him. Their father had recently been knighted for service to the crown—a euphemism for loaning Prinny a large sum of money that would likely never be repaid—gaining them limited entrée into society. But they had little understanding of acceptable behavior. They didn't even recognize snubs.

"My lord, you look positively dazzling tonight," gushed one—he didn't bother identifying which.

"Complete to a shade," concurred her sister.

"So distinguished!"

"A person of dashing consequence."

"Bang up to the echo."

"A veritable tulip!"

He nearly cringed, for while he took pains with his dress, he disliked the excesses too many sprigs espoused. And these cant phrases should never be uttered by ladies, especially in public. But he remained silent. The twins rarely allowed anyone to edge a word into their chatter.

"We are so delighted to see you."

"And thrilled to receive this invitation from dear, dear Lady Ormsport."

"It must have been your doing."

"We have to thank you."

"Papa even bought us new gowns for the occasion."

"What do you think? Are they not the most marvelous creations?"

Two pairs of brown eyes gazed expectantly at him. He couldn't resist such an opening. Their antics had worn thin long ago. Lifting his quizzing glass, he examined each girl at leisure, finally releasing a despondent sigh. "One must indeed marvel. So much decoration obscures the underlying fabric. But you should remind your modiste that elegance demands simpler lines."

They blanched, falling back a pace at the blow. He turned away, regretting the necessity for the set-down. But they were incapable of discerning hints. If they took his words to heart, he had just done them a considerable favor. But their future was out of his hands.

So what should he do about finding a wife? His mother's candidates were impossible; she had a knack for choosing the most inane chits available. Yet none of the girls staging come-outs this Season appealed to him. Perhaps he should make a tour of the shires . . .

*No, no, no!* What a ridiculous idea. Despite his present boredom, he loved town. His wife must be socially adept, for she would join him at the apex of the polite world. And she must be intelligent. Debating with Elizabeth had been invigorating, for she brought refreshing views to any discussion.

Perhaps attending the intellectual soirees would allow him to meet more educated ladies. Or would that damage his credit?

"That blue becomes you, Lady Cunningham," he commented in passing. "And please commend Miss Letitia's maid. Waves frame her face better than ringlets, emphasizing her beauty and charm."

"Thank you, my lord. Your taste is impeccable, as always." She nearly simpered.

He moved on, though half of his escort stayed behind, praising Miss Letitia's looks and filling her dance card. The girl deserved the attention. As the seventh of eight daughters, her dowry was small by London standards. Perhaps now she would find a congenial match.

He automatically smiled at several gossips, but his thoughts were far removed from the ballroom. His wife must also place his welfare above her own. He could not abide selfish chits like Elizabeth's sister Cecilia, who had nearly trapped him into matrimony. Granted, Fosdale had been behind that scheme, but her willingness to go along with the plan was hard to forgive.

"That is a remarkable cravat, Lord Sedgewick." Lord Pinter quivered, apparently with excitement. He had lost much of his hair while at Oxford. To distract attention from an unflattering wig and beanpole figure, he enhanced his physique with every possible form of padding, becoming the archetype for Cruikshank's most cutting parody on the excesses of dandies. "What do you call it?"

"Variation on an original theme."

The lad's face fell into his own amateurish creation. "I don't suppose you would demonstrate it."

"Perhaps when you are more adept. In the meantime, practice the Oriental a few hundred times. Until you've mastered that, there is little point in trying something more intricate."

He sighed as Pinter moved off. All this toadying was becoming a bore. Perhaps doing something startling might recapture his usual amusement—replacing the tassels on his boots with jeweled fobs, maybe, or adding a lace flounce to his waistcoat. How many cubs would follow suit? How outrageous could he become before someone dared point out how ridiculous it all was?

But he set the thought aside. Jeremy Orville had just arrived. He had been looking for the lad all evening, but this was one conversation he did not care to share with others. Turning to the remaining puppies, he frowned.

"Hartford can provide introductions to Lady Harriet. She is our newest diamond." He gestured across the ballroom.

They took the hint. Even those who did not head for Hartford melted away.

"A word in private, Orville," he intoned, drawing the

lad into an alcove as music soared above the babbling crowd.

"My lord!"

"Has no one taught you discretion?" he drawled.

"I don't—"

Sedge ignored the protest and raised his quizzing glass, knowing it would magnify his icy glare. "Your reputation is in jeopardy, Orville. Society's standards might sometimes seem contradictory, but you are in no position to ignore them."

"What—"

He dropped his voice to a murmur that no one but Orville could hear. "Comparing Miss Higgins to a bulldog was an acceptable insult, but no gentleman would suggest she is suited only to whoring on the streets. Yet I would think you merely gauche had your comments been made privately to friends, or even in your club. But you voiced them to an opera dancer within hearing of a dozen others. A gentleman does not disparage members of his own class to outsiders. If you cannot control your tongue, either cease drinking or remove yourself from town."

He reddened. "I did not realize—"

"No one ever does. I know you are irritated with the girl, for she embarrassed you in public. But the circumstances were unintentional, and no one is demanding you wed her, in any case. Thus her appearance and her reputation are not your concern. Trying to destroy her will redound upon you."

"My apologies."

"Apologies are worthless unless you learn from the mistake. If you cultivate spiteful thoughts, they will spill out whenever your control loosens, reducing your consequence."

Sparing him further discourse, Sedge returned to the business of revelry. How had he become society's conscience? He had enjoyed taking Brummell's place as an arbiter of fashion, but he had never asked to judge behavior as well as dress. Keeping the sprigs out of trouble was becoming tedious. He had to constantly ponder his impressions and judgments, for the power society had placed in his hands was all too easy to abuse. And it set him apart, placing a small but very real gulf between him and the rest of the polite world.

He shivered. Eyes seemed to bore through his back, showering him with disapproval. Yet a glance around the ballroom revealed none but the usual figures.

Unexpectedly, memories of that companion washed over him, raising a ridiculous amount of heat. He should not have related the incident, though it made a delightful story. But recalling it incited new unruliness in his body. He would have to leave early and pass the remainder of the evening with his mistress.

# Chapter Three

Almont did not join Lord Sedgewick on his promenade around the ballroom. He exchanged gossip with several dowagers, then approached Joanna's alcove as the waltz drew to a close. "Miss Patterson. And Lady Harriet. How beautiful you are tonight."

Harriet giggled.

"An angel clad in gossamer and crowned in gold, whose eyes surpass the color of the sky and glisten with the luster of fine pearls," he continued.

"You flatter me, my lord." She simpered.

Joanna grimaced. Flattery didn't begin to describe the butter boat Almont was dumping over Harriet's head. She'd not heard such fustian since her brother Jeremy had tried to turn her up sweet after destroying her newest gown—a significant crime, for two years had elapsed since she'd acquired the previous one.

But was it truly fustian? She bit her lip in confusion as he uttered a dozen more compliments and Harriet fluttered her lashes. Society's facade of ennui made it difficult to sound sincere. Almont might spout this nonsense to every girl in town. Or he might have singled Harriet out for his attentions. She couldn't tell.

"I believe this is my set," he concluded.

"So it is," agreed Joanna. The musicians signaled a country dance.

She watched as Almont led Harriet out. He was precisely the sort of suitor Wicksfield would approve, yet he made Joanna uneasy. How was she to discover if he truly cared?

But thought of Almont fled as she again spotted Lord Sedgewick. His elegant form attracted her eyes, even when she tried to ignore him. And she wasn't the only one. Half the other guests also watched his promenade about the ballroom.

Why did he draw so many eyes? What set him apart from everyone else, including the other dandies?

She frowned, trying to shape her impressions into words. He exuded an air that went beyond the clothes he wore. Polished but not shiny? Elegant but understated? Confident? Nothing seemed to fit. But he commanded attention. Her eyes would have strayed to him even if they had not met earlier. He cut such a perfect figure that everyone else seemed either overdressed or slightly shabby.

Too bad his behavior was less elegant than his appearance. Her frown deepened when he turned his glass on the Silverton twins. She had always considered quizzing to be hostile. And Lord Sedgewick's use of the glass was more aggressive than most. Whatever he said reduced the pair to white-faced vapors. They fled the room the moment he moved on. She gritted her teeth. The girls might be brash, but that was no excuse to humiliate them in public. Under their rough edges, they were quite sweet.

Lord Sedgewick was a perfect example of why power was dangerous. Society had placed him on a pedestal, allowing him to dictate fashion and behavior. So he did. But using power arbitrarily was abusive. He cared little for how his actions affected others, apparently wielding it for his own satisfaction.

He exchanged greetings with others, the quizzing glass in constant use. But no one else seemed distressed. She had almost decided that she had misjudged him when he delivered a devastating set-down to Mr. Orville. Or so she assumed from the lad's reaction.

*Why do you keep doubting yourself? You were right the first time.* He had ridiculed her despite knowing nothing about her. He had been appallingly rude to the Silvertons. And now he had attacked a pleasant, well-behaved young gentleman. If Orville had done something worthy of public censure, surely Lady Beatrice would have heard. The woman knew everything that happened in town and much of what happened in the countryside.

Odious man.

Her father had taught her to judge people by their behavior. Membership in the upper class did not automatically make a person worthy of respect. In fact, he held noblemen to a higher standard than others, claiming that their exalted positions demanded more responsibility.

Yet society found that concept alien. They judged solely on birth. Fortune could raise or lower esteem, but never move one outside the boundaries of class. Power was theirs by right, to be exercised however they chose.

Every day brought new reminders that she neither belonged here nor understood those who did. Her mother might have been raised a lady, but her training had lacked the finer nuances of fashion and manners. Joanna's was even worse.

"What did young Orville do?" demanded Lady Trotter.

Joanna shrugged.

"It must be licentious," intoned Lady Debenham from her other side. "I would have heard if he'd been gaming to excess."

"Do you think he debauched an innocent?" Lady Trotter fluttered her fan.

"No. He pays little attention to the eligibles. Perhaps he seduced another man's mistress." She frowned.

Joanna ignored their speculation, her eyes again following Lord Sedgewick. Only when he stopped to chat with a group of ladies did she wrest her gaze away. But she could hear snatches of their conversation whenever the music softened.

"Lady Daphne is an outrageous flirt," declared a stout matron, setting her turban's feathers aflutter as she shook her head.

"Only with Henley." Lord Sedgewick sighed affectedly. "Young love. They were quite pink-cheeked after a turn in the garden just now."

Joanna glanced at the couple in question. Though not

partnering each other, they had contrived to be in the same set. Their scorching glances heated the ballroom and recalled the feel of Lord Sedgewick's body pressed firmly against her own.

"You must agree that Lutterworth's pique was warranted." Lord Sedgewick's voice again cut through the music—or did everyone pause when he opened his mouth, creating a pocket of silence?

When music again drowned out his voice, Lady Debenham picked up the thread.

"Once he accepted Brumford, Lutterworth should never have brought his daughter to town. No girl in her right mind would prefer so dour a man to a fashionable dandy. Now he's had to forbid Lastmark's calls and castigate him for his public attentions."

Joanna ignored her. The tale had been on every tongue since she had arrived in London. Lord Sedgewick's repetition confirmed that he was merely another shallow society creature. How could he tolerate discussing the same things month after month, for years on end? Had he no substance at all? London gossip already bored her to tears, for conversation at the vicarage had always been lively.

Yet she should not be surprised. Society itself was shallow, so it would naturally elevate a shallow man to its apex. And her personal preferences didn't count, for she would never belong here. Harriet's ignorance fit this world better than her own education.

She tried to turn her thoughts to duty, but her eyes continued to stray toward Lord Sedgewick. His quizzing glass remained in constant use, punctuating his words, magnifying any disapproval, judging each person who joined the crowd around him. He seemed so aware of everyone in the ballroom that she was amazed he had not yet pounced on her to demand that she leave. The fact that she remained invisible to him proved she was beyond even the fringes of society.

Harriet's return interrupted her reflections. "This is the best ball yet!" she exclaimed the moment Almont moved on.

"Control yourself," Joanna reminded her. "Displaying emotion is uncouth."

"I know, but I cannot help it. Lord Almont paid me the most delicious compliments. My hair is spun from pure gold. My eyes rival the crown jewels' largest sapphires. I have the grace of a swan and the voice of an angel."

"I suspect he flatters all the ladies."

"You mean he lied?" Her face twisted into a pout.

"No. You are very pretty, as you well know. And your voice is pure and sweet. But his mention of it means nothing. He heaped great praise on Miss Washburn's watercolors at last night's rout and complimented Lady Edith's horsemanship the day before." In recalling those incidents, her hope that he might offer for Harriet faded. The man was an incorrigible flirt. Only now did she realize that these memories must have underlain her impression of insincerity, vindicating her intuition.

"So I should enjoy his attentions but not take him seriously?"

Joanna nodded.

"What fun! I wonder if Lord Kensington will be as nice. Or Mr. Craven. He was quite sweet when we arrived. As was Mr. Singleton, though his story about his cousin's dog was too, too funny. He made me laugh out loud, and after you warned me not to. But he treats me like a diamond. Do you suppose all the gentlemen will do so?"

"I'm sure they will."

Lady Wicksfield joined them, introducing the Marchioness of Glendale and her son Reginald, Lord Ellisham. Ellisham seemed ready to bolt. Harriet would receive no compliments from this one, serious or otherwise. He had cringed upon hearing her giddy chatter as they approached. Yet his mother's eyes had actually warmed at Harriet's incautious words.

"Such a lovely, unspoiled child," said Lady Glendale to Lady Wicksfield.

"Yet versed in all the graces. You should hear her sing—angelic, the gentlemen always say. She brought tears to Almont's eyes only yesterday."

"Like my cousin, Julia, don't you think, Reginald?"

"Perhaps." Ellisham's wooden voice stripped all gaiety from the conversation, but Joanna could not repine. Lady Wicksfield's lie had her gritting her teeth. No one in London had heard Harriet sing.

Ellisham stepped away.

"Reginald!" hissed Lady Glendale under her breath.

He halted. "Have you a set free, Lady Harriet?" he asked stiffly, barely suppressing his irritation.

"Alas, her card is full," Joanna replied before Lady Wicksfield could commit the solecism of giving him a set already promised to another. He must be wealthy as well as heir to a marquessate. Lady Wicksfield glared even as relief flashed in Ellisham's eyes.

"Perhaps another time," he said.

Lady Glendale and Lady Wicksfield exchanged glances, then backed off to talk privately.

"That would be lovely." Harriet flashed a brilliant smile.

"Until then."

"Which will be when pigs take to the skies and hell has frozen over," Joanna murmured as Harriet turned to greet Lord Hartford.

Ellisham's eyes flew to Joanna's face, halting his escape. She reddened. A freak pause as everyone inhaled at once had allowed her words to carry.

"How prescient." His face broke into a grin. Within moments they were both laughing.

"Forgive me," she begged once she caught her breath. "That was intolerably rude."

"But true. How did you know?"

"Your eyes tell me that you faced a choice between escorting your mother to this ball and being drawn and quartered. I expect the decision proved difficult."

"That sums it up quite nicely. I have little use for this sort of thing." He raised his brows. "I fear I did not catch your name."

"Not surprising, since no one gave it. Miss Joanna Patterson, companion and chaperon to Lady Harriet—which makes my lapse of manners even worse, for one of my duties is to correct her behavior."

"Is that a problem?"

"Not really, but she is very young—barely seventeen—so she does not always think before speaking."

"And is somewhat hen-witted, I expect. Don't lie," he added over her protest. "Mother would not have introduced her otherwise."

Which explained her reaction to Harriet's prattle. Joanna nodded. "But she is very sweet, and quite sensible about the things she knows. So far she is unfamiliar with London."

"Then why bring her out so young?"

"I did not question Lord Wicksfield when he hired me," she said primly.

"Of course. Mother cannot have thought I might be interested in so young a chit. I am twice her age." He sighed.

"Perhaps she introduced you at the request of Lady Wicksfield."

"No. It was the other way round. Girls are not the only ones afflicted with matchmaking mothers. She has been pressing me for years. Every Season is worse than the last."

"Which explains why you would rather not have come this evening."

"Exactly. I hate being paraded about like a prime stallion."

"Why? It is little different than what girls face. Most are offered up as comely brood-mares. Perhaps we should hold the Season in Tattersall's auction ring and be done with it."

"I do believe I am shocked!" Yet his eyes twinkled with merriment. "But also intrigued. You are a most original lady."

"Hardly. I have merely misplaced the curb that should be controlling my tongue. If I wish to retain my position, I had best recover it quickly."

Mr. Singleton escorted Harriet out for a quadrille. Hartford left, taking the three young men he had introduced with him. Joanna swallowed a surge of guilt. She would have to quiz him about his latest protégés.

"Do you enjoy life as a companion?" asked Lord Ellisham, relaxing into a more natural stance.

"Very much, though I doubt most positions would prove this congenial. Since I must accompany Harriet, I get to attend all manner of entertainments, and have even received permission to enter the sacred halls of Almack's tomorrow. The experience will stand me in good stead in the future."

"And why is that?"

"Once Harriet has no further need of me, I will take up a post as governess to Sir Brandon Paxton's daughters—Lord Wicksfield convinced him to hold it for me. Preparing girls for a Season will be easier now that I have experienced one for myself."

"Is that truly the life you want?" he asked, a frown on his face.

"Teaching young ladies is an interesting challenge that will put my education to good use," she said, skirting the question. "But tell me something of yourself, my lord. Why is your mother pressing so hard?"

"I would think that was obvious. I am heir to the marquessate. She started parading chits before me ten years ago."

"Are you the stubborn sort who opposes all coercion?"

"Not really, though her pressure is annoying enough to make anyone balk. But she refuses to accept that some men are not meant for marriage. I should make an abominable husband, so why should I inflict myself on some poor, unwitting girl? My brother will see after the succession, so she has no need for hysteria."

"I see. You are certainly old enough to know your own mind and heart. My condolences on having to fend off her schemes. Have you considered leaving town during the Season?"

He laughed. "Yes. I've also considered making a Grand Tour now that the Continent is finally at peace. I've always wanted to visit Paris and Italy."

They fell into a discussion of Italian art and architecture, then drifted into talk of more esoteric places. Not until the music stopped did Joanna realize how long they had spoken.

"You had best move on," she said, sighing now that

the interlude was over. "You don't want to appear enamored of a mere companion."

"I wouldn't mind, if it were true. This has been a most enjoyable conversation. And if I stay another minute, I can speak with Lady Harriet, thus leaving the impression that I have awaited her. It can only help her reputation."

"Are you sure you wish to risk your own?"

But Harriet was already greeting him. He paid her a light compliment, bent briefly over her hand, then was gone.

The rest of the evening passed in a blur. Lord Sedgewick had left while she talked with Ellisham. Harriet's giddy excitement increased until Joanna had to remove her from the ballroom.

"Control yourself," she snapped when they had reached the relative safety of an empty antechamber. "Do you wish to give people a disgust of you? How could you embrace a gentleman in the middle of the ballroom?"

"B-but I was laughing so hard I could hardly stand. Should I have collapsed to the floor?"

"Of course not, Harriet." She paused to soften her tone. "You must master your emotions. Falling into uncontrolled mirth can destroy you. Yes, Mr. Craven can be exceedingly droll. But society reveres elegance and sangfroid. Anything approaching hysteria is gauche and low-class. You must cultivate moderation."

"I cannot even laugh?"

"Moderation, Harriet. A smile. A polite titter. These are acceptable. Mr. Craven knows that. It was naughty of him to goad you so far, but you have to accept responsibility for yourself. Excess sensibility will do you no good at all. You know what is at stake this Season. Look closely at the other girls. They do not exhibit vulgar emotions no matter what happens." Harriet was white-faced, her distress over the set-down raising a memory of the Silvertons. Joanna stifled a surge of guilt. At least no one else would witness this scold, and the reminder was necessary.

"Forgive me, Joanna," begged Harriet, sniffing. "But why must I hide so natural an activity as laughing?"

"Because society expects it. I do not make the rules. I merely teach them. If you wish to find a husband, then you must mind your manners." Poor Harriet. She had very little time to attach anyone, let alone the high-placed lord her father expected. "There is nothing wrong with laughter in private. Or tears. Or even anger. But you cannot afford to display such emotions in public."

"I will try harder."

And she had. The rest of the evening had passed in reasonable comfort. Lady Wicksfield was ecstatic when they returned home.

"You have done well," she said, following Harriet into the girl's bedchamber. "Lord Almont is increasingly attentive. But Ellisham is an even bigger catch. If only you had danced with him."

Joanna stared Harriet into silence before facing Lady Wicksfield. "It would have damaged her reputation beyond repair if she had given him a set promised to another—no matter how insignificant the original gentleman is."

"Yes, well . . ." She huffed for a moment, then set her irritation aside. "We will hold a set for him at Almack's tomorrow. A waltz would be perfect. No one will expect you to fill those slots, but Ellisham's credit is high enough that the patronesses will certainly present him as a suitable partner."

"You forget Harriet's age, my lady. The patronesses will never grant her permission on her first visit. Nor is Ellisham likely to choose a waltz as his first set with anyone. It would raise speculation he would not approve."

"Then we will save him a quadrille," said Lady Wicksfield firmly. "You will see to it, Miss Patterson."

Joanna sighed, but she had to warn them to look elsewhere. "Do not expect too much from this contact. I spoke with Lord Ellisham while Harriet was dancing, and I doubt he is interested in marriage."

"No gentleman ever is." Lady Wicksfield glared. "But he has no choice. He has a duty to secure the succession. His mother will see that he performs it. We must make sure that he chooses Harriet."

Harriet frowned. "But—"

"Go to sleep, dear," Lady Wicksfield interrupted her. "It is early days yet."

Joanna was willing to drop the subject. Ellisham was capable of handling his own affairs. And since she doubted that he would dance attendance on Harriet, she had nothing to worry about.

But Lady Wicksfield waved Joanna into her sitting room, determined to make her point. "You will see that Harriet attaches Ellisham," she ordered. "His title and wealth will save us from ruin."

"We have a better chance of attaching Almont," she countered stonily. "He is actively seeking a wife and shows an increasing partiality for Harriet. Whatever Lady Glendale's vows, Ellisham is opposed to marriage. Nor would he suit Harriet, being too old and too impatient to deal with her megrims."

"She will adjust, just as other ladies have learned to adjust. Marriage in our class is always a matter of convenience, so pay attention to what is important. Wicksfield expects the best title and fortune available."

Joanna tried to nod, but her head refused to move. "Lord Wicksfield gave me very explicit instructions, my lady. He needs a suitor who can help him obtain the loan he requires, but he also demands that the gentleman suit Harriet. He will not approve the match unless she is content. Almont may prove to be such a man, and it is possible that Ellisham might offer Harriet the support she needs. Or the ideal suitor may not yet have appeared. It is too early to discount anyone."

Lady Wicksfield frowned, fury boiling behind her eyes. But Joanna held the ultimate authority. She finally sighed.

"Very well. We will discount no one—including Ellisham." Waving Joanna away, she summoned her maid.

Joanna crawled into bed, but lay awake long into the night, staring at the ceiling. Where had the urge to protect Ellisham come from? He needed no help.

She reviewed their conversation, finally relaxing in relief. While she had enjoyed talking with him, there had been no physical attraction—certainly none of the awareness and gawky awkwardness she had suffered with Lord Sedgewick. It was too bad that Ellisham was not a lady, for their minds were quite alike. He could have made a very good friend.

Lady Wicksfield was going to be a problem. She had no patience for her husband's plans, which would not restore his fortune for several years. The woman cared for no one but herself, and would gladly sell Harriet if it would benefit her.

Lord Wicksfield must have known that, which explained the unusual power he had placed in a mere companion's hands.

*Help me wield it wisely*, she prayed.

The right husband would bring Harriet great happiness. But in the wrong hands, she would suffer. She lacked the confidence to control her own emotional state.

# Chapter Four

❧

Sedge glowered at Husby as the butler admitted him to Glendale House. His mother's summons had been unwelcome, for he rarely arose before noon. Yet here he was at only half past eleven, presenting himself for what could only be another lecture on setting up his nursery. Hardly unexpected, but why couldn't she at least have waited until a decent hour?

Yet he hid his frustration when he entered the drawing room.

"Here you are at last," exclaimed Lady Glendale, setting aside her needlework. "I despaired of seeing you today."

"You could hardly expect me to be awake, let alone dressed at the ridiculous hour of nine," he drawled, leaning casually against the mantel.

"If you didn't play cards until dawn, that would not be a problem."

He nearly corrected her, for he had gone to Jenny's after leaving the ball—and devil take that woman for making it necessary; it had required most of the night to get her out of his system—but he caught himself in time. His mother had often used deliberate misstatements to trip her sons into revealing childhood pranks, but he no longer owed her an explanation of his activities.

He deliberately relaxed. "Since I am in no danger of losing my fortune on the turn of a card or toss of a die, how I pass my time is not your concern, madam." He delivered the set-down in the same icy tone he had used on Jeremy Orville. He was well into his thirty-second year, long past his majority. It was time she recognized that fact.

"Perhaps not, though—" She sighed in obvious frustration when he lifted his quizzing glass. "That is not why I wished to see you. We have finally settled Reggie."

"Oh?"

"I introduced him to Lady Harriet Selwick last night—her mother attended school with my youngest sister, then managed to snare Wicksfield, who was the catch of that Season. Lady Wicksfield is all that is proper, so we can be sure that Lady Harriet will make a conformable wife. Reggie was so struck by her beauty that he waited for an entire set to speak with her a second time—unfortunately, her dance card was full before we managed the introduction."

"Waited to speak?" The incredulity was not feigned. Not only was the girl barely out of the schoolroom, but Reggie had long declared that he would remain single. Perhaps his reticence merely sought distance from their mother's pressure, but infatuation with a chit half his age seemed ridiculous.

"I saw him with my own eyes. He had not anticipated her arrival, so the shock of finding a new angel suddenly in our midst piqued his interest."

"The blonde with the rosebuds and lace on her gown?" They could not be talking about the same child. She didn't look a day over fifteen. Reggie wasn't stupid.

"You noticed her." Her satisfaction increased his irritation.

"I notice everyone. I would have attributed the gown to Madame Francine if not for the lace."

"You are impossible." She released one of her long-suffering sighs. "But you must rejoice that Reggie is settled at last—and to a girl of impeccable breeding. Now we must see to your future."

"There is no need. If Reggie is truly settled, then the succession is assured." Not that he believed for a moment that Reggie was serious. But arguing with her was not in his own interest. "You must be pleased with your success. Now you can return to the Close."

"How absurd! Reggie cannot shoulder the entire responsibility for the future. What if something happened to him? You know how I feel about your cousin. Allowing the marquessate to fall into the hands of a fribble is intolerable."

"Then you should do everything in your power to keep it out of my hands, for my reputation is exactly the same."

"That may be true—though I cannot understand why you insist on prancing about like a silly nodcock; it can only court disdain—but you are nothing like your cousin. We both know you are reasonably intelligent, so direct that intelligence to the future. You must wed, Sedgewick. I believe the Washburn girl would suit you quite well."

"Do you?" he drawled. "I cannot imagine why."

"She is lovely."

"And hasn't two thoughts to rub together."

"Then what about Miss Avery? She can conduct an intelligent conversation."

"Perhaps I should consider her. She has sworn to die a spinster, but she might be willing to accept her own establishment and a sizable allowance if I vowed to leave her alone."

"You jest."

"Not at all. She has turned down two dozen offers already, including a duke and two earls. Her brother has given up on her. She must be all of four-and-twenty."

"So was Elizabeth, but that did not prevent Symington from wedding her."

"Leave it, Mother. I have no interest in Miss Avery or anyone else."

"Only because you refuse to consider them. What objection could you have to Miss Heathmark?"

"I cannot distinguish her from my horse."

Lady Glendale pinched her mouth into a disapproving line. "That was unkind, Sedgewick."

"This entire subject is unkind. I will not wed until I

find a lady I can live with in comfort. No amount of pressure will speed the process."

"Nonsense. You are merely stubborn, having become so accustomed to opposing my wishes that you no longer look about you. But if you require beauty, then consider Miss Mason."

"She giggles."

"Miss Cunningham is more sober."

"With eight older siblings who relegated her to silence, she never learned to converse."

"Lady Edith Harwood?"

"Irrevocably selfish."

"Lady Constance Bowlin?"

"Are you so desperate that you would accept someone smarter than you?" He snapped his mouth closed at her shudder, furious that irritation had loosened his tongue. She was determined to retain her power and position after her husband died—a looming event, for the man's health was rapidly failing—which explained why she sponsored only the most conformable misses. But she believed her schemes remained secret.

"Miss Delaney?"

"When did you decide that Irish stock might suit? Perhaps I should consider her. I would derive great pleasure from watching you swallow your pride long enough to welcome her into the family."

"You are correct. She would never do."

"But not because she is Irish," he said, raising his quizzing glass. "She will not do because she displays no sense and less style. Now enough of this. I will eventually wed, but in my own time and for my own pleasure."

"Very well." The agreement was meaningless, as they both knew. She would never abandon her campaign. "In the meantime, I am holding a dinner party next week and will expect you to attend."

He caught a flash of cunning in her eye. So this was not the usual confrontation after all. Elizabeth had feared that she would take matters into her own hands. Was she actually willing to compromise him into marriage?

His temper shattered. "That will not be possible." He

headed for the door. "I have business at Meadowbanks that will keep me from town at least that long. Nor will I tolerate further meddling in my affairs. If you persist, I will spend the remainder of the Season in Paris."

Without waiting for a reply, he left.

Cursing his mother and every other matchmaker in town, he threw himself into his carriage, grateful that the curtains would keep him out of the public eye. He could not hope to carry off his usual sangfroid in this mood.

He had claimed business in the heat of the moment, but leaving town was an excellent idea. By accompanying Randolph to Cumberland, he had missed his usual spring retreat. Housing Elizabeth at Glendale Close until the Season began had been expedient, but Randolph had begged him to stay with her lest Lady Glendale's hauteur ruin Elizabeth's sweet character.

So he had not visited Meadowbanks in six months. His steward was a capable man, of course, but he needed to check the books. And he needed to relax. Perhaps his hectic spring explained why this Season seemed sadly flat.

Rapping on the roof, he ordered his coachman to Piccadilly. There were stops he must make before he could leave town.

Sedge was rounding a bookshelf in Hatchard's when voices halted him.

"Papa will never give in," whispered one. "He owes Brumford a fortune, but Brumford will cancel the debt in exchange for my hand."

Miss Lutterworth, Sedge identified. He had suspected some such scheme, but confirmation raised enough fury to choke him. He despised fathers who sold their daughters—particularly to cruel men like Brumford. Preventing such unions had been a personal crusade for fifteen years, though he rarely worked in the open.

"Then we must elope," replied Mr. Lastmark. "I know it is scandalous, but waiting until you are of age is hopeless. I haven't the means to rescue your father myself."

"I wouldn't allow you to pay his debts," she said seriously. "Most are gaming vowels. I've always suspected something odd behind them, for Brumford swore I would regret turning him down last year."

Sedge left them to their planning. Kensington was headed in their direction, so he struck up a conversation to give the pair time to part. Only after Miss Lutterworth rejoined her maid, did he collect his own books and leave.

Half an hour later he was sauntering along Bond Street when a frowning woman erupted from a shop, oblivious to the crowds hurrying by. The resulting collision was inevitable. He caught the victim, preventing a second collision with a passing carriage. The moment she was firmly on her feet, he grabbed the cause of the accident.

"You again!" It was the same bird-witted companion who had cost him last night's sleep. "Idiot!" He shook her. "If you wish to survive, pay attention to where you are going." A surge of lust washed over him, increasing his fury. What could he possibly find enticing about this woman? Thank God he was leaving town. He needed time to regain his senses.

"I . . . you . . . how did you—" Her face blushed crimson.

He gritted his teeth. "What is the point of wearing spectacles when you never look at anything?" he demanded as more heat pooled in his loins. He dropped his hands lest they do something stupid. Forcing a precarious control over his temper, he donned his most languid expression. "You must be newly arrived. Had you been here any time, you would already be planted in the churchyard."

"Arrogant fool!" she hissed.

"I really must insist that you bring an escort next time you venture out. We cannot have you endangering your betters. In the meantime, I will escort you home."

She recoiled. "You will not!"

Her obvious aversion brought his temper back to the boil. "Devil take it, woman. How dare you argue with me? I am only trying to protect you."

"I don't need your protection. I am perfectly happy with my own. Now step aside."

That look of haughty disapproval might have been intimidating if she'd had an ounce of intelligence to back it up—and if her cheeks weren't blazing like beacons. But he saw little need to explain in words of one syllable that she had misinterpreted his intentions.

*Not that you would mind,* whispered a voice in his head.

He jumped. Where had *that* thought come from? Raising his glass, he quizzed her thoroughly, ignoring her sputtered protests. He could recall every curve of the delectable body tucked under that uninspired gown.

She slapped the glass out of his hand. "How dare you pass judgment on someone you don't even know?"

"I have eyes," he snapped.

"Eyes are useless without a brain to interpret what they see. Society must be worthless indeed to have elevated so condescending a toad to the pinnacle of power."

He grabbed her shoulders through a haze of red mist. "How dare you insult your betters?" he demanded, shaking her again—and backing into the victim, who abandoned her grumbled complaints to shout obscenities at him. "Have you wit enough to remember your own name?"

"I've more wit than you, thank God. Maybe you can afford to waste your life in pompous posturings and petty prattle, but I must make my own way in the world. Now unhand me before my reputation is sullied by contact with a fool."

Burning heat climbed his face. What the devil was he doing? Fighting down his temper, he took stock of the situation. Mrs. Stanhope was cursing at the top of her lungs, drawing every eye on Bond Street. His public facade was long gone, and shaking had pulled the woman close enough that he appeared to be embracing her. Arguing with an imbecile over her mental capacity was ridiculous. Doing so in public was worse. Why had he allowed her ravings to destroy his control—all of his control, he admitted as another wave of lust engulfed him.

Never in his life had he appeared so foolish. And it was all her fault.

Donning the tattered remnants of his composure, he dropped his hands. It was past time to leave town. This ridiculous attraction called his sanity into question and threatened his reputation with ruin.

"If you don't wish to draw unfavorable notice, then pay attention to your surroundings," he growled. "Next time I'll deliver you to Bedlam, where you belong." Giving her no chance to respond, he headed for his rooms.

Joanna castigated herself as Lord Sedgewick strode away. How had she tumbled into another bumblebroth? After yesterday, she had vowed to be more careful. Yet barely twenty-four hours later, she had fallen into a new abstraction that again had drawn his attention.

Why did it have to be him? She had run Harriet's errands every day since arriving in town. Not once had she created a scandal, except when he was in the vicinity.

She had no excuse. Granted, she was plagued by problems, not least of which was Harriet's penchant for ruining gloves and stockings. But pondering solutions should not have blinded her to her surroundings. Not until she'd crashed into that woman had she recalled where she was.

She was grateful that someone had prevented a worse disaster, but did it have to be Lord Sedgewick? His look of horror at recognizing her had left her incoherent, stammering and stuttering until even she was not sure what she had been trying to say. Her performance had flustered her so badly that she'd compounded the problem by blurting out mortifying insults. Why hadn't the street opened up to swallow her?

The echo of her words raised new blushes. She could hardly blame him for losing his temper. How could she have been so stupid? And this was only the beginning. They were attending Almack's tonight. If he recognized her, he would delight in exposing her foibles. What would Lady Wicksfield do if Joanna was ejected?

But even fear could not hold her attention for long. Her arms throbbed where he had grasped her, and not from pain. Up close, he left her breathless. Now she

knew why he seemed so different from other gentlemen.
His dandy airs covered a burning masculinity that few
men possessed. It simmered just beneath the surface,
flaring when he was angry into a force that could over-
power anyone.

She shivered, appalled at her reaction. How could she
respond to an arrogant lord of limited intelligence and
less regard for her feelings? A lord who would grant
precedence to pond scum over her. A lord who could
destroy Harriet with a word, and might well do so to
avenge his damaged dignity. He would not forgive this
debacle any time soon.

Forgetting to apologize to the woman she had
knocked down, who was still screeching complaints, she
headed home.

All afternoon she debated whether to reveal her stupidity to Lady Wicksfield, though in the end, she remained silent. Nothing would prevent Lord Sedgewick
from ruining her if he chose to do so, but there was a
chance that he would not recognize her. While he had
examined her more closely this time, he would hardly
expect to find her at Almack's, and she doubted whether
he paid attention to minions even there. On the other
hand, confessing her trouble might well cost her both
this position and the governess post that awaited her,
for Lady Wicksfield would immediately report it to the
earl. Who would entrust their daughters to a woman
whose head was in the clouds?

Once they left for Almack's, she had no time to brood.
Containing Harriet's excitement required all her
attention.

"I can't believe we are nearly there!" the girl gasped,
spotting the entrance as they joined the line of carriages
inching along King Street. "I can hardly wait to behold
its magnificence. How much grander will it be than Lady
Ormsport's ballroom?"

"Calm yourself, Harriet," Joanna reminded her. "Remember society's watchwords—elegance and ennui. You
must keep your face and voice under control. Lady Hartford claims that Almack's is neat but unembellished and

that the refreshments are quite frugal. We have discussed this before."

"Of course." Harriet clasped her hands tightly in her lap. "But it seems strange."

"Not at all. This is not a private ball. We must pay admission. The cachet of Almack's is the exclusive company, for even money and position will not guarantee receiving the voucher that allows one to purchase a subscription. The patronesses require exceptional conduct and a spotless reputation. You can lose that voucher if your behavior displeases them, so mind your manners. Do not complain about anything, and never compare this to other gatherings. Do you understand why?"

She nodded. "If they do not like me, I will not be allowed to return."

"Exactly." At least one lesson had taken root. "Straighten your gloves and get ready," she added as the carriage stopped at the door.

The street was jammed, but she hardly saw the other vehicles. This was the moment of truth, the moment when she learned whether her latest lapse would condemn her. If she were refused admittance, Lady Wicksfield would have to send her back to the vicarage.

But her fears proved groundless—so far. And the ballroom was more sumptuous than she had expected. Great columns marched down the long walls. Five large windows overlooked King Street, each covered with rich draperies. Londoners might think it plain, but to eyes accustomed to a village vicarage, it was magnificent.

Harriet was soon surrounded by her court. Her dance card rapidly filled. Lady Wicksfield abandoned them to gossip with her friends.

But Joanna's mind kept wandering. Her eyes snapped toward the doorway whenever a gentleman appeared, irritating her, though she could not seem to stop.

*Concentrate on business,* she admonished herself when she realized she was again staring at the entrance. She would fall into some new debacle at this rate. Already she had nearly allowed Harriet to chatter unchecked. But despite her best intentions, she did not relax until the patronesses barred the doors at eleven. Not even Lord Sedgewick could gain admittance now.

His absence was noted.

"He hasn't missed a subscription ball in years," said Lady Debenham. "Has he fallen ill?" She sounded thoroughly out of sorts at having to ask.

"I heard he received an unexpected visitor," swore Lady Horseley.

Lady Beatrice shook her head. "So gullible. You should know better than to believe rumors."

Joanna nearly burst into laughter at London's premier gossip warning someone against rumors.

"I suppose you know differently?"

"Of course. He left for his estate at two o'clock this afternoon. He *said* he had business, but the real reason was an argument with his mother."

Her listeners broke into confused murmurs of shock, condemnation, and support. Joanna sidled away, fearful that someone might notice her relief. He was gone. By the time he returned, he would have forgotten their encounters.

The current set finished. Almont escorted Harriet back to her side, then moved off to find his next partner.

"Lady Harriet," said Lord Ellisham, appearing seemingly from nowhere. "That gown makes your eyes even bluer."

Harriet smiled. "How nice of you to notice."

"Have you any country dances free?"

Her face fell. "Not a one, my lord."

"Perhaps another day." He waited until Mr. Craven distracted her attention before smiling at Joanna. "I thought that might be the case."

"You are a complete hand, my lord." Then she blushed at being so forward. "Forgive me, I cannot seem to do anything lately that is not either gauche or mortifying—usually both."

"That particular lapse was hardly deserving of notice."

"The others were not. I am amazed I was allowed in here tonight."

"Oh?"

His eyes conveyed curiosity and sympathy. Before she

could stop, she blurted out the very facts she had sought
to hide. "I have drawn unfavorable attention from the
most arrogant gentleman in town. If he were here, I
would doubtless be out in the street by now."

"For what crime, if I might be so bold?"

"It was quite inadvertent—though he read me such a
scold that I am still quaking. He believes me a candidate
for Bedlam and ordered me not to leave the house again
without a keeper."

"Heavens!"

"Exactly. I had just purchased some gloves for Harriet—she ruined three pair in a single week—and was
pondering how to prevent further carelessness, when I
bumped into the most vulgar matron, if her language is
any judge. But I must believe that she exaggerated her
grievance, for this gentleman prevented her from falling
into the street or sustaining the slightest injury. And she
shared at least half the blame. She was striding along
Bond Street at so great a rate that she outpaced Lord
Osbourne's new curricle, and you must know how he
drives."

"Quite." His lips twitched. "Springs his horses without
offering up so much as a prayer for those in his path."

"Exactly. You would have thought she was fleeing a
mob, so why that odious man blamed me, I cannot say.
He shook me until my teeth rattled, then castigated me
for any number of crimes without allowing me a single
word in my own defense."

"What about the woman?"

"She was screeching her woes to the world and raining
curses on both our heads, but he completely ignored her.
After heaping any number of insults onto my shoulders,
he strode off in high dudgeon."

"A trying encounter, to be sure." He chuckled. "Did
you recognize the lady?"

"Not in the least, though she was wearing the most
outrageous hat I have ever laid eyes on."

"And a cloak lined in ermine, I'll be bound," he
interrupted.

"How did you know?"

"She moves like a man-of-war under full sail in a raging gale, venting her pique on anything she finds annoying. Her name is Mrs. Stanhope. Although her breeding is acceptable, she married a cit and has been unbearably obnoxious ever since her daughter was refused admission to Almack's. Picturing her knocked into the street is the most delightful image to come my way in some time. I wish I could have seen it." He gave in and laughed.

"I take it she is not one of your favorite people."

"Hardly. We have exchanged words on more than one occasion. Did she read you a scold once the gentleman departed?"

She could feel her face heat at the memory. "Oh, dear. I'm afraid I left without a word myself. I was so furious that I forgot she was there."

Ellisham laughed even harder. "How priceless. Ignored by everyone! But who, pray tell, was the gentleman?"

"An arrogant, overbearing meddler who seems to believe he is better than everyone else. He already made me into a laughingstock over yesterday's confrontation. What he will do this time, I have no idea. I suspect that nothing pleases him."

"What happened yesterday?"

She blushed. "Another of my scrapes. I don't know why I thought myself capable of chaperoning Harriet. I cannot pass a week without getting into trouble."

"I can't imagine how."

"My mind fixes on its thoughts, leaving me oblivious to my surroundings. I hope I do not draw censure onto Harriet's head."

"You will not."

She glanced up in surprise.

"I will not allow it."

"Thank you. My bumblebroths are mortifying enough without involving others."

"So what happened yesterday?"

"A dog." She sighed. "Two boys were tormenting it. In my haste to stop them, I failed to see an approaching carriage. The man dragged me out from in front of it." She bit her lip. "I must admit that he did chase off the boys and return Maximillian to his owner. But he made considerable sport of me last night, so I cannot feel properly grateful."

"Dear Lord. You cannot mean Sedge!"

"Lord Sedgewick Wylie. Someone identified him while he pilloried me. Odious fool."

His laughter was drawing attention, so he stifled it, growing quite red-faced in the process. "Beyond priceless. You are a pearl, indeed, my dear. I never thought to find anyone capable of criticizing Sedge—or of destroying his uncanny control." His eyes lit with speculation.

"Pardon me," she said stiffly. "But his character is quite lacking—not that I should be ripping up his conduct when he is not present to defend himself, but it is no more than he did to me. A more presumptuous man I've yet to meet."

Another chuckle escaped. "I must apologize for his lack of tact, Miss Patterson. Believe me, he is anything but odious. Nor is he particularly arrogant, though he does occasionally play that role in public. Perhaps you will give him a chance to redeem himself."

"Another of his slaves. I suppose he is your closest friend," she said, then blushed.

"In a way. He is my brother."

She jumped, dropping her head to hide another blush. "I see my tongue has again betrayed me. Forgive me."

"Of course. But you needn't flee." She was inching away. "I find it refreshing that someone does not dote on him. People have practically worshipped him since Brummell left."

"Why?"

His eyes grew serious. "It started with the cubs. Boys in town for the first time often choose older mentors to mimic, copying dress, manners, interests, even those unique little habits we all have. It serves an admirable purpose if the models are honorable, for it allows the lads to quickly fit in. Brummell was the pattern card for many years—in fact, Sedge was one of his followers when he came down from Oxford. But Brummell was getting rather long in the tooth even before he fled his creditors, so many cubs preferred Sedge. He has a great deal of fashion sense. Frankly, I would rather people followed his lead than some of the more flamboyant dressers."

"Yes, he does manage to look elegant even when reading one a scold."

"He is now the most powerful arbiter of fashion in town, and unlike others, he feels the responsibility of his position, keeping an eye on his imitators. When one of them is headed for trouble, he can often deflect him. Like young Orville last night. The cub has been denigrating ladies to his opera dancers. Sedge set him straight."

"Laudable," was all she said, though he could have been gentler about how he had gone about it. Mr. Orville had nearly collapsed in full view of two hundred members of society.

"You don't sound convinced. Believe me, Brummell never lifted a finger to help his imitators. Like many who rise above their station, he became more arrogant than any nobleman. And his gaming was legendary, providing an unfortunate example for many young men. That is what ultimately destroyed him."

Ellisham dropped the subject of his brother, instead launching a humorous tale about his aunt's companion, whose duties included walking four dogs in the park every morning. She was a poor-spirited creature, which the dogs knew full well. Unable to assert herself even to a terrier, she invariably became entangled in leads.

"She is not the same aunt who owns Maximillian," he added when she had finished laughing.

"That is obvious. Four terriers would dispose of that hairy rat for breakfast. Was he badly injured?"

"One small cut. He's suffered worse." He related several of the dog's exploits.

By the time the music ceased, she was again relaxed. Whatever his brother's faults, Lord Ellisham was fascinating.

"I've hovered here long enough to satisfy my mother," he concluded. "We must chat again sometime. Nod in my direction when Lady Harriet's card is full, so I needn't waste time squiring the chit. She does not impress me as being endowed with an excess of intelligence."

"A polite way of saying she is a pea-goose," she agreed. "She really does need a husband who can take care of her."

"But not me."

"I know. All other considerations aside, she would drive you to distraction in an hour."

Joanna lay awake long into the night, recalling that conversation. She could not believe that Lord Sedgewick was the benign person Ellisham described. Nor could she forget his angry eyes. They had started as light blue, but rapidly hardened into icy gray. When she finally succumbed to sleep, they slid into her dreams, pinning her down while he castigated her for every muddle she'd walked into in eight-and-twenty years.

Yet as the hours passed, they softened, brightening into a brilliant blue that twinkled with Reggie's humor.

# Chapter Five

Sedge returned to London at the height of the fashionable hour, slipping into his rooms with no one the wiser. Nine days had elapsed since he had fled his mother's sitting room, but the journey had helped. He was calmer than he had been all Season.

Randolph's estate adjoined Meadowbanks. The two evenings he had spent there had relaxed him as much as escaping London. His friends glowed with happiness. They had heard from Elizabeth's mother and brother, who seemed eager to heal the family breach, removing a weight from Elizabeth's shoulders.

He had spent the rest of his time considering the qualities he wanted in a wife. Besides being intelligent, she must be reasonably pretty, with a refined sense of style and the skills to organize any entertainment. He would have to buy a town house and become a host if he wished to maintain his social position. The sprigs would turn to younger mentors in a few more years anyway, but marriage would hasten that process. Young bucks rarely accepted direction from staid married men.

Thus he needed an educated hostess. He doubted that such a paragon could be found among the girls making their bows to society, so he must consider ladies nearer his own age—but not spinsters. Women who had long been on the shelf usually had shortcomings he could not accept. Widows would be better. The late war had created a goodly number. He would begin looking at the better-born among them.

It was good to be back in London. He changed

clothes, then sorted a mountain of invitations during dinner. One of the drawbacks of his position was being asked to every event in town, so ten days of mail seemed overwhelming—events held while he'd been gone, balls honoring assorted mushrooms, card parties, musicales, a dozen routs, two Venetian breakfasts, an expedition to Richmond, another to Hampton Court. The heap of discards grew. By the time he reached the apple tart, he was arranging the remaining invitations by date.

Tonight he would appear briefly at Lady Stafford's rout, stay an hour at the Cunningham ball, pass another hour at the Barhampton ball, then drop by White's for a few hands of cards.

But that agenda did not last very long. His mother pounced on him within moments of his arrival at Lady Cunningham's. "I must speak with you, Sedgewick."

"Leave it," he drawled. "I've no wish to endure another of your scolds, and certainly not in so public a place."

"It's Reginald." She compressed her lips, inhaled deeply several times, then pulled him behind a potted palm. "Thank heaven you have returned. I've been terrified that he would disgrace his breeding before you could talk some sense into him. He actually refused my summons this morning!"

"I thought he was settled." His tone deliberately needled her, though given her penchant for criticism, who could blame Reggie for avoiding another confrontation?

"As did I. He has been dangling after Lady Harriet for nearly a fortnight, staying at her side through two sets every evening, calling on her three times, and driving her in the park twice. Even Mr. Lastmark's attentions to Miss Lutterworth were not as blatant."

She paused for a deep breath. "You will not have heard that tale, Sedgewick. It is the most shocking thing! Lady Beatrice claims they have eloped. The Lutterworths have not appeared in two days, and Brumford was scowling on Bond Street yesterday."

"I know." Her digression was hardly a surprise. She never ignored scandal, even when in the throes of her own hysteria. "At least they escaped safely. I had feared Miss Lutterworth might balk at the end."

"You knew what they were planning?" Her voice squeaked with indignation.

He smiled. She had lost all control over her face. "She would have suffered greatly with Brumford."

"That makes no difference."

"It makes every difference." His voice hardened. "Had I interfered, I would have been as guilty as Lutterworth of selling the chit to a vile swine."

For once, she understood. "You had nothing to do with Cousin Caroline's death, Sedgewick. It has been fifteen years. Let it rest."

"I could have prevented her marriage." He choked off the words. There was no point in raising the issue again, though the memories remained fresh. He alone had understood both Lufrond's vicious nature and the threats that had forced Caroline into the match. But he had remained silent, unwilling to admit that he had spent a weekend in London when he was supposed to be in school, and even more loath to confess to eavesdropping on Lufrond in a brothel or to witnessing his uncle's mad losses in an unsavory gaming hell. So his uncle had sold Caroline to Lufrond. Six months later, she had died, ostensibly from a fall down the stairs.

His mother frowned, also recalling that tragedy, for Caroline had been a family favorite. Her abstracted expression reminded him of that woman who'd embarrassed him so badly before he left town. Had she managed to kill herself yet?

The question raised new memories of crushing that delectable body against his own. Perhaps he should visit Jenny tonight instead of going to White's. To distract himself, he returned to his mother's original complaint. "What is wrong with Lady Harriet—aside from her age?"

"Nothing. She is sweet and would make a perfect marchioness. But I realized yesterday that Reggie pays her no heed."

"Stays at her side, calls, driving—"

"He spends all his time talking to the girl's companion," she spat, interrupting. "He is infatuated with that witch!"

"Infatuated." He quizzed her thoroughly. "With a companion."

"How dare you treat me like one of your witless imitators."

"You are making less sense than they do."

"I am serious. How can he consider any companion, let alone that one! Her breeding is appalling. Granted, there is a remote connection to Wicksfield, but her father is a vicar in a parish so small he cannot earn more than twenty pounds a year. One of her brothers is apprenticed to a blacksmith. And her morals are outrageous. Lady Horseley heard that she's been jilted twice, and Lady Wicksfield admits that some very havy-cavy doings led to her parents' marriage. What does he see in her? Even her clothes are dowdy."

"Do not turn this into a Cheltenham tragedy, Mother," he said soothingly. "Reggie knows what he owes to the title. I cannot believe he would form an ineligible attachment."

"Then you are naïve!" she snapped. "I have seen his face when he looks at her. He has allowed an unscrupulous fortune hunter to dig in her claws. You must get rid of her."

"Me?"

"You. He refuses to listen to me. In fact he called me the most vile names when I mentioned her yesterday. We cannot allow the marquessate to fall into the hands of an encroaching mushroom. Aside from her breeding, she is too old to produce an heir."

"How old is she?" For the first time he felt a ripple of unease. Like Prinny, Reggie preferred older women. His mistresses had all been over forty.

"She must be nearly thirty. And her manners are appalling. Why only last night, I heard her order Lady Wicksfield to summon their carriage. Her employer! I don't know what threat she is using, but she runs that household. You must speak with Reggie. Make him recognize that she cares only for his title and wealth."

"Very well. I will talk to him."

"Thank you. Do so immediately. He is with her now."

"Where?"

"Just beyond the young men hovering around Lady Harriet. Near the terrace door."

He glanced around the palm. Reggie was facing him, his face alight with laughter. Even from this distance, he looked younger than his thirty-four years. Younger and happier.

His heart sank through the floor. Reggie's expression matched the looks that Randolph had exchanged with Elizabeth at dinner last night. How could he be so foolish?

The woman's back was turned, though her shoulders shook with laughter. How had she caught Reggie in her snare? Her hair was plain brown, pulled into a simple knot at her neck. A square of lace served as a spinster's cap. Her high-necked gown was merely serviceable. Yet she had captivated one of the Marriage Mart's prizes.

She must be beautiful and witty as well as scheming. A formidable adversary. So why could he raise no image of the woman?

He should never have left town. If he had stayed, he would have noticed that Reggie was heading for trouble. Working his way around the room, he exchanged greetings, quizzed an importunate sprig, and mildly cut a matron whose amorous antics were becoming too public.

"Can you spare me a moment, Reggie?" he asked quietly once he reached his brother.

Reggie jumped. "When did you return?"

"This afternoon."

"May I present Miss Joanna Patterson? Joanna, my brother."

Shock stalled his heart. Spectacles. Pert nose. Unbecoming blush spreading past her hairline. "We have met," he said coldly, even as his reaction confirmed that her bosom was anything but average. Was that what interested Reggie? It couldn't be her mind.

"M-my lord."

"A modest improvement in gowns since Bond Street." He deliberately quizzed her bodice, pleased when she flushed even brighter.

"H-how d-dare—"

"Too bad your mind hasn't improved."

"I could say the same, my arrogant lord," she snapped, finding her tongue. "Do you enjoy inflicting p-pain on p-people? How p-petty. No wonder Maximillian tried to b-bite you."

"Your position is already precarious, Miss Patterson," he said through clenched teeth, keeping his public facade intact with an effort. "Shall I send you back to the country where you belong?"

She blanched, making him curse under his breath. He had not meant to threaten her unless it was the only way to separate her from Reggie. But her lack of sense was obvious. She slowly nodded. "I overestimated your consequence, my lord. The measure of a man is the stature of those he considers his enemies."

The shaft hit home. But responding would trigger his temper—again. He could not survive another lapse into fury. It was miracle that he had yet to hear comment on their confrontation in Bond Street.

He maintained his dignity by turning to Reggie. "If I might have a word with you?" The situation could not be as serious as his mother thought. Reggie would never give her heart to an idiot, so he must be interested in less honorable activities. Something about Miss Patterson kindled unbelievable lust.

He gritted his teeth as Reggie whispered into her ear before bidding her a fond farewell.

"I've never seen you so rude, Sedge," said Reggie when they had reached an antechamber.

"I dislike encroaching mushrooms, especially schemers."

"Since when do you condemn without facts? Joanna is neither encroaching nor a mushroom. She is Lord Wicksfield's cousin, Sir Nigel Patterson's niece, and is related to many other noble families."

"Which still leaves her well below your touch, Reggie," he insisted, though her breeding was far better than their mother had claimed. "Stay away from her."

"How dare you dictate my friends!"

"I am serious, Reggie." He abandoned his usual indolence, for it served no purpose now. "I will not allow a fortune hunter to defile this family. Either leave her alone, or I will ruin her. I am amazed society has not already done so. Her behavior is appalling."

"I never expected you to become Mother's lapdog. I suppose she recruited you because I refused to heed her latest summons."

Sedge paced the room. "She expressed her concern. How could she not? But I act on my own and always have." He glared.

"This is unbelievable." Reggie ran both hands through his hair. "When Joanna described you, I thought she exaggerated, but it seems I do not truly know you, Sedge. Arrogant, presumptuous, and overbearing was how she put it. Also impossible to please. To that I must add credulous and stupid."

"Why? Because I refuse to sit idly by and watch you succumb to the wiles of a brainless mushroom?"

"Make up your mind. How can someone be both scheming and stupid?"

"She has bewitched you. How can you tolerate that stammer?"

"Joanna is right," he said, shaking his head. "Your arrogance is growing worse. Not only do you make ridiculous assumptions—and jump to the same erroneous conclusions that Crossbridge does—but you then try to force those notions down everyone's throat."

"How dare you compare me to Crossbridge?" he demanded. The man had been his nemesis for years, displaying no sense and less understanding.

"Because it fits. Joanna is an intelligent, educated woman who only stammers when embarrassed. There is nothing about her character or her breeding that would ever tarnish the marquessate—not that it matters. You have forgotten that I have no interest in marriage, as she well knows. Her future is already settled. I don't particularly like it, but she is satisfied. And I have no say in it in any case. She is a dear friend, and will remain so, but no more."

"A friend," scoffed Sedge, his fears growing until they nearly choked him. Gentlemen did not befriend ladies, especially unmarried ladies outside their own families.

Granted, he was close to several females, though only because they were married to his real friends. But honest friendship was impossible, for male and female minds were far too different. So why was Reggie lying? He almost had the tone right, but his eyes betrayed him. And his willingness to lie proved that the situation was worse than he'd thought.

Reggie's brows snapped together, reminding him that he was exerting no control over his own face. His thoughts must have shown.

"If you do anything to hurt her, I *will* offer for her— after cutting you dead in the most public place I can find," Reggie growled. "Not that she would willingly accept me, but if the alternative were losing her job, she would have no choice."

"You are obsessed, just as Mother claimed." He had never heard such a load of fustian.

"I knew she put you up to this. Why deny it?"

"She is concerned, and who can blame her? You have put yourself in danger. Miss Patterson is not the first to pretend innocence while scheming to better her situation."

"You insult me with every word. Either drop the subject or name your seconds. If you wish to be helpful, convince Mother to go home. She needs a new pastime. Father has undoubtedly been working too hard again. Perhaps she can slow him down."

"She won't go as long as we remain unwed." Sedge sighed at the admission. "She still hopes to see you shackled to Lady Harriet. Supposedly the girl is sweet."

"She is. Also unspoiled and caring."

"So why not offer?"

"How many times must I say it before you believe me," he snapped. "I will never wed anyone, and certainly not the most brainless chit I've encountered in years. I doubt she could produce one astute thought, let alone two to rub together. But this is no place for serious discussion. Shall we retire to White's?"

"An excellent suggestion." And one that would keep Reggie out of Miss Patterson's clutches for tonight. Perhaps by morning he could devise a plan to separate them permanently.

Reggie could protest all he wanted, but his eyes told a different story. And no matter what his own intentions were, a schemer could easily trap him. Miss Patterson might be content to wait for an offer at the moment, but eventually she would take matters into her own hands. Reggie's insistence that she was intelligent merely made her more dangerous.

Joanna watched Reggie and Lord Sedgewick move away, irritated at her performance. Why did the man always tie her tongue in knots? It had been years since she had fallen apart over a simple introduction.

Of course, she had never been formally introduced to a man who already held her in contempt. Lord Sedgewick's fury clearly conveyed his revulsion that Reggie's friendship might bridge the gulf between her and society— not that she would allow it to.

She had no intention of exploiting him. One way or another, her place was in the country. She might have wed a squire if she had felt even budding friendship for either of the two who had offered. One had been a harsh man who criticized every word she uttered. The other had wanted a mother for his children so he could remain in Gloucester with his mistress. Life as a governess seemed preferable.

Assuming she could pursue it. Lord Sedgewick's antagonism could ruin her. Though his suspicions were wrong, her pitiful stammering made her seem guilty of misconduct. And she had again let her temper explode into insults, giving him yet another grievance. If he had not already heard the jokes about their confrontation in Bond Street, he soon would. Her only luck was that so far no one knew the identity of the woman.

But she pushed the problem aside. Imagining disaster would merely distract her from duty. At least Reggie must now admit his brother's arrogance. He had been praising the man for days, almost convincing her that her initial impression had been wrong. But no more. Lord Sedgewick would never suit Harriet, no matter what Reggie thought—though to be fair, he had never actually suggested it. Harriet needed emotional support, not an arrogant lord with an explosive temper, a knack for jumping to hasty, erroneous conclusions, and an exaggerated belief in his own importance.

But this was not the time to quibble. Mr. Wethersby was leading Harriet into the next set. The girl was more animated than she had been in weeks.

Joanna bit her lip, cursing herself for allowing Reggie to distract her from business. Only now did she realize how often Mr. Wethersby had escorted Harriet in recent days. Allowing him to dance attendance on her had apparently given him the wrong impression. Even worse, Harriet appeared to harbor a *tendre* for the man.

*Now what?* She cursed her inattention. Again she had become blind to her surroundings.

Wethersby was ineligible. Aside from his age—he was barely three-and-twenty—his circumstances would never do. His income might support him comfortably, but he lacked both the fortune and title Lord Wicksfield expected. The earl would never approve.

So she must deflect his attentions and keep a closer eye on Harriet from now on. And she had to find out more about the girl's serious suitors.

*Stupid!* Why had she not asked Reggie's help? He could discover the facts behind the facades.

Harriet had four potentially serious suitors. Almont was the highest ranking. Lady Wicksfield adored him, demanding that Harriet choose between him and Reggie. But Joanna had reservations. Despite his constant attentions, he seemed abstracted. Did his apparent falseness arise from the contrived ennui demanded by society, or was he hiding something important? Perhaps he did not want a wife at all. He might be using Harriet to hold off his family's pressure. After all, Reggie had deflected his mother's demands by apparently dancing attendance on the girl. Unfortunately, that ploy was now exposed. Lord Sedgewick had seen through it in an instant.

The other suitors were even less likely. Lord Penleigh had the necessary title, but his fortune was merely decent, and he was more than twice Harriet's age. Mr.

Parkington was both wealthy and younger, but three older brothers and several nephews stood between him and a title. Lawrence Stoverson was clearly enamored, and his age of twenty-five made him seem approachable, but his fortune was only modest, and he grew quite irritated whenever anyone contradicted him. Not the sort to provide the support Harriet needed.

The music came to an end with no sign of Reggie—or of his brother, which was a relief. Harriet and Wethersby exchanged an intimate glance, reminding her of another unpleasant chore. Only pain could come of so unsuitable an attachment.

Again cursing her inattention, she coolly dismissed Wethersby, then welcomed Lord Penleigh, who had bespoken the next set. She would wait until they returned home before reminding Harriet of her duty. Hysterics were inevitable and might last some time. More than once, Harriet's sensibilities had left her bedridden.

But Wethersby must go. And not by way of a cut, which would tarnish Harriet, for there was no reason for a public set-down. Once Harriet accepted the reality of her position, Joanna could speak to Wethersby in private.

The price of her Season was steeper than she had expected.

# Chapter Six

∽

$F$ive days later, Joanna retreated to the corner of Lady Beatrice's drawing room, folding her hands primly in her lap. Harriet knew better than to open her mouth on morning calls unless addressed directly, so this portion of her day rarely posed problems. And she had even less concern today, since Lady Wicksfield had accompanied them. For the moment, gossip held sway over surreptitious shopping.

She hid a smile. Lord Wicksfield had warned her that the countess would find ways to overspend her allowance. Thus she had budgeted an amount to cover it. So far, Lady Wicksfield remained within it.

But her self-congratulation died under mortification as the memory of last night's ball sneaked back into her mind. How could she have been so foolish?

The ballroom had been suffocatingly warm, even with all the windows open. She was fetching the lemonade Harriet would need after finishing a sprightly reel when the girl's name had echoed from the far side of the refreshment room. Like a ninny, she'd turned to see who had spoken. But she hadn't stopped walking.

Heat again climbed her face. The moment of inattention had cost her dearly, for she'd collided with Lord Sedgewick in the doorway.

"Dear Lord, not you again," he'd drawled, pulling out a handkerchief. Lemonade stained his coat, his waistcoat, his pantaloons. It even spattered his cravat. When he raised his glass to glare at her, a dribble of lemonade distorted his view.

"I c-can't b-believe—" Her voice had died completely under the fury in his eyes.

"You are a menace to society, Miss Patterson."

"I didn't m-mean . . . I mean, I d-didn't see you."

"Why am I not surprised?" His voice remained languid, exhibiting the sangfroid he showed the world. But he exuded an intensity that left her reeling. "I suppose it is too much to expect you to leave town, but would you please stay out of the way? That potted palm near the entrance would provide an admirable barrier to protect us from your antics."

He'd retreated before she could wrap her tongue around a reply. He exchanged comments with numerous guests during his progress to the door, so she was unsurprised to hear the words *clumsy servant* buzzing through the room. Her own clothing had collected only two tiny drips, which increased her embarrassment.

Yet despite his fury, he had refrained from turning her into a laughingstock. She'd lain awake most of the night alternately cursing herself and pondering his actions. Why did she fall into scrapes only when he was nearby? And why had he not grabbed the opportunity to drive her from town—she knew he was scheming to end her friendship with Reggie.

Morning brought no answers, but she was determined that never again would he overset her to the point of stammering idiocy. Eight-and-twenty years of living should have built enough poise to face him down the next time they met. She had to do it for her own peace of mind. She was becoming obsessed with the man, watching for him everywhere, avoiding his vicinity lest she embarrass herself again. It was interfering with her duty to Harriet.

"The Lutterworths left town this morning," said Lady Beatrice, interrupting Joanna's memories.

"Hardly surprising," commented Lady Marchgate. "With his daughter gone and his reputation in tatters, he had little choice. And after Brumford's latest tirade, he probably feared for his safety."

Joanna returned to her brooding, having already heard about Brumford's attack on Lutterworth last night. He was so obsessed with Lutterworth's daughter that he'd had to be forcibly ejected from Brook's after uttering wild threats against Lutterworth and Lastmark. The incident revived some of her fears for Harriet.

Braxton was an impoverished baron who had been sniffing around Harriet for weeks. She had made the mistake of encouraging him before she discovered his circumstances, and he was furious over her change of heart. Had he developed the same obsession that plagued Brumford? Harriet was beautiful, sweet, kind, and had an air of fragility that appealed to many gentlemen. And society still believed that Wicksfield was wealthy.

How could she learn his motives without starting rumors that would harm them all? She had not seen Reggie since the Cunningham ball. Immediately after Lord Sedgewick had spirited him away, he had been summoned home to Glendale Close.

*Devil take the man*, she fumed for at least the hundredth time. What gave him the right to dictate his brother's friendships? Odious creature. She should have dumped the lemonade over his head.

Reggie had sent her a note before leaving, explaining the summons, but he had not known how long he would be away. She hoped he would return soon. Almont was poised to make an offer, but she had no way to investigate his background. She could not ask Wicksfield's help. Despite his vow to give Harriet a voice in her future, he would probably grab the first chance to resolve his own crisis, so she feared giving him an opportunity to change his instructions.

If only she knew someone else who could help!

She had put off speaking privately to Almont, hoping she could learn more about his circumstances before she had to make a decision. The Brumford imbroglio demonstrated that acceptance into society did not guarantee a man's character. An unscrupulous lord might pursue Harriet because she had no male protector in evidence. But at least she could acquit Almont of obsession. He sounded too insincere.

She stifled a sigh.

Even if Almont was serious, Harriet might refuse him. She was developing a surprising stubbornness and had already balked at avoiding Wethersby. Joanna's coolness had made him cautious, but he still demanded one set at every ball and continued to dance attendance on her. Joanna was afraid to press lest Harriet bolt. All she could do was pray that Reggie could either turn up information to make Wethersby acceptable or find a flaw that would convince Harriet to spurn him.

A wave of laughter swept the drawing room, startling her out of her thoughts. Honest laughter. Not the polite titters of elegant ladies.

"Not again!" exclaimed Lady Hartford.

"This very morning," confirmed Lady Debenham. "Lord Crossbridge has once more bared his peccadilloes to the world."

"But last time he was set up."

"Perhaps, though the implications were correct." She snorted inelegantly. "Crossbridge applies different standards to himself than to others. Despite pretending to be a strict judge of propriety, his own behavior is appallingly lax. And his judgment is worse."

"Quite true, alas," said Lady Beatrice. "I have never liked his self-righteousness."

"But what did he do now?" demanded Lady Stafford, who had arrived during the laughter.

Lady Horseley straightened, adopting a censorious tone. "As he had promised last evening, he brought me his copy of the *Botanical Magazine*, which contained a colored plate of the bee orchis. They are becoming quite rare."

"Not wildflowers!" gasped Lady Stafford, a hand to her throat. "How decadent! What is the world coming to?"

"Really, Penelope," hissed Lady Hartford. "You are doing it much too brown." But her face was alight with laughter.

Lady Beatrice's eyes gleamed.

"The magazine was perfectly innocuous, as you well know." Lady Horseley glared. "But when he tripped on entering my drawing room, he dropped it, allowing a print to flutter out—a most shocking print.''

"Not one of *those*!" Lady Stafford widened her eyes.

"Exactly."

"Appalling," agreed Lady Debenham. "How can so arrogant a prig justify having such a thing?"

"The poor man must have been terribly embarrassed," said Lady Hartford.''

"He turned red as Captain Harrington's uniform coat," confirmed Lady Horseley. "Claimed he'd never seen the cursed thing before, then accused Ellisham of tripping him to perpetrate another of Lord Sedgewick's pranks."

"Lord Sedgewick has made him a laughingstock more than once," Lady Debenham reminded her.

"But never without cause," said Lady Beatrice, a smile twitching the corners of her mouth.

"What will Crossbridge do now?" asked Lady Hartford. "Will he accost Lord Sedgewick at the Harwood ball tonight?"

"They might not be there," said Lady Beatrice. "Vauxhall's opening gala is tonight. We all know how Lord Sedgewick loves the gardens." Her smile more closely resembled a sneer.

"As does Crossbridge."

More knowing glances were exchanged.

Joanna ignored the subsequent chatter. Crossbridge's activities did not interest her. She did not even care that Lord Sedgewick, arbiter of fashion and manners, indulged in juvenile pranks.

Reggie was back. At last.


"We missed you, Reggie." Joanna smiled broadly when he joined her that evening. "I trust you encountered no trouble."

"Not at all. My father merely read me a new lecture on duty and responsibility." Anger flared briefly in his eyes, but mellowed into a warm smile. "You look enchanting."

"Fustian, Reggie. Don't waste your breath on flattery. I need your help."

He frowned. "Surely Sedge is not annoying you."

"The other way around, I fear." She blushed at the reminder of the lemonade episode. But Lord Sedgewick was watching her, so she refrained from explaining. This was not the ideal place to talk, but she must broach the subject before his brother spirited him away for another week. "Lord Wicksfield charged me with screening Harriet's suitors, but I know little beyond their public faces and fear that they may be hiding truths that would make them unsuitable."

"Such as?"

"If I knew that, I would not be asking."

"Forgive me for teasing. You are right that many facts are known only by other gentlemen. What do you look for in a suitor?"

"Lord Wicksfield is naturally concerned with family background and financial stability. But beyond that, I must find someone who will care for Harriet. Her ephemeral appearance is misleading, for she is not physically frail, but she is emotionally fragile. She needs a husband who can handle her megrims."

"I see." He drew her nearer the wall, lowering his voice. "Who is seriously courting her?"

"I know Almont means to make an offer. I've put him off in hopes of seeing you first. He strikes me as insincere."

"Astute of you. Almont needs to settle his succession—he recently had a falling-out with his brother, who is next in line. But he wants only an heir. He will invest no time or emotion in his wife, for his heart belongs to his mistress and their four children."

"Good heavens."

"He will offer Harriet his name, a large allowance, and the freedom to pursue her own interests once an heir is born. But that is all she can expect."

"She needs more—support during hysteria, tolerance for her mistakes, genuine affection."

"She won't get that from Almont. Who else might offer?"

"I am not sure. Lord Penleigh has been growing more particular."

"Good Lord. He's older than I am." He frowned. "His primary need is for a hostess. But he would expect her to arrange everything without help, whether for social occasions or political gatherings."

"I did not know he was active in politics."

"He is very involved in Parliament, and becoming more so each year. His mother currently serves as his hostess. He wishes to lessen her burden, but she strikes me as a lady who will cling to control until the day she dies—which could easily be twenty years or more; she is stubborn beyond belief."

She understood his hints. Penleigh would not care which woman ran his household. He lacked both the patience and the interest to train a wife or support her against his mother. Harriet would likely become Lady Penleigh's companion. "What about Mr. Parkington?"

"I doubt he is serious. He attaches himself to every new diamond, but he has yet to offer for anyone. His principal interest is horses. And since he has no title, I doubt he will wed without love."

"Which he shows no signs of feeling." And just as well. Harriet was terrified of riding. She would hardly enjoy a husband devoted to horses. No wonder she was cooler toward him than her other suitors. "What can you tell me of Mr. Stoverson?"

"Not much. He rarely visits the clubs. I've heard little against him, but I can ask. I believe we have mutual friends."

"And Mr. Wethersby?"

He sighed. "Like Stoverson, he is ten years my junior and moves in different circles."

"Can you find out his exact financial position? Harriet may have formed a *tendre* for him, but I doubt Lord Wicksfield will approve."

He met her eyes. "There is more to this than you are saying. What do you really wish to know?"

She glanced nervously at the crowd. "Call tomorrow morning, and I will tell you the whole story. This is not a propitious time."

"That sounds ominous." He frowned.

"Merely circumspect. London is too fond of gossip.

But what do you know of Mr. Reynolds and Lord George Sterne?"

He sighed. "When did they join her court?"

"The day you left."

"Dear Lord, I feel old. Reynolds is barely out of school, but he might be well suited. He is wealthy in his own right, is heir to the Earl of Bounty, and has close ties to the Marchioness of Woodvale."

"You sound uncertain, though. Is it only his age?"

"His father is venal. Not that it should matter. Reynolds refuses to go near the man. But the lad is very intelligent, so I must question whether he and Lady Harriet would really suit."

"I see. He would soon grow tired of her limited understanding."

"Or he might not. It would depend on how attached he is. As for Lord George, I find the man tedious beyond belief. We disagree on nearly everything. Since I avoid him, I cannot say whether he would suit. But Sedge would know. He keeps track of everyone."

"Do I?"

Joanna was hardly surprised that Lord Sedgewick had joined them, for she'd felt his eyes from the moment Reggie had arrived. But she blushed, wondering how much he'd heard. Despite his unexpected reticence over yesterday's clash, she didn't trust him to keep a secret. The man was too fond of gossip.

"Joanna was asking about Lord George Sterne. Would he make a convenable husband for Lady Harriet?"

Sedge raised his quizzing glass toward Harriet's set, pursing his lips as he examined her. "I shouldn't think so. He is a fastidious prig, while she seems rather flighty."

"So I feared." Joanna sighed, too concerned over Harriet's problems to feel nervous tonight. Success was looking grimmer every day. At the moment, Mr. Reynolds seemed the best choice, but she wasn't even sure he was serious, let alone what Harriet thought.

Lord Sedgewick turned to his brother. "Crossbridge has decided that you were behind this morning's embarrassment."

Reggie shrugged. "He blames both of us."

"I doubt it. I made peace with him two months ago. He knows I would not set him up again."

She looked at Reggie. "You refer to the incident at Lady Horseley's?"

He nodded.

"What exactly did he drop—between friends?"

"A rather suggestive drawing of a man and a woman." He winked. "But that is as much as I will say."

"If it was anything like the one my brother keeps in his desk, it was more than suggestive."

Reggie laughed. "I am shocked that you know of such things." His voice made a joke of the statement. "I am more shocked that you would snoop through your brother's effects. And I am appalled that a vicar's son would keep such a print where it might be found."

"As well you should be." Lord Sedgewick was not joking. "Mother is looking for you, Reggie. You had best find her before she stages a scene in public. She expected you to call upon your return."

Shrugging, Reggie excused himself.

Sedge turned a puzzled stare on Joanna. "You are not tongue-tied tonight."

"I am not embarrassed tonight."

"Don't you fear that I might ruin you?"

"Not in the least." She met his eyes. "It would hardly enhance your reputation to destroy someone from a lower class who poses no threat to your own—unless society considers lemonade a lethal weapon. I know you would gladly consign me to Hades, but since I am incapable of changing your opinion, it no longer matters. Thus I need not cringe when you appear." Unfortunately, her claims were false. His stares always made her feel guilty of some gross solecism. His very presence made her squirm. But she was determined to prove that she could control her voice and face, despite his renewed use of that dratted glass. "I do owe you an apology for last night, though, and my thanks for twice rescuing me from disaster."

"It was nothing." Having studied every inch of her costume, he turned his quizzing glass toward Harriet.

"Regardless of her age, she is rather young to be marrying."

"I agree, but her father wishes her to wed. My job is to screen her suitors and prevent her from forming unsuitable attachments."

That snapped his eyes to meet hers. "You?"

"If you are honestly shocked, then your opinion of me is lower than I thought. I fear your reputation for judging people to the inch must be overstated."

"Despite Reggie's claims to the contrary, you've given me little cause to consider you sensible."

Heat stained her cheeks. "Touché, my lord. You have indeed seen me at my worst, though I suspect your judgment is based on gender more than our brief acquaintance. Shallow beings rarely look past the surface."

"Are you not a female?"

"So are Lady Hartford, Lady Comstock, and Miss Washburn," she said, naming an intellectual, a gamester, and a brainless widgeon.

"Touché, yourself. So which of them is more like you? Until recently, I would have sworn it was Miss Washburn."

"It hardly matters, my lord. As Mary Wollstonecraft noted, a woman's sex even stands between her and rational converse."

"Ah, another of her radical devotees, I see."

"Hardly. The only radical notion I espouse is that women are as capable of rational thought as men—sometimes more so." Especially in his case. A rational man would hardly spend his days in vapid conversation.

"Perhaps you also agree with her comment that many men are capable of a tolerable understanding."

"Do you claim such an aptitude?" she dared, surprised to hear him counter her quote from *A Vindication of the Rights of Women* with a quote from *A Vindication of the Rights of Men*.

"Many believe so, though others might quibble."

She pursed her lips in thought. Reggie was right. Lord Sedgewick was quick-witted—which made his public persona more enigmatic than ever. "Perhaps we have both been guilty of judging on too little acquaintance. But why would an educated man choose to play the part of a mindless fribble?"

He flinched. "An odd question. I must wonder why you ask it."

"Rudeness. I spoke without thought, though the question itself is hardly odd. I will shortly assume a post as a governess. Training girls will be easier if I understand the society they must enter."

"An interesting ambition." His quizzing glass again examined her.

The music stopped, recalling her to duty. She had already passed too much time on conversation. "We can debate my ambitions another time, my lord. But for now, I must distract Lord Darnley. He is not a man I wish to see in Harriet's court."

"Quite unsuitable," he agreed. "But loath to take direction from women. With your permission, I will deal with him."

"Thank you."

Sedge left Darnley in the card room.

He had maintained his facade of aloof amusement during the entire confrontation with Miss Patterson, but it had been difficult. Every erotic dream he had suffered in recent days had risen up to torment him the moment he caught sight of her. It didn't help that Reggie had been right about her intelligence. When she was not in the throes of temper or embarrassed from dousing him with lemonade, she was a most intriguing woman.

The admission added to his turmoil, for Reggie was more enamored than even their mother had feared. He might claim simple friendship, but when he had arrived in the ballroom, his face had revealed the truth. His eyes had locked instantly onto Miss Patterson, joy stripping years from his countenance. He had all but ignored greetings in his haste to reach her side.

The sight had shocked Sedge to the core. The girl was not a beauty, but she had blushed becomingly, and the flirtatious light in her eyes made her seem the most desirable woman in the room. When he added her wit, intelligence, and a solid education, she became extremely dangerous.

He had never thought to see that look on Reggie's face and could only pray that the attachment had not passed beyond infatuation, for a hired chaperon of limited breeding was clearly ineligible to become Marchioness of Glendale. Surely Reggie was not blind to that reality. Pursuing her could only lead to pain.

Miss Patterson's emotions had been harder to gauge. He had surreptitiously watched her since returning to town—which was how he'd managed to collide with her last night; he had wanted to know if she was meeting someone in the refreshment room. She had flirted with no one else, yet he still did not know if she truly wanted Reggie or merely coveted one of the highest titles on the Marriage Mart.

Not that it mattered. She was a schemer, preying on Reggie's emotions in a way no other female had managed. A dangerous schemer, for she had the intelligence to adopt the ingenuous facade that hid her determination to leap above her station. Her tale of seeking a position was clever, but clearly false. She sought understanding of society only to hone the trap she was setting for Reggie.

Ignoring the voice protesting such arrogant assumptions, he whipped up his fury. If nothing else, it banished his unseemly lust.

Reggie's expectations attracted fortune hunters in droves—just as his own mystique did. Aside from taking elementary precautions to avoid being compromised, neither of them offered more than casual contempt to the creatures. But Miss Patterson had adopted a sneakier approach, hiding her ultimate goal behind a facade of friendship. That alone demonstrated her intelligence.

He exchanged laconic words with a friend, flirted lightly with Lady Jersey, and frowned young Cathcart into staying in the ballroom rather than slipping outdoors with Miss Cunningham. But his mind teased at the puzzle of Miss Patterson.

If she was merely a fortune hunter, he could probably buy her off. But if she cared for Reggie, opposition might make her dig in her heels. Revealing that a man of Reggie's rank could never offer for her could prompt a compromise.

Yet he did not truly fear compromise at this point, for she did not need to press the issue. Reggie was so tied in knots that he might toss propriety to the winds and actually make an offer.

So he must control Reggie. And he must assume that she had formed a *tendre* for his brother, making her the most dangerous of all the fortune hunters. Heading her off would be a challenge.

He would not underestimate her again.

# Chapter Seven

"Mother is in another of her takings." Harriet dropped wearily into a chair. "What am I to do, Joanna? She lectures me daily on duty and honor. Unless I attach a man of wealth and power, I will bring disgrace to a family whose reputation for sense and decorum has continued unblemished through five centuries."

"You are not the one threatening that reputation," Joanna reminded her. "Your father's own actions have brought him to this pass."

"But I have been designated to rescue him—as Mother reminds me daily. She interpreted Lord Ellisham's long absence as a sign of disinterest, so she is concentrating on Lord Almont. Why does she insist on him? Despite his incessant compliments, I cannot like the man, yet she is pressing me to bring him up to scratch."

"If he does not please you, then ignore him," Joanna said, grateful that she need not divulge her own reasons for disapproving Almont. Harriet had a history of revealing secrets when in the throes of excited chatter. Aside from the impropriety of an innocent girl discussing gentlemen's liaisons, it would do her no good to publicly insult Almont. "You know your father cares about your happiness as well as about solving his own problems. And now that Ellisham has returned, she may stop championing Almont."

"I don't see why. Ellisham pays me little heed."

"But she is unlikely to notice that. While it is true that Ellisham will make no offer, he can distract your mother. What do you think of Mr. Reynolds? He seems quite enamored."

Harriet stared at her foot. "I do not know. His dress is rather extreme."

"True, though he merely follows fashion as so many others do. And that will mitigate as he grows older." Last night's shirt points had resembled blinders, the impression enhanced by an enormous cravat that had thrust his chin halfway to the ceiling and had drawn a frown from Lord Sedgewick. "But he is sensible about most things."

"He is so educated that I fear to open my mouth lest I say something stupid."

"You need not be. Gentlemen do not expect ladies to be well-read."

"Most gentlemen feel that way," agreed Harriet. "Almont all but patted me on the head when I asked him to explain the difference between helping the war veterans from his village, which he approves, and helping the tenants evicted from his estate by an enclosure act, which he opposes. I'm not to fret over such complexities. But Mr. Reynolds is different. Lady Woodvale raised him, so he is accustomed to intellectual women."

"You have a point," she conceded, surprised by the astute observation. She had known that Harriet could be sensible, but now she wondered if the girl was smarter than anyone gave her credit for. Perhaps her frequent *faux pas* arose from immaturity rather than incompetence. "So we will not encourage Mr. Reynolds. But there are many other gentlemen. I am sure we can find one capable of satisfying both you and your father."

"No such paragon exists." Tears appeared in Harriet's eyes.

"Nonsense. The Season is not yet over. New gentlemen take note of you every day."

Harriet looked doubtful, and with her new suspicions of the girl's intellect, Joanna had to agree. While it was true that more gentlemen were drifting into Harriet's court, most were young bucks with no serious intentions. The older ones had been courting girls who'd accepted others, so there was little chance they would form a new attachment this Season.

"A breath of fresh air will drive away these megrims," Joanna said briskly, needing to remain optimistic. "Fetch your pelisse and that new bonnet. A walk will make you feel better."

Wicksfield House was only a block from Hyde Park. Joanna preferred walking in the morning, for carriages jammed the park during the fashionable hour. Today, a fresh breeze drove the soot and smells toward the city, leaving the sky clear over Mayfair. Birds sang merrily from shrubs and trees. Flowers nodded, saturating the air with their sweet nectar. A dog barked in the distance.

"This feels like home today," said Harriet wistfully.

"Are you not enjoying London?"

"Y-yes." Guilt flashed in her eyes. "The balls and theater are quite exciting. And I've never seen such elegant gowns." ·

"But?"

"I miss the Harper girls," she admitted, naming the squire's daughters. "And the open fields. I feel caged in town. The people are nicer at home, too. They never mind if I trip over a carpet or prefer Rose Parker's puddings to Cook's elegant cakes." Rose was a tenant. "In London, I can never relax. There are rules about everything, and Mama scolds when I make mistakes. You are more tolerant, but I know I will never keep it all straight."

She was right, conceded Joanna. Lady Wicksfield pounced on the slightest slips. "You are doing very well, Harriet. No one has said anything against you. And Lady Pressington's musical evening was quite successful. Lady Cowper swore you sang like an angel, and even Lady Jersey complimented you."

"Mama did not. She was furious that I changed songs without telling her."

"Your choice was better." They had held this discussion before, but Harriet still harbored doubts about her small rebellion. "Robert Burns is quite popular, and your selection reflected both your age and your sweet nature. Her suggestion would not have worked as well.

You cannot carry off teasing allusions to things you don't understand."

Harriet's forehead creased in concentration. "What are you talking about?"

"She wanted you to play the coquette, hoping Almont would respond with an offer. But that is not a role you could manage." In truth, Harriet's angelic performance had worked much better. Joanna had been deflecting him ever since.

Discussion ceased when a gentleman approached. Wethersby.

"Miss Patterson. Lady Harriet."

Harriet flushed.

His eyes dueled briefly with Joanna's, acknowledging her attempt to discourage him and his refusal to comply. Since this walk had been her own idea, there was no question of an assignation. Thus she nodded stiffly.

He turned to Harriet. "Will you be at the theater tonight?"

"Of course, my dear sir," she exclaimed before Joanna could stop her. "We will be in Lady Thurston's party. Do you know what we are to see?"

"Shakespeare's *Othello*, though you will find it rather tragic." He turned to accompany them as they resumed their walk. "But you will enjoy the farce. They are performing Sheridan's *School for Scandal*. I will make a point of visiting your box during the first interval."

"We will welcome you."

He cast another glance at Joanna, a twinkle lighting his eyes, though he kept his face rigidly neutral.

The path was too narrow to allow her to remain at Harriet's side, so she fell in behind them as Mr. Wethersby carefully outlined the plots of both plays. She was torn between gratitude and annoyance. He was making sure that Harriet enjoyed the evening—and doing it in a way that was not condescending. Yet in the very process of helping her, he was feeding her *tendre*.

Devil take the man! Did he not realize that he was placing Harriet in a difficult position? How could he expect to offer for an earl's daughter? Even discounting

Wicksfield's problems, Wethersby was merely a baron's younger son.

She nearly interrupted to claim a pressing errand, but something stayed her hand. He was speaking now of his home in Yorkshire, gently probing Harriet for her views on country and city life. After describing the estate he had recently inherited from an uncle, he allowed her to compare it with Wicksfield Manor.

Harriet had not been this relaxed since arriving in London. Her voice was more confident, lacking that note of uncertainty that usually made her sound on the brink of hysteria. Her hands flowed in natural gestures. And her comments again showed more awareness than usual. Was it fear and insecurity that made her seem so dull-witted? Since Joanna had met her just before leaving for London, she had no points of comparison. But if insecurity was responsible for her demeanor, then Wicksfield was doing her a vast disservice by presenting her now. As Lord Sedgewick had noted, she was far younger than her years—except with Wethersby.

She shivered.

"I must leave you now," he said regretfully. "Remaining longer would draw unwanted attention, despite the presence of the most estimable Miss Patterson."

He turned to face a crestfallen Harriet, allowing Joanna a view of his face. It reflected a level of caring she rarely saw in gentlemen. Not mindless infatuation, which half the bucks in town affected, but a warmth that ran much deeper. His eyes locked with Harriet's as he said his farewells.

Joanna automatically muttered conventional phrases, rocked to the core by the look they had just exchanged. Wethersby loved Harriet. Intensely and irrevocably. And she returned his feelings in full measure.

Disaster loomed. Unless Reggie turned up a secret fortune, the Honorable Jonathan Wethersby was in no position to help Wicksfield obtain a loan. She could not imagine the earl granting permission for a match. He might pay lip-service to allowing Harriet a voice in her future, but when faced with the reality of an offer, his own interests would come first.

Yet she had to admit that Harriet was not suited to the social whirl a gentleman of high standing would demand. The girl was uncomfortable in society, where she must think through every comment before speaking. As she had admitted only an hour ago, she preferred the country. Her inclinations would appall the high sticklers.

The admission placed a new burden on Joanna's shoulders. Honesty admitted that Harriet would be happiest with Wethersby. They had not met a single gentleman who would suit better—at least none that she had noticed, she admitted, guiltily aware that her own dereliction to duty had allowed this friendship to grow unchecked.

Silently blowing out a long breath, she faced the consequences. Not only would this match expose Wicksfield's problem to the world by forcing him to sell the town house and tighten his belt even further, but it would subject him to Lady Wicksfield's wrath. The countess combined limited understanding with a determination to get her own way that turned her into a harridan when she was crossed. In fact, Joanna now feared the woman had less intelligence than her daughter.

These suspicions were confirmed the moment they reached the house.

"Where have you been?" demanded Lady Wicksfield. "Ellisham called half an hour ago. When he discovered Harriet's absence, he left."

"We were walking in Hyde Park, Mama," said Harriet.

"How dare you leave when a gentleman might call? If you have thrown away a chance to snare a marquess's heir, I will never forgive you."

"It is well before calling hours, my lady," pointed out Joanna. "We could hardly have expected him." Though she should have known he would call early, if only to avoid Lady Wicksfield.

"He must wish to make an offer."

"I doubt it." How had Lady Wicksfield arrived at so absurd a conclusion? "All the gentlemen know that they must first speak to Lord Wicksfield. But even if his thoughts are moving that direction, he would hardly change his plans just because we were away when he called without warning."

It took several minutes to calm the woman's nerves, but at least Reggie's call would deflect her attention from Almont. She would prefer a marquess's heir to a baron, particularly since the Glendale fortune was larger.

If Lady Wicksfield publicly pursued Reggie, Almont might give up and choose someone else. Already the Season bored him. He wanted to settle his succession so he could return to his other family.

But nothing was certain, and even losing Almont would not resolve her growing problems. She had under-estimated Lady Wicksfield's ability to spend money— again betraying her naïveté, she admitted. The allowance for this Season had seemed enormous compared to a vicar's budget, but London prices were appalling. The funds would expire in another fortnight—sooner if Lady Wicksfield was hiding additional debts. So she must think. The earl would only consider Wethersby's suit if she found an alternate way to fill his empty purse.

Sedge slipped into an isolated corner of Hatchard's so he could relax his public face while pondering this latest information. He had enjoyed running into his friend Thomas, at least until that last *on-dit* had stabbed icy fear into his gut. Why had Reggie been paying a call at Wicksfield House at ten in the morning? That was long before acceptable calling hours. In fact, few people were even awake then—except servants.

Miss Patterson?

The cold spread. Reggie had spent four days out of town, during which their father had berated him for re-maining unwed—and probably for his attentions to Miss Patterson; their mother would have reported them. The moment he spotted her on his return, his face had filled with joy—as had hers, he admitted grimly. They had talked seriously for an entire set, then openly flirted when he'd joined them. Reggie had called on her at a time when her employer was likely to be asleep.

It was not a pretty picture.

So how could he save Reggie from making a mistake

he would rue for the rest of his life? Pressure was not
the answer. Their parents' tirades had prompted Reggie
to dig in his heels and deny even obvious truths. Sedge
doubted he could do any better, but he had to try.

"Miss Patterson." He rapidly donned his public facade
when the author of Reggie's troubles appeared around
a bookcase.

"My lord." She cocked her head, then grinned. "Now
why might London's most fatuous fribble be skulking in
the corner of a bookshop?"

"Hardly a fribble, Miss Patterson," he drawled. "I
work quite hard at what I do."

"And what might that be?"

"Ornamentation. Without my efforts, London would
be quite dull—ill-dressed men, dowdy women, even mis-
matched decor in drawing rooms and boudoirs." He
shivered theatrically. "Can you imagine the horror? It
took me an hour to dissuade Lady Duncan from adding
an orange tapestry to her scarlet drawing room. And
Lady Taverstock actually contemplated mixing delicate
French tables with Egyptian crocodile couches."

"A dreadful mistake, to be sure," she replied, apparently tongue in cheek. "Doing it more than a little
brown, I believe."

He stifled a chuckle. "Not at all. The world piles many
duties on my poor shoulders. In addition to staving off
esthetic nightmares, I must entertain a society larded
with courtcards, goosecaps, and totty-headed rattles.
Fortunately, society cooperates by providing me with
abundant stories."

"Like the empty-headed ninny who couldn't spot a
horse at ten paces?" Her voice had chilled.

She must have overheard that particular performance.
"I intended you no harm, Miss Patterson, and would
have changed nothing had I known you were listening.
Granted, you probably felt embarrassed, but no one
could have deduced your identity from my words. And
life is more pleasant if one can appreciate its humorous moments."

Her mouth twitched. "I suppose there is a certain ab-
surdity in discerning a minuscule mop like Maximillian

while remaining blind to a team of fifteen-hand carriage horses clattering across the cobblestones."

"I would have called them sixteen hands, myself."

"Of course. How blind of me."

He joined her laughter. "You see? Humor enlivens any day. Did you note Mr. Rosewood last evening?"

"Rosewood . . ." Her frown suddenly cleared. "Ah, the spotty-faced youth in the purple coat and flowered waistcoat. Is he the one who tripped Miss Applegate?"

"Twice. He entertains a passion for her, poor boy, though she was absent the day comely faces were awarded. To make amends for his clumsiness, he spirited her into the garden."

"It must have worked. They were blushing on return," she noted.

"All too well. He plans to make her an offer."

"At his age? He cannot be above nineteen."

He twirled his quizzing glass. "Will her father object? Given her looks and lack of dowry, she can hardly do better. But one must pity the poor girl."

"Why, if he truly cares?"

"Your ignorance is showing." He smiled. "Miss *Rose* Applegate to wed Mr. *Rose*wood. The world will think her a stutterer for the rest of her days."

She joined his laughter. "She will survive, though, for few people will use both names. I will reserve my sympathy for gentlemen whose parents encumbered them with monstrosities. Like Lester Lyle Leonard, Lord Lipping. Try saying that after a few glasses of Christmas punch."

"Cecil Sherman has the same problem. But you cannot always blame insensitive parents. Mr. Marblehead has wished for a title for years—you can imagine how his schoolmates plagued him."

"Probably no more than they plagued Peter Padden, the squire's son. To this day he cringes at any mention of puddings."

They shared a congenial smile, but Joanna soon grew serious. "This is an opportune meeting, my lord. I will not see Reggie this evening as we are promised to the theater. Would you ask him not to call tomorrow? Lady Wicksfield imputed the most ridiculous motives to him this morning. I would not wish her to do anything unscrupulous."

"Why did you not tell him before he left?" he asked.

"I was from home at the time." She pulled a book from the shelf. "I must hurry if we are to manage today's calls." And she was gone.

He frowned after her. The chit was the most accomplished actress he'd seen on or off a stage. She played the ingenuous companion to perfection, even using him to send a veiled message to her target.

Poor Reggie. He'd probably been caught before he realized his danger. She exuded an aura worthy of the Sirens. He felt it himself, though he refused to succumb. But for the first time, he could sympathize with Ulysses tied to his mast. Even knowing the danger she posed, he was tempted to test the waters.

Joanna paid little attention to the stage that evening. Nor did she turn her usual cool stare on Wethersby when he joined them. She was scanning the other boxes, hoping for inspiration. How was she to solve Wicksfield's problem?

Gossip claimed that Lord Northrup had made a fortune during the chaos following Waterloo. But other investors had lost equal fortunes by believing the wrong rumors. Even if the opportunity arose for another windfall, how did one decide which way to bet?

Lord Hartford made a tidy income from breeding and training hunters, but Wicksfield lacked expertise in that field. And building a successful stable took time.

Mr. Fulwood had returned from several years in India with a fortune, but again, that would not work for Wicksfield. Many men had left the country in search of riches, but few returned as nabobs. Disease, accidents, and failure took a steep toll.

Was anyone else willing to back a loan? It was a tricky question, for gentlemen drew a sharp line between business and friendship. She could not summon the courage to approach even Reggie with such a suggestion.

But thoughts of Reggie recalled her latest meeting with his brother. She almost wished he had remained furious with her. Acknowledging his wit made him far too intriguing.

She stifled a shudder. How could she entertain any liking for a man who despised her? He might have changed tactics, but he remained determined to destroy her friendship with Reggie. It was a fact she must never forget.

But she had. When he had smiled at her in Hatchard's, she had forgotten everything—which was incredibly stupid. Never again could she allow her judgment to waver. Matching wits with a fatuous fribble of uncertain temperament could only hurt Harriet.

Crossbridge entered a box across the theater, drawing her attention. The very proper Lady Hortense Leigh accompanied him, as did her parents.

"He is still furious over his recent embarrassment," whispered Lady Thurston to Lady Wicksfield, loudly enough that Joanna heard her in the rear of the box—evidence of a hearing problem she refused to acknowledge.

Most of the audience was also staring at him. Reggie's hints bore little resemblance to current gossip, which now suggested that the print depicted every perversion known to mankind. Young cubs mobbed Crossbridge, demanding to see the infamous illustration—and offering shocking sums for the privilege.

"How can he show his face in public?" demanded Lady Wicksfield.

"He has vowed vengeance on the culprit," said Lady Thurston.

"On Ellisham?"

"Ellisham was merely a pawn. He probably planted the print when he called on Crossbridge that morning. And why would he visit Lady Horseley if not to trip Crossbridge? Everyone knows he despises the lady. But Lord Sedgewick must have been behind the incident. He is the only man in town who could force Ellisham to behave so basely."

Joanna ignored their growing indignation. Crossbridge kept his eyes on the stage, blithely ignoring the avid stares of half the audience. How would it feel to be the object of so much curiosity? He must dread each new outing.

Yet she had to wonder how the illustration had gotten into that magazine. Both brothers had denied complicity. Despite rumors to the contrary, she believed them. Reggie would never have done so, and even the most avid gossips admitted that Lord Sedgewick had avoided Crossbridge this Season. So perhaps Crossbridge was not as staid as his public image implied. Most of society hid behind facades. Why not him?

Snatches of conversation drifted in from adjoining boxes, many describing Lord Sedgewick's earlier pranks against Crossbridge. Some were hilariously inventive, reminding her sharply of her brother Jeremy. Was that why she felt drawn to him? Maybe he exuded a faint air of home.

# Chapter Eight

❧

Joanna stared as she trailed Harriet and Lady Wicksfield into Lady Warburton's ballroom. The annual masquerade was a twenty-year-old tradition that offered innocent maidens the excitement of a costume ball while protecting them from the ribaldry common at the public masques. Only the highest sticklers received invitations.

Lady Warburton had turned the room into a forest glade for this year's festivities. Huge pots held trees whose outstretched fingers brushed the ceiling. Lanterns festooned their branches, supplementing the thousand candles blazing from sconces and chandeliers. Banks of flowers, thickets of ferns, and even a babbling brook adorned corners and alcoves. A wall of mirrors doubled the effect.

Beneath this canopy surged an incongruous assortment of characters—Romans and Greeks, gods and goddesses, rulers and rogues of every description, Shakespearean characters, knights and monks, cavaliers, courtiers, and ladies-in-waiting.

Joanna wrestled her face under control. She might not belong to this select company, but that was no excuse for behaving like an awestruck rustic.

Harriet's blue eyes danced with excitement from behind her mask. She was costumed as a dainty shepherdess, blonde ringlets framing her face, one hand clasping a token crook. Other shepherdesses glided through the crowd, but none surpassed her beauty.

In contrast, Joanna was clearly a chaperon. The plain brown domino covering her hair and gown made her nearly invisible amidst this riot of color. Her unmasked face also set her apart.

Lady Wicksfield dove into the crowd, zigzagging around clusters of gossips. The crush made it difficult for Joanna to keep up. More people jammed the ballroom than at any other event she had attended, though the first set had not yet begun.

"Parkington has a new pair of bays—"

She narrowly escaped being stabbed by a Roman centurion's sword.

"Lady Glendale canceled tomorrow's at-home. What do you suppose—"

A collision with Henry VIII's padded belly reminded her that she was just a clumsy country girl who didn't belong here. She should not allow gossip to distract her attention. Mortified, she mumbled an apology, her face flaming hotter when a ripping noise proved that she had stepped on someone's hem as she backed away.

By the time she escaped, a fat friar obscured Harriet. But a bright green scarf fluttered from the tall cap of the countess's lady-in-waiting costume, allowing her to continue in the right direction.

"Crossbridge may have to rusticate—"

She skirted a band of improbable pirates.

"—the bear was on the upper landing."

Exhaling in relief, she joined Harriet in a relatively clear alcove. The jostling seemed worse than usual, more evidence that she was nearly invisible tonight.

Within minutes, Harriet's court clustered around them, and Lady Wicksfield wandered off to gossip with two other ladies-in-waiting.

"No costume?" asked Reggie, startling her. She had not seen him approach.

"I am only a companion," she reminded him.

"Perhaps, but you would make a marvelous Boadicea. Far better than Miss Heathmark." He nodded toward one of the Season's failures. The girl's costume would hardly attract a suitor. It emphasized her boyish figure and grim visage. She appeared ready to run her sword through anyone who approached.

"Perhaps you should dance with her," Joanna suggested. "Attention from a conquering hero might soften her face." Reggie was dressed as Julius Caesar, choosing the armor of the war years rather than the flowing toga in which the man had died. He made a splendid general.

"You are the most kind-hearted lady I know, Joanna. How can I refuse so generous a request?"

"I am sure you could find a way if you wanted to."

"Perhaps." He paused. "I have the information you requested. Sedge gave me your message, but this is no place to talk, either."

"The trials of being a friend rather than family. But Lady Wicksfield's reaction to your call was too rapacious for comfort. I refuse to expose you to whatever scheme she may have devised."

"Thank you. She is as bad as my mother. Can you slip out during one of the sets? I will secure an antechamber."

"That should work." And it would give her a chance to discuss Lord Wicksfield's problem. A sleepless night had convinced her that she needed help if she was to find a solution. "The fourth set will be best. Harriet's card should be full by then."

As he moved off, she returned her attention to Harriet—but not soon enough. Lord Almont was leading the girl out for the first set. It the was second time in three days that he had claimed that important spot, which would firmly link their names in the eyes of society. Harriet's reputation could suffer when she turned him down.

But all Joanna could do was make sure it did not happen again. At least he had claimed only the one set. She would counter him by giving Wethersby two sets, including the supper dance. And she must let Almont know that an offer was unwelcome.

Sedge deliberately arrived late for the Warburton masquerade. His sojourn at Meadowbanks had convinced him that he must wed, but it had done little to relieve his ennui—unless it had returned because he was making no progress.

He had spoken to widows every day. Despite having to hide his motives from the eyes of everyone in society,

he believed that he had given each candidate a reasonable chance to attract his interest. His requirements were
simple enough, but so far he had found no one who
merited a second look.

Surprisingly, there was no single stumbling block. Now
that he was looking for it, he had found many ladies of
reasonable intelligence. Others were gracious hostesses,
possessed admirable style, or even espoused some of his
less public causes. But even those who seemed perfect
on paper left him feeling cold. Analyzing why added
new requirements to his list every day.

*Arrogant. Presumptuous. Impossible to please.*

Reggie's quote echoed in his ears. He could hear Miss
Patterson saying it, for she was not shy about speaking
her mind. Not that she was right. A man needed standards if he was to maintain his position. Was it his fault
that London's widows failed to meet those standards?
Everyone was too something . . .

Too stupid. But he could not endure stupidity. Yes,
he tolerated a great deal of it in town, but never in
private. His friends were well educated, as were their
wives. His own wife must fit into that group.

Too greedy. He expected to share his sizable fortune
with his wife. But he could not accept anyone whose eye
dwelt solely on his purse. Nor could he stomach reckless
gaming or spending. He'd already rejected two candidates because they seemed too fond of cards.

Too demanding. He wondered if the late husbands of
several widows had welcomed death as a release from
an unendurable existence. The women were harridans
who would make his life a misery if he made the mistake
of offering. Some reminded him too strongly of his
mother, who ruled the Close with an iron hand.

Yet he had to choose someone. He had already dismissed the young ladies and the older spinsters. Must he
search in the country after all? How could he judge social aplomb away from London?

But a larger problem was his mother. She would op-
pose anyone of resolution and intelligence, refusing to
relinquish her power without a fight. If Reggie remained
adamant, his own wife would produce a future marquess.

He might have to live at the Close for a time while the boy learned about his inheritance. Thus he must devise a way to blunt his mother's inevitable antagonism. And one of these days, he must discuss the future with Reggie. Was he truly serious, or was he merely reacting to their parents' demands?

But that was for later. First, he must approve Lady Warburton's masquerade. And there were still half a dozen widows to examine.

The receiving line was gone, though Lady Warburton would be hovering nearby, suffering agonies because he had not yet arrived. His power was getting out of hand. Setting fashion modes was one thing. But lately, his choice of entertainments was focusing either envy or scorn on society's hostesses. Two ladies had fallen into hysterics because he had left town last week rather than attend their balls. The situation was becoming absurd— and patently unfair to the losers. No man could attend everything.

He grimaced.

Thus he had an additional incentive for marriage. Once he wed, the bucks would choose a new icon from among London's beaux, and the hostesses would follow suit, for their regard stemmed from his ability to produce eligible gentlemen at Marriage Mart events. Where he went, others followed.

But that was for the future.

Mentally girding his loins for an evening of revelry, he climbed the stairs. As he reached the top, Reggie emerged from the ballroom and headed for the first antechamber, frowning when he found it occupied. Only then did he notice his brother.

Sedge suppressed his own frown. He had seen countless gentlemen go through the same motions, but he had not expected Reggie to be arranging an assignation. He could think of only one female who might be meeting him.

"I was beginning to think you weren't coming," said Reggie, joining him at the top of the stairs.

"If I had known you were looking for me, I would have arrived earlier. Is there a problem?"

"I am not sure. Mother has commanded that I wait on her at the ungodly hour of nine tomorrow."

His spirits lightened. "She also commanded my appearance, but all is postponed. Father summoned her home this afternoon, claiming a health crisis. She left at once."

Reggie paled. "You don't suppose he suffered another attack!"

"Of course not. We would all have been summoned in that case. He probably wants a personal report on your affair with Miss Patterson."

"I'm not—"

"I know. I believe you have no designs on the chit. Just watch out for traps."

"Joanna would never do anything underhanded. She is far too caring. In fact, she sent me to dance with Miss Heathmark an hour ago, suggesting that my attentions would soften the girl's expression enough to attract other partners. And she was right. Three cubs signed her card when our set was over."

"I'm not surprised."

Reggie sighed. "I doubt Father wants a simple report—he can get that by post. It is more likely that he wants a sympathetic audience for his ranting. I threatened to leave the country if he did not cease his demands."

"You didn't!" But the words stuck in this throat as a new arrival mounted the stairs. "Good God! What is she doing here?" He turned his most ferocious glare on his mistress.

Jenny LaRue was dressed—barely—as Aphrodite, her diaphanous costume revealing every inch of her notorious body. Another time, he might have appreciated the sight, but tonight fury obscured all else.

"I love your costume, Sedgie," she said breathlessly, tripping up the steps to his side. He was garbed as an Elizabethan courtier in padded trunk-hose, embroidered doublet, and narrow ruff. "Who is your friend?"

Jenny was not overly bright—her talents were purely physical—but he'd never dreamed she could be this stupid. "What are you doing here?" he demanded, ignoring the sudden confusion on her face. "How did you get in? Lady Warburton is very strict about who receives invitations to these affairs."

"B-but you invited me."

"Never."

"Of course you did!" Pouting, she pulled out a letter.

"This is a forgery." He handed it to Reggie. The writing was only vaguely similar to his and contained endearments he would never have uttered, let alone put on paper.

"Not his hand," agreed Reggie. "Someone hoaxed you, Miss LaRue. The question is who and why."

"Later," Sedge suggested. "We must get her out of here before anyone sees that costume."

"Damn you!" Her voice turned strident. "My invitation is just as good as yours. And what's wrong with my dress? It's a bloody masquerade, isn't it?"

"The invitation was also forged, Jenny." He ground his teeth at her language. What had he ever seen in this low-class wench? "Lady Warburton only welcomes society's highest sticklers. Both your profession and that costume make you ineligible."

"I will see her home and explain," offered Reggie, grasping Jenny's arm. "Did you wear a cloak, my dear?"

"Of course I did! It's windy." She pulled free of his grasp. "But I ain't goin' nowhere with no stranger."

"Jenny—"

"No. You won't ruin my evening. I've dreamed of this for days. If Lady Warburton asks me to leave, I'll go, but you're probably lying about her, too. You just want to hurt me."

Sedge ignored her, addressing Reggie over her head as his arm blocked her progress. She had to be half seas over to behave so recklessly, for she must know she would never find another protector if he denounced her. "Carry her if you have to. If she says another word, gag her. I will deal with the footmen who let her in." He didn't bother introducing Reggie. The less Jenny knew, the better. The situation was precarious enough already.

Footsteps approached from the ballroom, dropping his heart into his shoes. If Lady Warburton saw Jenny, his reputation would be in shreds. Everyone knew who paid her bills.

But the woman who appeared was worse. Miss Patterson had nearly reached the first antechamber when she spotted the group near the stairs. Her face lit with pleasure.

"Good heavens, it's Mary Jones!" she exclaimed, rushing up to throw her arms around Jenny's shoulders. "Or Mary Johnson, I should say. What are you doing in London? How is your family? Are you going home at last? Your father longs to see his grandchildren. He talks about them constantly. But why didn't you tell him you were accepted in the highest circles? He would be so proud!"

Sedge's heart stopped altogether. He would be a laughingstock by morning. Miss Patterson now had the perfect revenge for any embarrassment he might have caused her. She could turn the tables on him quite thoroughly. One word would convince her that he had invited Jenny. She already held him in contempt. And society would follow suit, of course. His history of playing pranks had finally circled back to bite him.

Jenny opened her mouth as his brain groped for some way to avert disaster. But the words that emerged were worse than any he had anticipated.

"Shut up," she hissed, her face twisting into an unrecognizable mask of terror. "You got the wrong horse by the tail. I ain't this Mary creature." Shoving Miss Patterson viciously aside, she raced down the stairs.

"Damn!" He reacted too late to save Miss Patterson from cracking her head against a baluster. "Catch her, Reggie. Find out what the devil is going on," he added, for Reggie was staring, his love clear in his horrified eyes. "I will look after this one."

He scooped Miss Patterson into his arms as Reggie reluctantly headed for the door. Her face was stark white in sharp contrast to her brown domino. Carrying her into an empty room, he laid her on a couch.

Her pallor and cold hands terrified him. How could he explain her injury? Claiming that she had slipped would make her look clumsy and might affect her position. Yet the truth would precipitate the very scandal he was trying to avoid.

He slid back her hood and removed her spectacles, then unpinned her hair so he could examine the sizable lump on the back of her scalp. Though the bleeding was minimal, her breathing seemed labored.

Unfastening the domino, he pulled it away from her throat, then jerked the feathered cap from his head so he could press an ear to her chest. Her heart beat steadily. But still she lay like a corpse.

*Damnation!* he fumed, running his fingers through his hair. Why had she tried to snare Reggie? If she had not talked him into an assignation, neither of them would have been in the hallway. Miss Patterson would not be hurt, and he could have gotten Jenny away with no one the wiser.

"Wake up, damn you," he growled.

Reggie would be furious if she was seriously hurt. The look on his face matched those Sedge had often seen on Randolph's. Could he prevent Reggie from making a fool of himself, or had this affair already progressed too far? But speculation could wait until later, he reminded himself. How was he to explain her injury?

Her hands were icy. Chafing warmed them but did nothing to awaken her. Shaking made no difference. Nor did cursing. He was ready to swallow his pride and fetch help when the color finally seeped back into her face.

She stirred. "What—" Her face snapped into a frown.

"Lie quiet, Miss Patterson," he suggested, finally able to banish the most pressing fears. "You fell and bumped your head."

"Fell?" She frowned, blinking several times. Her eyes were an unexpectedly rich brown now that spectacles did not obscure them. "Where is Mary? Why has she treated her parents so badly?"

"You mistook Miss LaRue for someone else," he said, inexplicably protecting her from the sordid side of society. Jenny must be hiding a serious fall from grace. Was she better born than anyone knew? But why then had her accent lapsed so badly?

"Hardly. Mary was my closest friend for years." Her

voice slurred, as if she were only half conscious. "We did everything together. Another person might share her face—after all, I've not seen her in quite a while—but I could never mistake the scar on her shoulder. I put it there when we were ten. We weren't supposed to be out on the church roof, so when I heard Papa coming, I told her to jump, then pushed her off when she balked. She landed badly, but she forgave me long ago, so why wouldn't she talk to me?"

She sounded bewildered. He could feel heat climbing his face as he tried to compose a reply. "This is no time for conversation," he finally declared. "I will fetch Lady Wicksfield to look after you."

"No!"

He glared.

"You have done enough, my lord." Finally wide awake, she struggled to rise.

"You should rest longer." But he helped her sit, supporting her shoulders when her face paled. His hand shook with the contact, infuriating him. How could he feel attraction at a time like this?

"I will be fine in a moment." She tilted her head toward the ballroom, then exhaled in relief. "The same set. Was I unconscious for long?"

"Only a few minutes."

"Excellent. Leave me now. I will compose myself, then rejoin Harriet."

Torn between her obvious lucidity and an ingrained belief that head injuries should be treated with the utmost caution, he hesitated. He had no authority over her, but Reggie would be furious if anything happened to her. Despite his distaste for the connection, he owed Reggie for dealing with Jenny.

He was still debating when a voice erupted from the doorway.

"Scandalous!"

*Dear Lord!* It was Mrs. Drummond-Burrell, the most disapproving of the Almack's patronesses. Lady Horseley and Princess Esterhazy crowded behind her. Each was appropriately robed as a Fury.

Mortification burned his face. This was far worse than if Jenny had reached the ballroom.

He was alone with a female, a situation he would never have allowed with anyone from his own class. Yet Miss Patterson was gentry. The facts of her breeding paraded relentlessly through his mind: Cousin to Lord Wicksfield, niece to a baronet, remoter connections to Sweetwater, the Earl of Mossbank, and Lord Wellspring. Not only was his presence in this room a personal insult, but she might lose her current and any future jobs.

He glanced at her and cringed. His arm remained around her shoulders. Her domino gaped, exposing her gown's bodice. Her hair tumbled wildly about her shoulders—his flush deepened as he recognized the allure of that curtain of hair. Even if he were not responsible for her dishevelment, the appearance of impropriety was enough to condemn her.

But his guilt was clear. His hands had opened her clothing and unpinned her hair. His cap sat beside her spectacles on the table. His arm still absorbed her heat.

There was but one redress. Rage dimmed his vision, but he set his face into a fatuous smile.

"Hardly scandalous," he drawled, "though I am as clumsy as the greenest cub this evening. I actually knocked Joanna into the wall as I spirited her from the ballroom. But you may wish us happy, for despite my stammers and blunders, she has done me the honor of accepting my hand." He held their eyes lest Miss Patterson's shock belie his statement. Her instinctive recoil had already bruised his side. But for the moment, he was too numb to think beyond salvaging their reputations.

The Furies offered the expected congratulations—none sounding sincere. His head whirled and his stomach churned, adding to his discomfort. Somehow he found himself sheltering Miss Patterson from view as she twisted her hair into place. His *sotto voce* admonition to be quiet must have worked, for she uttered no word.

But he could feel her growing fury as he escorted her back to the ballroom, followed by three of the most vicious gossips in London. And he could not blame her. He had just stolen her from the man she loved. At least her reaction mitigated one fear. If she were strictly a fortune hunter, she would have welcomed him. But his spirits sank even further with the admission, for this situation was far worse.

# Chapter Nine

$\backsim$

Joanna stumbled, only her grip on Lord Sedgewick's arm keeping her upright. Her head spun dizzily.

"Smile!" he growled as they approached the ballroom, three gushing ladies firmly in tow.

She risked a quick glance at his face. Despite the upward tilt of his mouth, he was furious. His eyes had faded to icy gray, though the rakish tilt of his cap and the feather curled over his brow hid them from all but the closest scrutiny. Fine lines clustered at their corners, matching others near his nose and chin. His tone would have sent a dog scurrying for cover.

The ladies swept past as he paused to survey the crowd. Gasps sped across the room. Eyes and quizzing glasses snapped to attention.

She swayed, spots dimming her sight.

"It's too late to swoon," he advised dryly, widening his smile even as his arm stiffened. He radiated tension in palpable waves.

"This is absurd," she hissed, finally able to force words from her mouth. "I cannot—"

"Do you wish to be unemployed, my dear?"

"But why—"

"Enough. This is no time to debate. The least thought should reveal our position. If not, I will explain later. For now, you will express delight over our betrothal and refer any questions to me."

He was quivering with rage, so she abandoned her protests. They would straighten out this mess when they were under less scrutiny. In the meantime, she would play out the farce, if only to avoid embarrassing him yet again.

Descending the stairs, they circled the ballroom, exchanging pleasantries and accepting congratulations. Her mouth stiffened from false smiles. Shock joined forces with the bump on her head, pounding pain into her temples until she wanted to scream.

If only she could escape. The usual cloud of perfumes gagged her. Tinted haze danced before her eyes, occasionally pierced by improbable figures. An armored knight. A turbaned prince. Madame Pompadour's foothigh coiffure. Cleopatra. Only her mounting dizziness seemed real. Her increasing desire to be held was even more unreal. She clamped down on any sign of attraction, knowing it grew only from her spiraling weakness.

When the music stopped, she dropped his arm, duty finally jolting her from her lethargy.

"I must return to Harriet."

"Her mother can look after her. We must dance the next set."

She abandoned her frigid smile. "Chaperons don't dance."

"Betrothed young ladies do."

"I am neither young nor a lady. Nor will I wed you." Ignoring his frigid eyes, she doggedly continued. "Lady Wicksfield cannot look after Harriet. She is undoubtedly in the card room. Would you have me abandon my charge?"

"Like it or not, we are betrothed, so your first duty is to me. I will not tolerate a scene. You will allow me to partner you in this waltz."

His rage was growing. But she could not give in, despite the increasing difficulty of stringing thoughts together. "Honor makes its own demands, sir—as you should know, since you are the first to criticize any lack of it. I vowed to chaperon Harriet. Would you see an innocent ruined because I left her to her own devices? Even this very proper ballroom can be unsafe." She gestured. Appropriately robed as Beelzebub, Lord Darnley was heading toward the alcove where Wethersby had just returned Harriet.

"Contrary wench, aren't you!" he snapped. Taking a deep breath, he murmured a few words to Lord Hartford, then grabbed her hand. "Thomas will look after her. We need to talk. Since leaving would cause more speculation than is already in evidence, we will dance."

"Very well."

"Thank you." His voice mocked her acquiescence. "Quit craning your neck. Thomas has already sent Darnley away. I expect her card is full in any case, so smile."

She glanced briefly into those furious eyes before dropping her gaze to his ruff. "Why are you doing this to me?"

"*To* you?" His scorn banished another wave of lethargy. "Do you understand nothing? We were discovered alone in a compromising position. Refusing to wed would tarnish my reputation and destroy yours."

"By all means, let us keep your exalted position intact," she said, glaring. "Never mind that you might harm me in the process." The words poured out, even as she tried to stop them. But though he stiffened, he maintained his smile.

"Do you wish to be dismissed from your post without a reference?" he demanded. "I could survive walking away, but you would not."

She cringed, but he had a point. Who would hire a governess with a ruined reputation?

"Smile," he reminded her. "I will call on you tomorrow at eleven. We will wed immediately. This will be no more than a nine-day wonder if you can manage to appear pleased. I don't know why that should be difficult. I am considered quite a catch."

"You odious, arrogant—"

"Enough, Miss Patterson. You are not stupid—"

"Which is why your conceit leaves me cold. I prefer my life the way it is, not that you care. All that matters is that you remain firmly ensconced on your pedestal." She tried to pull away, but his grip tightened.

"Smile!" he snapped. "Talking here is obviously pointless. I will call on you at eleven." He swung her into a complicated turn, his face twisted into false pleasure.

His silence was a relief. Her pounding head deadened the music. His words seemed unreal. The evening was unreal. The very idea of marriage was unreal. Surely there was some way to escape. If only she could think.

The swirl of the dance was creating a pretense of intimacy even more unreal than the rest. His broad shoulders promised strength. His hand burned into her back, contrasting with that icy stare. The constant turning increased her dizziness. If only she could rest against that hard chest and know his powerful arms would protect her. But she would find no succor there. However much he despised her, he would blindly follow the dictates of the shallow world in which he lived, ignoring the emptiness that would result. And how could she complain? The only support honor demanded was his name.

A new wave of nausea engulfed her. Faces flashed past. Ghoulish faces. Shocked faces. Skeptical faces. Hostile faces. The music beat against her temples—on and on and on. Would this set never end?

Yet its end proved worse. He led her to her alcove, bowed over her hand, then departed. She wanted to flee, to lie down, to go back to the moment when she had left the ballroom to meet Reggie. But she could not move.

People deluged her. Some offered congratulations. Others slyly demanded to know how she had brought one of society's most elusive bachelors up to scratch. Everyone made it clear that she was too far beneath his touch to attract genuine interest.

Cursing him for abandoning her to a task he knew she could never handle, she tried to turn the topic—without success. Hiding the truth tied her tongue in knots until she could barely utter a word. Her smile cracked more than once. When Reggie appeared to lead her into the next waltz, she nearly fainted from relief.

"I cannot think of a better wife for Sedge," he said once the music started.

"Please," she begged. "No more platitudes. I will shatter if I must keep up this pretense another minute."

"I understand. But that was not politeness, Joanna. I

have long wracked my brains for a way to bring you together. Deep inside where it counts, you are exactly alike."

"Is that why you've spoken of him so often?"

"Of course." He met her eye. "Surely you saw through such a weak strategy."

"I thought you were trying to match him with Harriet. They are both somewhat lack-witted."

"Never. Sedge may play that role in public, but he is extremely intelligent, taking firsts in all his courses at Oxford. And you are just as smart. I welcome you as a sister." His eyes were clear, revealing his earnestness.

"I cannot think of a better brother," she admitted. "But I was not referring to learning. I suspect he reads widely. Yet he demonstrates little common sense. Why would he accept a lifetime of misery when explaining the circumstances could have avoided it? His credit is such that everyone would listen, but he made no attempt to explain, for he is too selfish to consider anything but his own precious reputation. God forbid that anyone should entertain suspicions of him."

"Relax, Joanna. You are in shock, and who can blame you? Your head must be devilish sore. But please set aside your fears. In time, you will admit that fate has been kind."

"You are placing a comfortable face on an impossible situation, Reggie. You must know that he hates me."

"He is in shock, and at least as furious as you. But do not misinterpret that as hatred. He does not know you."

"Stop making excuses. He has disliked me since our first meeting. Tonight's fiasco merely makes it worse." Her voice broke.

"Joanna—" He stopped whatever he had started to say and tried again. "Do you hate him?"

She sighed but managed to keep that hideous smile in place. "No, though I can find little in him to like. He is arrogant, quick to judge, too willing to criticize others, and he makes no attempt to consider the consequences of his actions. There must be some way to escape this trap. Marriage can only bring disaster."

"What happened? I escorted Miss LaRue away and

questioned her—she was tricked into coming here this evening." He scowled. "But that is another story. What prompted his offer?"

"Hardly an offer. He announced a betrothal without even warning me. High-handed fool!"

"Relax, Joanna. What happened?"

She unclenched her jaw. "I regained my senses in an antechamber. Since there was no real damage, I tried to send him away. But he was still arguing the need when Mrs. Drummond-Burrell appeared, accompanied by Lady Horseley and Princess Esterhazy."

"Good God! Those are the most judgmental harridans in town."

"Exactly. But not unreasonable. They would have gladly looked after me if only he had explained. But he didn't even try! He made some inane comment about knocking me into a wall, then announced that I had accepted him. I thought gentlemen despised lying. Surely the ultimate arbiter of manners and fashion should not be doing so."

"He would never willingly lie, so there must be more to the tale. How long were you unconscious?"

"Only a few minutes."

"Had he checked your injuries?"

"Of course. He is not incompetent."

His smile widened. "So he must have disturbed your hair. And he probably removed your spectacles. Anything else?"

"He loosened my domino and helped me sit up." She dropped her eyes but could feel a blush staining her cheeks.

"Forget your own knowledge for the moment. What did the ladies see when they arrived?"

Her blush deepened.

"That bad? I notice that the angle of Sedge's hat has changed and his hair is a mess. He only disturbs it when he is upset, though few people are aware of it."

"I admit the scene may have appeared suggestive, but surely they would have understood if he had explained. An accident that left me unconscious required at least a cursory examination. And he only had his arm around me because I nearly swooned when I sat up."

He laughed. "That might have worked with Lady Sefton or some of the others. But Lady Horseley believes the worst of everyone, and Mrs. Drummond-Burrell is one of Mother's closest friends. Knowing how badly Mother wants Sedge to wed, she would never have allowed such an opportunity to pass."

"So he must wed someone far beneath his touch, whom he dislikes, solely because your mother wishes to set up a nursery?"

"Please do not judge so harshly. And consider your own situation, Joanna. You will be ruined unless you marry him."

She would be ruined anyway. Tears threatened, but she blinked them away. He was right. Not even a merchant would hire a ruined spinster to teach his daughters. "Poor Papa," she murmured. "He will never understand. I don't know how I can face him."

"He knows society's rules as well as I do. And he will see the benefits. After all, Sedge is considered the biggest catch on the Marriage Mart."

"So he informed me." Her icy tones brought a flush to Reggie's cheeks. "Papa has no aspirations to society. He has long condemned marriages of convenience, so I know exactly how he will feel about this one. And what about your parents? No matter how badly they wish to see him wed, they will hardly welcome me. I am amazed that your mother has not already swooped out to halt this farce. She was appalled enough when she realized that we were friends."

"She isn't here." The music swirled to a close. "We will talk later," he said, leading her back to her alcove. "Try to accept the inevitable, Joanna. I truly believe that this will be a good match. And you have one firm supporter. I welcome you into the family with all my heart."

"Thank you, Reggie. Perhaps that will be enough." The words were merely formality, for she knew it would not be.

"You have remained on view long enough," he contin-

ued as another wave of people converged on her corner.
"I will escort you home."

He was as good as his word, easily persuading Lady
Wicksfield to leave. He bantered lightheartedly with
Harriet for the entire journey, deflecting all questions.

But Joanna knew that he had merely postponed the
inevitable. Lady Wicksfield was angrier than ever before.
Only her hope of snaring Reggie was restraining her
temper.

Even as he fended off a barrage of impertinent questions, Sedge kept one eye on Reggie's waltz with Miss
Patterson. The future appeared worse than ever.

She was more relaxed than he had seen her all evening, sharing genuine smiles and warm glances with his
brother.

The knot in his stomach tightened when Reggie burst
into laughter. Every smile hammered the truth into his
head. She had been on her way to meet Reggie. They
shared a rapport enjoyed by few married couples. The
sparks flashing between them were unmistakable.

Fate had certainly landed him a facer this time. How
could he wed a woman who was in love with his brother?
He tried to imagine undressing her, touching her, leading
her to bed . . .

He couldn't do it. Despite that enticing body—which
continued to raise his interest, he admitted grimly, grateful that Elizabethan trunk-hose hid the evidence—bed-
ding her seemed incestuous. Why hadn't he let Reggie
tend her injury?

The answer was obvious, of course. He had ordered
Reggie away because he'd recognized his brother's attraction and wanted to prevent it from growing. Reggie
had accepted because he'd realized that Sedge was too
angry to remove Jenny without creating a scandalous
scene.

He suppressed a new grimace. He had never believed
Jenny could be so stupid. Another wave of fury swept over
him, making it difficult to accept Lady Marchgate's felicitations.

He ejected Jenny from his mind. She would receive

her *congé* from his secretary in the morning. He would have dismissed her anyway after tonight's fiasco, but now he had no choice. He believed in marital fidelity—even under these circumstances.

Somehow, he must overcome his distaste. Neither of them could counter fate. His own reputation would recover if he refused, but he could not ruin hers. If he failed to take her to wife, she would wind up as a courtesan. No other job would be open.

He slipped into the refreshment room so he could no longer see her dancing with Reggie. He had until eleven o'clock to accept this abrupt change in his life. Looking for a lady who would suit him the way Elizabeth suited Randolph was no longer possible.

Miss Patterson had none of the attributes he had sought in a wife. Her breeding was minimal. She was a stuttering rustic with few social graces, who would likely embarrass him at every turn. He doubted if she could successfully plan refreshments for an afternoon of callers, let alone arrange a dinner or ball. Her wardrobe demonstrated a woeful lack of style. Even her wit and intelligence would bring him no pleasure, for it was too closely allied with her scheming.

The reminder bit painfully into his stomach. How long could he remain loyal to a wife who loved his brother?

Rage again flared. If Miss Patterson had not plotted to snare Reggie, he would not be in this fix.

# *Chapter Ten*

～

Reggie escorted Lady Wicksfield to the door, heaping a last round of compliments on Harriet before leaving.

Joanna knew he hoped to soften the anger that had kept Lady Wicksfield tight-lipped since leaving the ballroom, but the task was hopeless. The moment Harriet started upstairs, Lady Wicksfield ordered Joanna into the drawing room.

"How dare you abandon your sworn duty!" she snapped.

"I didn't—"

But she ignored the protest. "I am appalled, Miss Patterson. Appalled! Only a greedy upstart would take advantage of our favor to feather her own nest. I warned Wicksfield that allowing a low-born rustic into society would lead to trouble. Hovering on the fringes of the polite world was bound to give you ideas. And I was right."

"You were wrong, my lady."

"Enough of your insolence, girl," she hissed, discarding any pretense of gentility. "I've seen how you flirt with the gentlemen, and I've watched you steer the most eligible suitors away from Harriet—distracting Lord Ellisham, deflecting Lord Almont. Did you think your wiles went unnoticed? You vowed to see her settled, yet you have prevented her from making a match."

"You wrong m—"

Again she overrode the protest. "Wicksfield will receive a full report of your perfidy. Entrusting our future to an inexperienced fortune hunter was a grave error.

But you will get your comeuppance. Even Lord Sedgewick cannot force society to accept you—especially when people learn how you betrayed us."

"I betrayed nothing." She glared at her erstwhile employer. "I have carried out Wicksfield's orders to the letter. Do you really believe I want this? Wedding Lord Sedgewick must lead to disaster. The only schemers this evening were your brainless friends, whose meddling is forcing me into an untenable future."

Lady Wicksfield's snort filled the drawing room. "Don't bother uttering your pathetic excuses. Your actions speak for themselves. I find your morals questionable, your honor nonexistent, and your character odiously selfish. Lord Sedgewick is far too high in the instep to look twice at so lowly a creature, so you must have trapped him. But your greed is futile, for you cannot be stupid enough to expect a place in society. He will likely lock you away in the country."

Joanna clamped her mouth shut, for argument was useless. Lady Wicksfield would never accept the truth because she assumed that everyone shared her own greed. But her wariness increased when Lady Wicksfield's eyes gleamed with sudden cunning.

"But your future may be less bleak than I thought," the countess said, smiling. "My support will assure society's acceptance, just as it got you into Almack's. I will overlook your betrayal, provided you immediately see Harriet settled. Since you are adept at bringing a powerful lord up to scratch, you should have no trouble arranging a match for her. I will expect Lord Ellisham's offer within the week. If you fail, I will destroy you."

The woman wanted Harriet betrothed so that she would not have to chaperon the girl. Her return to London had revived friendships with old schoolmates whose acceptance had exaggerated her opinion of her own social standing. How could she claim more power than even Lord Sedgewick wielded?

And an even stronger motive was pride. Lord Sedgewick outranked all of Harriet's suitors except Reggie. Lady Wicksfield would feel insulted if a mere companion took precedence over her own daughter. But she must have realized that Reggie would never willingly offer.

"You misunderstand, my lady," she said, forcing cordiality into her voice. "Lord Sedgewick's offer arose from chivalry. If I could escape marriage without damaging his reputation, I would gladly do so. Never would I knowingly trap any gentleman, for an unwilling union must become intolerable. Requesting that I snare another is so dishonorable that I cannot believe you are serious."

"You dare to call me dishonorable?" Lady Wicksfield's voice rose to a screech. "Ungrateful, encroaching liar! How can you contaminate society with your presence? You tricked us from the beginning, throwing yourself on Wicksfield's mercy, wheedling until he gave you more authority than he gave his own wife! I cannot even buy a packet of pins without your approval! When I think of how I begged Lady Cowper for your Almack's voucher, I could weep."

"This discussion is pointless." Joanna interrupted the tirade. "You are deliberately twisting facts. Wicksfield approached me to chaperon Harriet, which I have done to the best of my ability"—she ignored the guilt over her conversations with Reggie; without his help, her job would have been impossible—"rescuing her from potential scandal any number of times. Wicksfield's judgment is sound, as your behavior proves. You are blind when it comes to Harriet's suitors. Ellisham will never wed, and Almont's affections are reserved for his mistress. Yet despite knowing that Wicksfield places Harriet's interests beside his own, you continue to pursue gentlemen who would make her miserable. He will not be pleased by your scheming. Nor will society."

She departed while Lady Wicksfield was still gasping for breath.

The future looked grim indeed. Lord Sedgewick had demanded an immediate wedding, so she must first convince him to wait. She needed time to think if they were to avoid disaster. Lady Wicksfield might wield no social clout, but she was right about one thing. Society would never accept her.

She pressed her pounding temples, trying to ease the pain enough to clear her mind. Everything that had happened since her fall was a blur of color, scent, and sound. The only vivid images she retained were Lord Sedgewick's furious eyes and Reggie's satisfied smile. But no one else had welcomed news of this betrothal. Shock, scorn, and ridicule had underlain the social smiles and insincere felicitations. Everyone assumed she had trapped him. Once shock subsided and the gossipmongers started working, things would be worse.

No one would believe her protests. No one would accept his explanations. Gentlemen of Lord Sedgewick's stature did not offer for companions, no matter how many great houses they could claim kinship to. Society would always see her as a fortune hunter who had grabbed a chance to escape servitude. No one cared that she had twice eschewed marriage to a wealthy man. No fortune could offset the misery of living with someone who did not want her.

Blinking away tears, she stared into the garden. Reggie claimed that his brother was a loving, caring man with interests unknown to society. She could accept that, though she doubted he would squander his caring on her. But what Reggie refused to believe was that Lord Sedgewick found her disgusting. Tonight's fury may have grown from the situation, but his underlying disdain was real. Even while laughing together at Hatchard's, she had sensed his antipathy.

Reading him was surprisingly easy. She had watched him closely since his return to town, trying to anticipate any retaliation for exposing him to ridicule in Bond Street that day. No matter what face he presented to the world, she always knew when he was pleased, bored, angry, or scornful, as he usually was around her. The keys were his eyes and his aura of passionate virility.

His eyes varied from flat gray to bright blue, their color reflecting his mood. Most of the time, they were a light blue-gray—dull when he was bored, sparkling when something piqued his interest. Pleasure intensified the blue, while anger leeched it away, leaving only gray.

His aura revealed the intensity of his emotions—absent

if he was bored or mildly irritated, powerful enough that she had trouble breathing if he was hiding excitement, hatred, or rage.

Tonight, he had already been furious when she'd arrived in the hallway—sensing him had drawn her attention to the group by the stairs. Mary's skimpy costume was probably responsible, for the ultimate arbiter of fashion would be appalled that anyone might wear such a gown to a society ball.

Not that the impropriety surprised Joanna. Mary had never been particularly bright, often doing and saying things inappropriate to the occasion. Her elopement with an actor from a traveling theater company had shocked the neighborhood, though it was typical of her starts. And it seemed to have turned out well.

But she digressed. Sedgewick's anger had overwhelmed him when Mrs. Drummond-Burrell appeared, scrambling his thinking; he should have known that his credit could turn aside any criticism. Even after he'd controlled his face, the fury still simmered. Their waltz had been horrid. His eyes had been harsh gray, as flat as slate. His turbulence had beat against her in the most concentrated burst she had ever felt.

He had held her in contempt since their first unfortunate meeting. His only reason for approaching her since then had been to terminate her friendship with Reggie. Now they faced an impossible future made worse by his social position. So lofty an arbiter of fashion could never accept a mere companion.

If she were lucky, he would install her in a remote cottage and forget about her. But she doubted that would happen. Reggie would never wed, so Lord Sedgewick must secure the succession. He was not a man who shirked duty—as this betrothal proved. But intimacy with a man who disliked the very sight of her might be too much to bear.

And their future might be even worse. Society was a shallow institution, which meant that loyalties could change in an instant. Few had repined when Brummell's debts sent him fleeing the country. They had merely turned to Lord Sedgewick for leadership. They could just as quickly abandon him.

This was getting her nowhere, she conceded, climbing into bed as the clock in the hall struck three—not that she had any chance of sleeping. Past mistakes could not be remedied, but the future could yet be changed. Somehow she must escape this trap. His position in society was at stake. As was happiness for both of them.

She had eight hours to devise a way.

Sedge forced his feet up the steps to White's. He had discarded his costume, but this was not an evening for retiring early. He must behave as normally as possible lest he betray his fury over this twist of fate. Besides, allowing time to brood would make carrying out his duty even harder. He must see this episode to a conclusion before second thoughts drove him to dishonor.

But he could not halt his mind. Even as he exchanged greetings and answered a new round of questions, it turned over every scrap of memory, searching for a way out.

How had he fallen into this trap? And why? Someone had hoaxed Jenny into attending the masquerade. She hadn't the brains to plan such a scheme on her own, and her writing was so poor that she was incapable of forging that letter. Was Miss Patterson somehow involved? The chit knew Jenny, and her protestations were ridiculous. No one would prefer servitude over a luxurious life of social prominence.

*Except Elizabeth,* his conscience reminded him. *She would have refused a duke's heir if she had not loved him.*

But that was irrelevant. If Miss Patterson was anything like Elizabeth, she would have repudiated him in the middle of the ballroom. Loudly and firmly.

He shivered.

Yet what could she have hoped to accomplish by tricking Jenny? Her goal had been to attach Reggie. Creating a scene might have maneuvered Reggie into compromising her, but only if she'd known in advance when and where all the players would be in position.

*Stupid!*

His mind was clearly muddled. Miss Patterson had nothing to do with Jenny. She had been on her way to meet Reggie at the time. The confrontation with Jenny had actually prevented that meeting.

As he accepted felicitations from Rathbone, relief thawed the edges of the ice encasing his heart. Wedding the chit would be difficult enough without suspecting that she had precipitated this mess. Her attachment to Reggie was a large enough hurdle.

So who had tricked Jenny? Could it have been Lord Peter Barnhard? Lord Peter had tried to lure her into his bed more than once, and he must know that Sedge would dismiss her after this stunt.

"Lord Sedgewick." A deep flush marred Crossbridge's face.

Of course. He should have guessed the truth sooner, but he'd honestly thought the baron had learned some prudence after nearly destroying Randolph's betrothal. "What the devil do you want now?" he snapped. "Haven't you done enough damage?"

Crossbridge paled but held his ground. "Then I was right. Miss LaRue somehow instigated your betrothal."

Sedge glared.

Crossbridge plowed heavily ahead. "I owe you far more than an apology. I not only blamed you for planting that print, but actually accused Ellisham of tripping me."

"I told you we had nothing to do with it," he said coldly.

"Quite. But I did not listen. In my arrogance, I tricked Miss LaRue into attending the masquerade, hoping to embarrass you, but I never expected the situation to spin out of control."

"You never do. But how do you know what happened?" A witness could explain Miss Patterson's dishevelment and provide an escape. "Were you watching?"

"Ellisham told me," he said, killing that flash of hope. "You were gone before I realized that something had gone awry with my plan. I was debating what to do when Ellisham dragged me outside to demand an explana-

tion—he'd recognized my hand on the letter to Jenny. I
was appalled to discover what had happened, and even
more so when I realized that I had tucked that print in
the magazine myself. It was on my desk when my
mother called . . ." He blushed deeper than before.
"There are not apologies enough to atone for my mistakes, but I cannot allow you to blame someone else for
my dishonor."

"Damn you, Crossbridge!" The curse burst out.
"Didn't you vow just two months ago that you were
through jumping to conclusions? Only Lady Elizabeth's
brush with death saved Symington from your meddling.
I doubt I will be so lucky."

"I am unfit for society," agreed Crossbridge, hanging
his head. "I will leave within the week. Perhaps a year
or two on the Continent will redeem me."

"Somehow I doubt it. You are the most incompetent
fool I know." He snapped his jaw shut, appalled at losing
his temper so thoroughly. At this rate, he would have
no reputation left to salvage.

Crossbridge sighed. "I cannot blame you for being
upset, but I had to confess before leaving. Ellisham
feared you might fault Miss Patterson. She is as much a
victim as you are, and is less capable of bearing it. But
good may yet come of this. You are very alike."

"Good-bye, Crossbridge. I cannot think we have anything further to say." He ignored the baron's parting
comment. The man's judgment was hopelessly impaired.

Pausing to erase any new signs of fury, he headed
for the gaming room and a high-stakes match of piquet.
Concentration won him a substantial sum, but did little
to improve his temper.

Nor did three hours of tossing and turning. He would
have been better served to have gone to Doctor's Common himself instead of sending his secretary.


"My lord." Miss Patterson turned from her pose before the fireplace, her voice freezing the air of the drawing room.

"Miss Patterson." Circles under her eyes attested to
little or no sleep. Obviously she favored this match no

more than he, though they had no choice. Yet what sort of future faced them? She would meet Reggie often, but marriage would place a permanent bar against ever wedding him.

He pushed the image aside. Emotion would make this day even more difficult, so he would concentrate on honor. Once he had satisfied its demands, he could consider the next step.

"The arrangements are complete," he announced. "I will return at two. We will wed at half past, then retire to Glendale House."

"Why?"

"I can hardly move you into Albany." He glared at her. "Females are not allowed."

"Th-that is not what I m-meant." Her face flushed an unbecoming red. "Why are you forcing me into m-marriage? You d-despise me, as does everyone else. Since I can only embarrass you, there is no point in sacrificing yourself. You know your reputation will recover if I disappear. My mother can use my help—I have eight younger siblings. Or if you b-believe that my presence would harm Father, then lend me enough to buy a c-cottage in a remote spot. I can change my name to guard against the unlikely event that someone might have heard mine."

"Have you no thought for honor?" he demanded, angrier than ever. By the time she stammered to a halt, he was quivering with the overpowering urge to throttle her. "Am I to set you up like a cast-off mistress, allowing the world to believe that I ruined you in truth? No, Miss Patterson, you will see this through. If you behave yourself and refrain from embarrassing me for the remainder of the Season, you may retire to my estate. But not until you have removed every last trace of scandal from this imbroglio. I will not be jilted on top of everything else. Do you understand?"

She collapsed into a chair, her face now stark white. "Yes, my lord. I understand that your arrogance is worse than I had imagined. You care only for your precious reputation. What a pity. You fight to retain the devotion of fools and prigs whose only use is to inflate your considerable vanity. Don't you understand how worthless their opinions are? They would turn on you in an instant if a more intriguing mentor appeared. Yet you will force us both into misery in the dubious name of honor."

"Dubious?" he spat. She had no concept of the demands placed on every member of the world in which he lived.

*She speaks tru—*

*No!* He stifled the voice, whipping up his fury to hold it at bay. His task was difficult enough without entertaining doubts. She was raising questions he dared not consider.

"Honor is what separates a gentleman from the masses," he stated firmly.

"True honor, perhaps. But the gentleman's code you swear by is no more honorable than selling carp as lobster. Honor should not inflict misery. Can you not set aside your stubbornness long enough to admit that a moment of embarrassment is preferable to a lifetime of pain?"

He loomed over her, fighting back the urge to strike out. What the devil was wrong with him? Again he had nearly come to blows with her despite his hatred of anyone who abused women. He needed to conclude this meeting quickly before he lost what little control remained over his temper.

"Pack your things, Miss Patterson. I will return at two and will expect to find you ready. You needn't bother with clothing. Mademoiselle Jeanette will wait upon you at four to fashion a decent wardrobe. We will attend the opera this evening."

"But—"

"Stop fighting fate," he growled, recognizing the very arrogance she decried, but unable to stop it. The alternative was shaking her until her teeth rattled. "I have listened to enough of your prattle. You will act the happy bride, starting now. Tomorrow you will be at home to callers. We will remain in town for the remainder of the Season, participating in all events." He turned to leave. "Until two, my dear."

"If you wish anyone to believe us happy, you had best

improve your own countenance," she snapped, rising to glare at him. "You sound as if someone were forcing broken glass down your throat."

Sweeping out, she left him standing in the drawing room—cursing.

Joanna covered her face with both hands, forcing back tears. Crying would accomplish nothing.

*Odious, arrogant beast!* she fumed, pacing the floor of her bedchamber—not that it provided enough room to work off her fury. She suspected that it was usually assigned to Wicksfield's valet. Even her space at the overcrowded vicarage had been larger.

How could she face society? Lord Sedgewick's fury confirmed her inadequacy. She had nearly collapsed when he'd loomed over her; his height and breadth actually made her feel fragile. Yet knowing they would be miserable and knowing she lacked any attribute that might make her acceptable, he remained obdurate.

*Stupid man!* How could he believe honor was more important than truth, duty more demanding than comfort? How could he expect to pass off a wife who lacked beauty, breeding, fortune, or charm? No one with any sense would believe him.

His insistence had already driven nails into the coffin of this marriage. Before they had even exchanged vows, they were doomed.

# Chapter Eleven

❦

Joanna walked through her wedding in a trance. Only three images remained in memory afterward—Reggie's smile as he took his place in support of his brother, the dead tone of Lord Sedgewick's vows, and the icy lips that had briefly touched hers at the end.

Her dread increased when he escorted her to the office to sign the register. His arm quivered beneath her hand. He radiated a fury that nearly buckled her knees. Leaving the church alone with him was the hardest thing she had ever done.

"My mother should return in a day or two," he announced as they drove to Glendale House. "We will pass the remainder of the afternoon with the modiste, so now is the time to resolve any questions."

"Do you mean that your parents don't even know of this?"

"I wrote them this morning, apprising them of the facts. We will not mention them again. In six hours our tale must sound believable."

She blinked. "What tale is that?" She remembered little of the masquerade beyond her efforts to remain on her feet without losing control of her stomach.

"Pay attention this time," he snapped. "I dislike repeating myself."

"Then make sure your audience is attentive! I was barely conscious last evening—as you, of all people, should know."

He inhaled deeply, deliberately relaxing his fists. "I must beg your pardon, my dear. Snapping at you was unconscionable even without the injury. Does your head still ache?"

"Some. But at least I am in no danger of fainting today." Pain flashed in his eyes, bringing satisfaction. "And the nausea has lessened. As long as you refrain from forcing me into another waltz, I should be all right."

He flinched. "Very well. Our history is quite simple. We formed a deep and lasting attachment from the moment Reggie introduced us. Carried away by the romantic atmosphere at Lady Warburton's masquerade, I impulsively begged for your hand rather than waiting to call upon you in the usual manner. You accepted. When Mrs. Drummond-Burrell's innuendo offered an excuse to wed immediately, we jumped at the chance. We are both well beyond the age of consent, and gathering our respective families would have caused intolerable delay."

"How impetuous of us."

"You aren't the only one suffering the slings and arrows of outrageous fortune, Lady Sedgewick." Flat gray eyes bored into hers, proving she had pushed him too far. "If we have any hope of carrying this off, you must cease baiting me. At the moment, anything that hurts me reflects badly on you, and vice versa. Do you understand?"

"Yes, my lord." But his quote startled her. He rarely relaxed his facade enough to expose even a basic education. Reggie claimed that he let down his guard only with close friends and family. Despite the farcical ceremony so recently concluded, she fit neither category, so his fury was clearly getting the best of him.

He turned away. "You need explain nothing further. Our private life is of no concern to others."

"But why would anyone believe such rubbish?" she asked, honestly perplexed. "You look like death walking, and I cannot appear much better."

"By the time we reach the opera house, we must both contrive the proper expression. Whether people believe the tale is irrelevant. They will accept whatever image we display. By next year, they will have forgotten anything else."

He spoke the truth, as she knew all too well. Public persona rarely matched real character, but society cared only for surface appearances, accepting shallow posturings as truth and ignoring the double standard that implied. Many clung to that surface, needing its safety to frame their world. With enough repetition, people would believe anything—even that Lord Sedgewick's judgment surpassed everyone else's.

"Very well. I will try not to embarrass you, but you know how pressure affects me."

He shuddered. "We must contrive a way to cure that, but for now, we have arrived. Smile. Gossips like Lady Beatrice learn much of their news from modistes and servants, so watch your tongue."

Glendale House was the largest in Grosvenor Square, occupying the same frontage as five average houses. She tried not to stare at the marble walls and Corinthian columns decorating its opulent hall. A magnificent split staircase provided access to two wings. What had she gotten into? This grandeur was more typical of country estates. The Glendale wealth must be greater than she had imagined.

Lord Sedgewick introduced the butler and housekeeper, but spared her a formal welcome from the rest of the staff.

She felt more out of place with every step as he led her upstairs. Each new feature was more elegant than the last, overwhelming her senses. Intricately carved banisters, ornate ceiling, a life-size statue of Zeus on the landing, smaller sculptures in exquisite niches . . . marble flowed into polished paneling as they continued up a second flight. By the time they reached the upper floor, she was trembling so badly that she stumbled, knocking a Chinese vase from a table.

"Oh, no!" Shattering glass nearly drowned her exclamation.

"Are you hurt?" Lord Sedgewick's hold kept her upright.

Tears threatened to fall. "Forgive me, my lord."

He stared for what felt like hours, but was probably only an instant, then tucked her arm firmly through his own. "Of course. This has been a difficult day, and you are not yet recovered from your fall."

"That is not what I m-meant. I should have warned you that I am prone to c-clumsiness," she admitted, wishing she had thought to reveal that failing earlier. Perhaps it would have convinced him to forgo this disaster.

His arm stiffened, but his voice remained calm. "We will contrive to cope." He inhaled deeply several times, then opened a door. "This will be your bedchamber, with your dressing room through here."

She flushed, for his words raised the specter of marriage duties.

He continued without pause. "On this side is our sitting room. My room lies beyond. The modiste awaits us in the sitting room. Are you ready?"

She managed a nod. He was outwardly ignoring her confession, though his intensity had increased. Or perhaps he was merely postponing a confrontation until the modiste left.

Mademoiselle Jeanette had brought three assistants and what seemed like mountains of fabric.

"This is Lady Sedgewick," he announced, leading her into the center of the room. "She needs a complete wardrobe."

"*Oui,* my lord. We will start with the most urgent." Her snapping fingers sent an assistant scurrying. "An afternoon gown, a walking dress, and an evening gown for the opera."

Joanna nearly gasped at the splendid clothing produced for his approval—no one asked her opinion, but that hardly surprised her. The lemon afternoon gown was of finer fabric than anything Harriet owned. Guessing the cost made her cringe. The sprigged muslin walking dress included a matching green pelisse. But the rose silk opera gown left her speechless. Delicate embroidery traced the low-cut bodice before flowing across the skirt and around the flounce. It was as elegant as anything she had seen.

"Excellent," said Lord Sedgewick. "Lucy can manage the fittings while we check your pattern cards."

Lucy dragged Joanna into her room and stripped her.

"*Mais oui*," she exclaimed when Joanna stood numbly before her clad only in a corset and shift. "I feared that we would need to do much alteration. But that other gown, it did not show you to advantage. I should have known the monsieur would never misjudge size."

Michelle's cough closed her mouth on further discourse. Only then did Joanna realize that Mademoiselle Jeanette must also have outfitted Sedgewick's mistresses. She stifled the memory of Mary's costume. Sometime during the wee hours of the morning, she had realized Mary's position. It explained her furious denial and also why she had never brought her family to Cavuscul Hill. They were probably figments of her imagination. Had her marriage also been false, or had her husband abandoned her? But how typical of Mary to hide her failure, even if doing so meant cutting off the very people who loved her most.

She banished Mary from her mind.

How had Sedgewick known her measurements? Her clothing was shapeless. Yet he had held her more than once. She doubted that he had noticed her figure last night, but there had been that first meeting. He had jerked her out of harm's way so quickly that she had been pressed against his body for several seconds. But why would he remember the encounter so clearly? She couldn't have made a favorable impression, especially since she was so much taller than Mary. If that was the sort of companion he preferred, she was in bigger trouble than she'd thought.

She stifled Mary's image yet again, concentrating on her own size and weight. She was not petite, so their encounters had revealed Sedgewick's unexpected strength. How had he managed to lift her?

Lucy flung the afternoon gown over her head, recalling her to the present. She must practice appearing content.

"It is beautiful," she said, trying to keep the awe from her voice.

"*Merci*, but it needs adjusting." She tucked and pinned, then whipped the gown off and handed it to

Michelle, who immediately sat down to make the alterations.

Ten minutes later, they had disposed of the other two, and Lucy began the interminable process of measuring her in every conceivable direction. She then threw a wrapper around her and ordered her back to the sitting room. Lucy remained to work on the opera gown.

"There you are, my dear," said Lord Sedgewick, smiling warmly when she appeared in the doorway. "Tell me what you think of these designs."

She nearly stumbled at the affection in his voice. Any man who could act this well belonged on a stage. Only his gray eyes revealed the truth.

"This should do for tomorrow's ball," he continued. "It is not as elegant as some, but it will be easy to make up."

"Lovely," she said, surprised that he considered Jeanette's problems. "Perhaps in a willow green silk."

That startled a genuine smile from him—and a flash of twinkling blue that closed her throat. "Perfect. With lace edging the neckline and hem."

She nodded.

"Excellent. Now for the other ball gowns . . ." He picked up a dozen cards.

Joanna bit back a protest. The Season was so advanced, she could hardly need all this.

But the comment died unspoken. The ultimate arbiter of fashion would care for appearance more than anyone else. Never would he allow his wife to appear in anything but the best. As he had reminded her only an hour ago, any lack in her appearance or behavior would reflect poorly on him.

Shivers raised the hair on her arms. She knew little of the nuances of fashion. How was she to manage without embarrassing him? She hardly knew what to wear for which event. Harriet's maid had dressed the girl. Her own choices had been among three gowns that varied only in color.

This was another aspect of her changed status that she had not considered, though it was too late to back out.

Had he deliberately rushed her into marriage before she could develop even colder feet?

His touch broke through her abstraction. She had been murmuring agreement to every question without taking in anything he said. But now he leaned forward to reach another stack of cards, setting his hand on her shoulder.

"Do you ride?" he whispered into her ear.

"Yes."

"Cross-country?"

She nodded.

"You will want two or three habits," he said aloud. "These for use in town, and this for the country." Again he dove into details with Jeanette.

Blinking, she realized that an enormous mound of fabric had been set aside, along with dozens of pattern cards. Jeanette's order book was rapidly filling as she noted details.

"Nightrails." He lifted another stack of cards.

Joanna blushed.

On and on it went. She was ready to collapse by the time Lucy returned with the completed gowns. Whipping off the wrapper, the girl flung the opera gown over her head. Only the fact that Sedgewick was bent over yet another pattern card kept her from swooning.

"*Magnifique*, Lady Sedgewick," exclaimed Jeanette as Lucy fastened the last pin. "I love dressing beautiful women."

Joanna nearly protested, but Sedgewick's stunned expression stopped her. It was his most honest face yet. His eyes were actually blue—brilliant blue; heart-stopping blue; the warmest blue she had ever seen.

"As usual, you have outdone yourself, Jeanette," he drawled. "I believe we have accomplished enough for today. Will eleven be suitable for delivering the ball gown?"

"*Oui.*"

Joanna held her tongue until Jeanette and her assistants had gone. Then she turned on her husband. "You expect her to make up a ball gown by morning?"

His voice froze her marrow now that they were alone.

No trace of blue remained. "It is a simple design, and she will have half a dozen women working on it. We have no choice, as you would realize if you took a moment to think. You must have a ball gown by tomorrow night. Since you must also be at home to callers, morning is the only time you can schedule a fitting. And you had best be prepared for a crowd. Nearly everyone in town will call tomorrow. We will drive out for the fashionable hour, then dine here before attending Lady Jersey's rout and the Stafford ball."

"So much."

"And all of it essential." He paused as if searching for words, finally shaking his head. "It grows late. Morton will be waiting to dress your hair. We dine in half an hour."

"Morton?" Somehow she got the question out. It would be fatal to let him cow her, for allowing him to play the dictator would eliminate any hope of a comfortable future.

"Your maid." He left. But at least this solved the problem of choosing proper dress.

Sedge stared blindly at the stage, deaf to Mozart's *Cóssi Fan Tutte*. Duty, honor, and determination had carried him through the last twenty-four hours, helped by the numbness that had descended at Mrs. Drummond-Burrell's first gasp of shock. But the numbness was wearing off.

How was he to survive this disaster?

There were a few bright spots, of course. She cleaned up quite nicely, her body even more delectable than he had surmised. But thinking about that would only lead to frustration. He had felt a burst of healthy lust when Lucy first called attention to the fit of this gown. It hugged her bosom to bare an enticing swell of breast, then swirled teasingly around long legs. The effect was now enhanced by an elegant hairstyle and the pearls he had presented before dinner.

A shiver had shaken her shoulders as he'd fastened the clasp. Desire? Or regret that he was not Reggie?

The question doused his own desire in a cold bucket

of memories—laughter erasing ten years of care from Reggie's face; the love and concern blazing from Reggie's eyes when she fell; her own eyes locked on Reggie's soulful gaze as they twirled around Lady Warburton's ballroom. It was the first time Reggie had waltzed all Season. But the most painful image of all was their wedding. She had looked at Reggie during the entire ceremony.

So her desirability sliced new pain through his heart, though at least her appearance made his tale seem believable. But he could not bear intimacy with a woman who should have wed his brother. Nor could he bed a woman who wished him out of her life.

Her intelligence was acute, yet befriending her could only lead to frustration. Despite avoiding the indiscriminate raking some of his friends enjoyed, he was a healthy male who already felt a strong tug toward that delectable body. Spending time in her company would only make it worse, fostering a mental war that would tear him apart.

Her reluctance to wed him still rankled, though he was convinced that she did not understand the consequences of refusing him. She had no concept of how lonely her life would be once society ostracized her. She might not have been born to its ballrooms and drawing rooms, but she had depended on society's good will for her support. Without a position, she would have nothing.

The curtain rang down on the first act. He had arranged for his closest friends to call during this interval, filling the box to keep the curious and catty at bay until his wife found her footing.

*His wife.* The phrase sent a shudder down his back. If only Randolph were in town. His good sense might help him through this trial. His own mind was in such chaos that he could hardly think. Nothing could penetrate the pain and anger engendered by trapping himself through his own stupidity.

But Randolph was out of reach. And now that the moment of truth was at hand, new fears paralyzed him. She stammered whenever she was nervous. The problem intensified with embarrassment—an inevitable product of stammering, even if nothing else happened. And she admitted to clumsiness—which explained how she had managed to splash lemonade on every piece of clothing he had been wearing that night. He had frozen upon hearing her confession, though only now was he realizing the potential consequences. Reggie had also hinted that she sometimes forgot her surroundings, worsening her other problems. Charm might relax her, but he was too nervous to attempt it. Fear of her mistakes threatened his own control.

But he must persevere, he reminded himself. No matter how bad the ordeal became, he must make the best of it if he was to salvage their place in society. If he failed to pull this off, he might as well put a gun to his head. He could not tolerate becoming an object of ridicule.

Stifling a shudder, he set an expression of pride on his face and welcomed the first callers.

Joanna nearly jumped out of her skin when the first rap sounded on the door to their box. The sight of Lord and Lady Hartford did little to calm her nerves, though both had helped her introduce Harriet into society, and Lady Hartford had stood up for her in church.

"You must still be in shock," Lady Hartford said, drawing her aside. Hartford was distracting Sedgewick.

"Does it show?"

"Not at all, but Sedge told us what really happened, so I know exactly how you feel. I was also forced into marriage because of an inadvertent compromise. My first public appearance was terrifying."

"How did that happen?" The question slipped out without thought. She stammered an apology, but Lady Hartford was already laughing.

"A stranger passed out in my lap in the mail coach. One of the other passengers assumed we were wed, so after the coach crashed, I regained consciousness to find us sharing a bed."

"Good heavens!"

"My feelings exactly."

"You seem reconciled to your fate." She blushed at

so personal an observation, chiding herself for speaking without thought.

But Lady Hartford merely smiled. "More than reconciled. We soon fell in love. But it was initially a shock, for my background is the same as yours—connection to noble families but born to a country vicar. So hold your head high and remember that your breeding is as good as many in society and better than some. Are you aware that Lady Jersey's grandfather was a banker? Her parents eloped, as did she."

"But she's an Almack's patroness."

"Exactly. She held her head up and convinced everyone that she was just as good as they were. Granted, her grandfather's fortune helped, but if you look, you will find skeletons in a great many society attics."

Joanna relaxed a trifle, which was probably Lady Hartford's intent, but she could not pursue the subject. Already the box was jammed with callers, many of whom examined her suspiciously. By the time the last one left, her face was stiff from smiling, and nervous terror left her a wreck. How was she to survive another interval?

"You did quite well," said Sedgewick.

"None of them believed this charade," she countered.

"Probably not. These were close friends who know me too well. But they understand the need to establish you. The next interval will bring people who will be less supportive and more curious. But if you continue as you started, they will accept our fiction."

He turned back to the stage, though she doubted if he was paying any more attention than she was. If someone had asked the name of tonight's offering, she could not have identified it. She had barely survived his friends—now that he'd identified them, she realized that they had been kind; curious rather than cutting, and anxious to set her at ease.

She suppressed a shudder, for she remained in view of the world. There was more fiction being played out tonight than Sedgewick had admitted even to those he called close friends. His reactions went beyond the need to put a good face on a marriage of convenience. Most aristocratic marriages lacked emotional attachment, so their situation was hardly unique. Husbands displayed little beyond indifference for their wives.

But in only a few hours, Sedgewick's dislike had hardened, so he must recognize her unsuitability. He could have accepted the daughter of an earl or of another marquess. But being forced to wed the daughter of a vicar was too much.

He was trying to hide his revulsion, but it was evident. His intensity had nearly overwhelmed her as he turned from closing the door behind the last caller. She had detected it more than once in the carriage while they waited to alight at the theater. Now his death grip on the chair arms and the rigidity of his shoulders revealed his growing turmoil.

Yet he managed to hide it in company—far better than she hid her own emotions. How did he do it? It had to be more than mere acting. Could it be his clothes?

Staring blindly at the stage, she considered his appearance. His coat was a rich wine red that added color to cheeks even paler than fashion demanded. His cravat sported a new arrangement that had drawn comment from every gentleman who had called. He had combed his hair into deliberate dishevelment, allowing the release of running agitated fingers through it. Perhaps that was his secret—dressing to distract the eye.

And he had helped her as well. Her gown was a deep rose that added warmth to her own face. The double strand of pearls at her throat formed a contrast that enhanced that effect. And he had deliberately complimented her appearance to improve her confidence. As a result, she had stuttered far less than nervousness generally produced. She doubted any of it was coincidence.

But clothes could not cover everything. By the end of the third interval, she no longer made any pretense of watching the stage, though she thought the performers had moved on to the evening's second offering. Her head pounded. More than one cutting comment had reached her ears, though always spoken too softly for Sedgewick to hear. It boded ill for tomorrow. He would not be in the drawing room, for his presence would admit that he did not trust her.

Either he sensed her growing strain or was suffering himself. He rose to leave, choosing a moment when action drew every eye to the stage. His carriage awaited them outside.

"Sleep well," he ordered as he escorted her upstairs at Glendale House. "Tomorrow will be worse, though the most sensational rumors should have run their course by the time we reach Lady Jersey's. And by next week, a new scandal should push this into memory."

Depositing her at her door, he continued to his own room. She did not know whether to be relieved or insulted that he was apparently not interested in consummating their union.

Neither, she decided an hour later as she stared at the canopy over her bed. Postponing it merely increased her dread—and not just of marriage duties. Now that she had time to think, she was terrified. How was she to survive a future tied to society's leader? She did not belong here. She knew less about the *ton* than most aristocratic ten-year-olds. Even her recent sojourn on the fringes of London society had seemed alien, so how was she to manage a lifetime in town?

# Chapter Twelve

～

Four days later Joanna entered Almack's on Sedgewick's arm. For the first time since their marriage, eyes
did not dissect their expressions the moment they arrived. The worst was past.

At least in public. She felt as though she had aged ten
years. Not because of Sedgewick's continuing anger, for
she had soon realized that it was not aimed at her, but
from the stress of being the focus of attention wherever
she went. And the suspicion and antagonism she faced
was far worse than what Crossbridge had endured last
week. He belonged. She did not.

That fact had been confirmed on her first full day as
a wife. Her at-home had been the most uncomfortable
afternoon of her life. Callers had packed the enormous
drawing room. Few of them believed Sedgewick's tale.
Even fewer considered her an acceptable addition to the
*haut ton.*

Cuts disguised as compliments predominated. Lady
Wicksfield's blatant absence was duly noted. Lady Thurston dropped any pretense of cordiality as she repeated
Lady Wicksfield's claims that Joanna had schemed to
attach a wealthy gentleman while thwarting Harriet's
chances of making a match. A dozen heads had nodded
in agreement as the vitriol poured forth.

Yet she'd had supporters. Lady Hartford had arrived
early, staying all afternoon. And Lady Thurston had
barely finished denouncing her when Reggie arrived—
had he been listening from the next room?

"Welcome to the family, my dear," he had said after

cutting Lady Thurston dead. His voice had carried to every corner, curbing all conversation. "As I mentioned when I first presented you to Sedge, you are birds of a feather. We are delighted that he recognized it. Sometimes he focuses so closely on dress that he misses the character beneath the facade."

"You do him an injustice," she had replied, dutifully supporting her husband. "He is far more knowing than many believe."

"Obviously." He had laughed. But his words had caused a discernible shift in the women's attitudes. He had thrown down a gauntlet that no one had been willing to pick up.

So she was tolerated, and she could only thank Reggie's sincere delight. Sedgewick's credit probably helped, but even his friends remained cool, withholding their full approval for now.

She wondered if Sedgewick realized that Reggie's credit was more responsible for her acceptance than his own. If he was as astute as Reggie claimed, he must. As she had feared, their marriage had diminished his standing. Lady Wicksfield's charges, which circulated with new details every day, made him appear gullible at best. The effect was apparent even to her untutored eyes. Several of his followers had already defected. The pain was undoubtedly feeding his continued fury.

His anger had not dimmed since the masquerade, emerging as frigid orders about the day's schedule when they were alone. He dictated her wardrobe, instructed her on the most minute details of behavior, chastised every slip, and filled every hour with activity. At times she wanted to scream at him, but only once had she lashed back.

"Must you wear spectacles every waking moment?" he'd demanded when they were returning from Hyde Park that afternoon.

"Yes, if I wish to see beyond the end of my nose. Would you prefer that I mistake Lady Horseley for Mrs. Arlington?" she'd asked, naming bitter enemies.

"You exaggerate."

"Hardly. You may have perfect eyesight, but some of us are not so lucky."

He had given her the strangest look. Only later had she wondered if his constant use of a quizzing glass covered his own weak vision. Not that it mattered.

He had ignored her spectacles this evening, and she had dutifully followed his other orders. He was the acknowledged expert about those things she did not know. She suppressed a nagging suspicion that shoving her into the *ton* was partly a game to test his power. He could have used the excuse of a wedding trip to retire to the country where he could teach her what she needed to know away from prying eyes. But he had not, raising her fears of mortifying him. Despite the fact that he had not yet commented on her clumsiness, they both knew that she was unworthy. His only acknowledgment of her confession was the tight hold he retained on her arm in public—a hold that had saved her from falling more than once.

But for the moment, society seemed willing to play his game. He had accompanied her to routs, balls, the fashionable hour in Hyde Park, and a Venetian breakfast, displaying a discreet infatuation that hid his true feelings. He'd waltzed twice with her at every ball and kept her close most of every evening. She danced other sets only with Reggie or one of his friends. But his hovering would diminish tonight. The patronesses frowned on couples who lived in each other's pockets. Now that society's surprise had faded, she could no longer expect his protection.

And that was good. She had come to enjoy hanging on his arm, which was dangerous. Admiring him could only make her situation worse, for his antipathy remained. His public regard was merely an act, a fact she must never forget.

"Smile," he growled, as they began their promenade through the ballroom.

"I am," she murmured, nodding at Lady Cowper.

He acknowledged Lady Beatrice and the Cunninghams, then raised his quizzing glass. "You look enchanting tonight, Miss Washburn. Madame Celeste has done you proud. Those who appreciate beauty will delight in the change," he added to her mother.

"It does become her," agreed Lady Washburn. "But why Celeste? She does not dress your wife."

"Of course not. Both Celeste and Jeanette are *artistes,* but each creates a markedly different style. Celeste turns petite young girls into breathtaking angels. Jeanette works better with regal beauties such as Lady Sedgewick." He bestowed a smile on the pair. "We must draw attention to Miss Washburn's new look. I will partner her for a set. Perhaps the third."

"Thank you, my lord," said Lady Washburn, barely restraining herself from kissing his feet. "We would be honored."

Joanna ignored his compliment, knowing it arose from the role he was playing, but his arrogance irritated her. "Why do you sound so condescending?" she murmured as they moved away. "You are haughtier than an emperor."

He raised one brow, but surprised her by answering. For once his tone lacked any trace of anger. "Society has seen fit to set me on a pedestal, so why should I not exercise that power? You must admit that the girl's wardrobe was appalling."

"True. I rarely see gowns with so many ribbons and ruffles."

"Exactly. Her mother's taste is atrocious, but the girl is of good character and deserves a decent match. So I recommended Madame Celeste, warning Lady Washburn to give Celeste free rein. As a result, Miss Washburn now appears gracious and pretty. Dancing with her will draw attention to that change."

"A worthy scheme," she admitted. His taste was impeccable. Perhaps Reggie was not blinded by family loyalty after all. Now that she considered it, the Silverton twins had adopted simpler styles and more demure behavior after his brutal set-down at Lady Ormsport's ball, and several of the most flamboyant cubs had toned down their attire after an encounter with Sedgewick's quizzing glass. Rather than dictating fashion, he was helping newcomers present their best faces to the world. Just as he was doing with her, she admitted. She had never looked better. And her confidence was rising as she learned more about the nuances of behavior.

But how would his diminished credit affect this crusade? That bored drawl could not hide his satisfaction at standing atop that lofty pedestal—a flash of blue eyes had accompanied the words. But wedding so far beneath him was bound to topple him off. How much blame would he place on her shoulders?

He continued their promenade, drawling greetings, quizzing guests, shaking his head at Mr. Cathcart's attempt to replicate the arrangement of his cravat, and frowning at Lord Pinter's buttons, which were a handspan across and embroidered with pansies and butterflies. Mothers exhaled in relief when he smiled at their daughters. His tail of sprigs mimicked every gesture.

But despite their seemingly casual meander, she felt judgmental, like an officer inspecting the troops. So when he paused to speak with a friend, she continued on without him, smiling when she reached Lady Hartford.

"You seem relaxed tonight," Lady Hartford said.

"What a gorgeous gown!" exclaimed her companion before Joanna could respond.

"Thank you." It was the most ornate she had yet worn, with crape *rouleaux* around the neck, sleeves, and both scalloped flounces. Seed pearls and crape roses further embellished it, but with a restraint that made it appear elegant rather than fussy.

"This is Mrs. Caristoke," said Lady Hartford, realizing that Joanna had not met her friend.

"Forgive me for missing your at-home, but my son has been ill. My years on the American frontier make it difficult to leave him to nurses at such a time."

"I cannot blame you," said Joanna, but here was yet another unusual wife of one of Sedgewick's friends. Was Reggie encouraging them to reveal oddities in their pasts to make her feel more at home?"

"Did you hear about Crossbridge?" asked Lady Hartford.

"He left this morning for a belated Grand Tour," said Joanna.

"*Very* belated. He is well past thirty." Lady Hartford laughed. "But it seems he'd hidden that print himself—slipped it out of sight when his mother came to call—so he needs to rusticate for a spell."

"He didn't!" exclaimed Mrs. Caristoke.

"Sedge told Thomas he did, swearing Crossbridge confessed the whole." She laughed.

"I can see why he left, though. He'd made quite a cake of himself over the affair."

"Speaking of making a cake of oneself, you should have attended the fashionable hour, Alice," said Lady Hartford. "Miss Delaney managed to fall out of her phaeton without even overturning it, landing with the most stupendous splash in the Serpentine."

"The poor thing," said Mrs. Caristoke. "She might have drowned."

"I doubt it." Joanna shrugged. "The water is very shallow at that point. But why was she driving horses at all, let alone a team she could not control?"

"It is a family trait," said Lady Hartford. "At least she is not as reckless as her brother. If that dog had not appeared, she would have managed quite nicely."

"But there are always dogs in the park," pointed out Mrs. Caristoke.

Joanna let them chatter. She had been surprised at Sedgewick's reaction—though considering their own early encounters, she should not have been. They had arrived on the scene immediately after the Hartfords. Sedgewick had abandoned all trace of arrogance, helping the girl out of the lake and wrapping her in the rug he carried in his phaeton. His actions had salvaged whatever pride she had left. Not until Hartford had calmed her runaway team and found a gentleman to drive her home did Sedgewick return to their phaeton. He was a good man to have around in an emergency.

The realization opened another crack in his facade. London's premier dandy ignored both potential danger and his own clothing when a situation called for clear-headed action. It set him apart from the other dandies who had happened by. Most had remained at a fastidious distance, exchanging droll quips as they quizzed Miss Delaney's dripping bosom.

She continued to mull Sedgewick's contradictory nature as she talked with other ladies. Why had an intelligent, capable, clear-headed man chosen to hide behind a facade of fatuous conceit? He had evaded the question when she had first posed it, but learning the answer was important if she hoped to understand him. What benefit did he derive from playing this role? It was clear that he greatly enjoyed his social position—which boded ill for the future. But she suspected that society's acclaim provided more than mere pleasure. If he needed it to feel worthwhile, what would he do to the person who destroyed it?

"Why does Sedgewick pretend to be a care-for-naught yet rush to rescue anyone in trouble?" she asked Reggie when he led her out for a waltz an hour later.

"I cannot say, though it may be his way of poking fun at society's more ridiculous notions." He swung her into a complex series of turns. "You dance divinely. Not many ladies can manage that particular step."

She hadn't known she could, either, never having tried it before, but he was an exceptional dancer. "Thank you, but don't change the subject. What notions?"

"Many members of society are shallow creatures who truly care only for style and gossip. They assume that all dandies share their thinking. Sedge never cared what people thought of him until Brummell left. But after the other dandies turned to him for sartorial leadership, he changed, exaggerating the fatuous arrogance until he became almost a caricature. His real interests are known only to a few close friends."

"But why?"

"I am not sure, though perhaps hiding his interests allows him to relax. He has been under pressure at home since an early age—we both were. Father expects perfection and absolute obedience to his will. He has belabored my responsibilities as heir since I was old enough to talk, and Sedge was expected to excel in other ways—firsts in all his studies, brilliant career in government or the military, strict adherence to Father's standards of

behavior. Sedge balked, especially after inheriting a fortune from our grandmother. But Father always punishes
the slightest deviation from his wishes—especially the
pranks Sedge used to indulge in. He nearly got sent to
the Peninsula a few years ago, where he probably would
have perished."

She gasped.

"I agree. A definite waste. Mother is little better, so
perhaps his facade maintains his privacy. I am not explaining it very well."

"Better than you think."

Lady Glendale had returned two days ago. Reggie's
revelations explained some of the undercurrents of that
meeting. Lady Glendale's welcome had been cold,
though Joanna could hardly blame the woman for that.
Not only had Sedgewick married beneath him, but he
had not even waited until his parents could attend the
wedding. Delaying two or three days would hardly have
made a difference in the gossip.

Now she realized that their nuptials must have widened a long-standing rift between Sedgewick and his parents. They would see this as yet another rebellion against
their authority, far more serious than his pranks and
wastrel pastimes.

"Do not look so grave, Joanna," begged Reggie,
swinging her into another complicated turn. "This is Almack's, seat of frivolous pleasure. The patronesses
would be appalled to espy a serious thought on the
premises."

She laughed. "How right you are, my friend. So tell
me what you think of Miss Washburn's new gown.
Sedgewick was admiring it earlier."

"Who am I to contradict the God of Fashion?" He
grinned. "And anything would be an improvement on
last night's creation. She looked like some odd sea creature, bristling with lace and green ribbons. The color
turned her face so sallow that she seemed downright
sickly."

They continued in this fashion for the remainder of
the set, allowing her to relax.

Sedgewick led her out two sets later. He seemed calmer this evening.

"Are you enjoying your triumph?" he asked after a lengthy silence.

"This has been more pleasant than I had expected, but I'd hardly call it a triumph."

"More than you might realize." His hand tightened, drawing her a full inch closer than decorum allowed—another way to demonstrate his supposed infatuation. "Every patroness has complimented your charming manners, and while Lady Wicksfield refuses to remain on the same side of the room as you, Lady Thurston actually defended you to Lady Horseley."

She pushed awareness of his masculinity aside, determined to remain light. "That only means that Reggie was lurking nearby. She must recover his good graces if she hopes to snare him for her daughter."

"Yes, he did mention that he'd cut the woman."

"Greed inspires odd alliances. Lady Wicksfield cannot be pleased that her bosom bow is pursuing an impossible goal instead of supporting her efforts to discredit me."

"Quite." He sidestepped one of the clumsier sprigs. "You seem more relaxed this evening."

"As do you," she said carefully. His intensity was down. Was his anger finally mitigating? His hand suddenly burned into her waist.

"Gossip is focusing on Miss Delaney. We have become old news, my dear."

"Just as you predicted." His eyes flared blue, then reverted to gray. Unsure what that meant, she fell silent. Passing so much time in his company actually made it harder to interpret his mood because she caught too many tiny changes.

She watched his eyes for the remainder of the set. They dimmed and brightened several times, though she detected no more blue. Was that an improvement? Or was he trying to decide how badly she was hurting his reputation? Wedding her had probably been similar to his rescues—a brief moment during which his code of honor superseded his fribble's role. But once the crisis passed, he usually resumed his normal activities. This time, consequences had intruded.

Harriet accosted her the moment Sedgewick moved off. "We must talk."

"Of course." She raised her brows. Harriet looked haggard tonight, with circles under her eyes and a furrow across her brow. "What is wrong?"

"Not here." Harriet's glance flicked toward Lady Wicksfield. "The retiring room. I will join you in a moment."

The retiring room was crowded, so she waited until Harriet appeared, then stepped into an antechamber.

Harriet followed. "You must help me," she begged, shutting the door.

"How?" If Lady Wicksfield had convinced Harriet to compromise Reggie, it would be just like the girl to expect cooperation.

"Mama is impossible." Harriet swallowed, fighting down tears. "She is demanding that I attach Lord Almont, but I cannot like the man, Joanna. He says all that is proper, but his mind is clearly elsewhere."

On his illicit family. But at least Lady Wicksfield had given up on Reggie. Cutting Lady Thurston and avoiding Lady Wicksfield had finally penetrated even her willful stupidity. "You would not be happy with Almont," she agreed. "Have you considered appealing to your father?"

She shuddered. "I cannot. I love Jonathan, but Father will never approve."

"Mr. Wethersby?" So her impressions had been right. And the girl's feelings must run deep if she was willing to defy her mother.

"Yes." She inhaled before continuing. "I know you do not care for him, but he is the most wonderful man. And he can support me in comfort. I have no wish to spend every Season in town. But Mama was appalled when I mentioned him as a suitor. She forbade him the house and refuses to let us dance."

"Control yourself, Harriet." The girl's voice had risen alarmingly. "Take a deep breath before you continue."

She complied. "Mama is determined. She is planning

an outing to Richmond next week and expects to wring a proposal from Almont before it ends. I fear she might do something outrageous."

"She might, though Almont would willingly make an offer on his own. He does not care whom he weds. I deflected him for several days before my marriage."

"Why did you—"

"Not now," begged Joanna, interrupting her. "I must think. Does Mr. Wethersby wish to offer?"

"Yes. We have discussed it, but he knows Mama will never agree. She was awful to him yesterday. I could not believe the names she called him. She must have questioned my maid, for no one else knew my feelings."

"Stop this, Harriet. If you start crying, everyone will know that something is amiss." Half of society must have spotted her *tendre*, for she wore her heart on her sleeve. Now that Lady Wicksfield was staying at Harriet's side, she was bound to notice.

"Jonathan wants to call on Papa," said Harriet, sniffing into a handkerchief. "But you know what he'll say. I asked Jonathan to speak with you before doing anything else. You are so smart, you are bound to think of a way."

"Your faith is misplaced. Your mother despises me, and your father must believe I betrayed him." She hadn't even managed to avoid her own unwanted marriage. How was she to help Harriet?

"Then we must elope," cried the girl. "I cannot live with Almont! I will die without Jonathan!"

"Absolutely not. Eloping would ruin you and harm your children."

Harriet stilled.

"Never forget that rash action can hurt both Jonathan and any children you produce," she repeated, pressing her advantage. "You must be very careful."

"As long as I can marry Jonathan."

"You must return to the ballroom. I will consider possible solutions, then speak with you tomorrow. When is this outing to Richmond?"

"Tuesday, unless it is raining."

"That gives us nearly a week. Avoid Almont in the meantime."

Harriet nodded and left.

Joanna stayed in the anteroom, pondering the situation. Despite Lady Wicksfield's antagonism, she still felt responsible for Harriet. Her own marriage did not negate her vow to see the girl settled.

But Lady Wicksfield would not accept Wethersby. He lacked the fortune she wanted. She paced the room, fruitlessly searching for a way out of the dilemma.

Excessive pride was the stumbling block. Wicksfield could recover without help. A loan would speed the process and salvage his pride, but he had other options. Could Sedgewick force Lady Wicksfield to accept Wethersby? A threat to make her a laughingstock might bring her round. If his wife proposed accepting Wethersby, Wicksfield might agree. It seemed improbable, but it was the best approach she could devise. Now all she had to do was convince Sedgewick to act.

She smiled. Four days ago, she would never have considered asking his help. But since their marriage, she had seen too many signs that he cared for others. Would a man who helped young people put their best foot forward do nothing while an innocent was forced into an intolerable marriage?

# Chapter Thirteen

❧

Sedge shut himself in the library. Reggie had headed for his mistress's shortly after dancing with Joanna. His mother had retired early, claiming a headache, which was just as well. He could not tolerate another of her tirades. But he hated the solitude of the night.

Sleeping was impossible. It would take hours before exhaustion overcame his mental turmoil. Fatigue tugged at his heels, but its only effect was to dull his thinking.

If only he could go to White's. Cards and conversation would distract him, but retreating to such a male bastion would expose his claims as the lies they were. No happily married man would leave his wife's bed only three days after the wedding. Exposing the truth would diminish his status even further.

He had been right about the cubs. Three of them had already defected, loath to hang on the tails of a married man—at least he hoped it was his married state that had driven them off. More vexing were the speculative glances from people whose usual demeanor ranged from respect to awe. So far the rumors had turned no one against him, but their very existence tarnished his reputation. Society had long embraced the adage *where there is smoke, there must be fire.* He had recited it often enough himself that he could hardly complain now that it was being used against him.

Most of the tales originated with Lady Wicksfield, who swore that Joanna had deliberately trapped him and had callously abandoned Lady Harriet after destroying the girl's chance to make a respectable match. The charges were so ludicrous that people merely laughed, but since they depicted him as inept, helpless, and stupid, he found them difficult to ignore.

He needed to devise a better defense . . .

But even his deteriorating reputation could not hold his thoughts tonight. They kept returning to the searing image of Reggie waltzing with Joanna. Faces alight. Intimate laughter.

The memory taunted him. She had been happy for that half hour. So different from her demeanor during their own set. Her eyes had probed behind his face, searching for something she could like.

She had never seen him as others did. Her voice echoed, reminding him that she no longer stammered with him because his opinion did not matter. The words had exposed his most secret fears, recalling all the other voices that had ridiculed him over the years: *You are merely a younger son . . . In the unlikely event I need your help, I will ask for it . . . Worthless . . . Failure . . . Incompetent . . . Fool . . .*

He could have tolerated indifference, but she had seen beneath his carefree shell to the emptiness within. His one achievement in thirty-one years was a precarious social position that would likely crash around his feet before much longer. Reggie was his only real family. His parents disdained everything about him, making no effort to understand him, for he was merely a necessary spare in case Reggie failed them. His estate ran as well in his absence as when he was there. His life was built on fantasy—as Joanna had seen. Tonight she had again probed his core. And again found nothing of value.

The shock of their sudden marriage had worn off, leaving him blue-deviled but unable to envision any improvement. Lust was consuming him, yet every time she danced with Reggie, he could see sparks flash between them, hardening his aversion to touching her. He wanted her to look at him like that—carefree, happy, her warmth igniting passion in both of their hearts.

He savagely shoved the thought aside. Better to wish for the moon. But turning back was impossible, and continuing as they were was too bleak to contemplate.

Somehow they must both set regret aside and address the future. Soon. Waltzing with her had made him frustratingly aware of her charms. The touch of her hand, the brush of her thigh . . .

He was rapidly losing his mind.

The first step was to talk. Time might mitigate her love for Reggie, but unless she hid her feelings in the meantime, gossip would claim a worse scandal. It didn't matter that Reggie would never cuckold any man, let alone his brother. Rumors would arise that would make the current ones look benign, pounding the final nail in the coffin containing both their reputations.

*You are such a fool,* hissed the voice, raising new shudders. *Why did you marry her, knowing how she felt?*

He frowned. Had there been another solution? But he could think of nothing acceptable. Claiming that she was betrothed to Reggie would have been cowardly, especially since Reggie had already denied any interest in her. And Mrs. Drummond-Burrell would never have believed the truth.

If only he had allowed Reggie to care for Joanna that night! Everyone would be happier—except his mother. He sighed. She had been appalled enough as it was.

"How could you allow that hussy to manipulate you into marriage?" she had demanded. At least Joanna had been changing for dinner when Lady Glendale stormed into the house.

"You mistake the matter, madam," he'd replied coldly, dragging her into the drawing room so she didn't treat the staff to a scene. "As I informed you in my letter, the fault was entirely my own. After injuring her—quite by accident—I partially disrobed her in checking the extent of the damage. The appearance of impropriety was too stark to ignore. But society believes this is a love match. I will not tolerate anyone claiming otherwise."

"No one can possibly believe such fustian—especially given your unconscionable haste."

He gritted his teeth, trying to forget her subsequent attack on Joanna's character, her breeding, and his own intelligence. She refused to accept that an immediate wedding had dissipated the scandal even faster than he'd expected. If he had delayed, Lady Wicksfield's tales would have fallen on fertile ground, allowing society to build the story into the *on-dit* of the Season. The resulting suspicions would have followed them for years.

Of course, one reason behind his haste had been to keep his mother away from the ceremony. Without saying a word, she could freeze a room faster than anyone he knew, and invariably did so when her orders were ignored.

Which brought him to his next problem. They could not remain in this house. He had moved to Albany ten years ago to escape his mother's scrutiny. Now there was even more need for privacy. So far, prudence had kept her silent. The marriage was a *fait accompli*, so any scandal would redound on the family. But sooner or later, she would ring a vicious peal over Joanna's head. He could not subject his wife to such a tirade. She had done nothing to deserve it.

The admission hurt, for he had not treated her as an innocent. Instead of retiring to Meadowbanks, he had forced her to remain in town and face the gossip. Her eyes had often accused him of pushing her into society to punish her. He should at least explain his reasoning. Leaving would revive gossip, undoing all his recent efforts. He would suffer more than she.

*Arrogant. Selfish.* Her voice echoed.

*No!* Society's respect might be false and empty, but it was all he had. He could not stand the pity of gentlemen who believed she had trapped him, or the disdain of ladies who thought he'd seduced her. His reputation was important. His position allowed him to help a great many people. Losing the good will of those who looked to him for advice and leadership would strip him of his only accomplishment.

Yet watching her face light up whenever Reggie appeared was equally intolerable. There had to be something that would earn her regard. Pouring himself a glass of brandy, he stared morosely into the lamp as the image of Joanna and Reggie flickered in its flame.

"My lord?" Joanna hesitated on the threshold.

"Come in." Fate was offering that private chat he needed.

"Thank you." She shut the door, then took her time about settling into a chair. "I wished to ask a favor, but I don't quite know how to begin."

Suspicion flared once more. Had she wed him because her father was in debt? Or a brother? He had not had time to investigate her family and suddenly realized that he knew nothing of her background beyond what his mother and Reggie had revealed. His mother's information was entirely negative, but she had never been a reliable source. Reggie's was entirely positive, but he was bedazzled. The truth probably lay somewhere between those extremes.

But the favor might have nothing to do with her family. Did she hope for an annulment so she could wed Reggie? Four days might have convinced her that a besotted husband was easier to control than a man already furious at fate.

His temper snapped. "You won't get an annulment, so don't bother asking for one. Nor will I send you off to the country. Flirting with Reggie will not change my mind, so you might as well quit. All it does is tarnish your reputation."

"What are you saying?" Her face was stark white.

"Your behavior is unacceptable, madam. How can I convince society that we are happily wed when you are warmer with him than with me?"

"Convincing them to believe a lie is impossible. Your eyes reveal the truth with every glance," she charged. "Reggie is caring and generous, while you can barely utter a civil word. Frankly, his honest welcome has done more to gain my acceptance than your vaunted credit. Why should I not enjoy talking to a gentleman who has gone out of his way to help me?"

"I'm sure he has," he said, hating his scathing tone but incapable of stopping it. Her charge stabbed pain into his very soul. "And he would gladly do more. I've seen the way he undresses you with his eyes—and so has everyone else."

"Hateful man." Tears shimmered on her lashes.

"Nothing satisfies you, does it? Stripping me of my home, my job, and any choice over my future wasn't enough. Now you would deprive me of my closest friend. How have you blinded the world to your selfishness?"

Remorse drove out anger, pain, and even his lingering regret. Only minutes after deciding that they needed a new start, he had reduced her to tears. His tirade was appalling, and too similar to those delivered by his parents.

She headed for the door, increasing his guilt.

"Forgive me, Joanna," he begged, deliberately addressing her by her given name for the first time. "I am upset, but you are not to blame. May I get you a sherry?"

She narrowed her gaze, suspicious of his sudden affability. "No, thank you. I obviously arrived at an inconvenient time."

"Sit down. Please," he added. "You must be as unsettled as I am." The admission surprised him, for he never bared his inner feelings. But she accepted a chair.

"This is not the first time you have castigated me," she said on a long sigh. "I suppose I shall grow accustomed to it."

"I hope not!" Her eyes widened at his tone. "I despise my parents' habit of criticizing me without verifying their charges."

"I see," she said, though he could hear her uncertainty.

"You wished a favor." He set his suspicions aside. *Find out the facts,* his conscience demanded. "Have I overlooked one of your needs?"

"Never!" Her shock was clear.

"Is it your family?"

"Of course not!"

"Again I must apologize. Many have begged me for favors, some even resorting to threats. Since I cannot imagine you are like those people, suppose you just explain the problem."

"It's Harriet. I promised to see her settled this Season and cannot honorably renege."

"A commendable attitude."

She relaxed fractionally. "She is in love with Mr. Wethersby, and he with her, but her mother has barred the door to him. Now that Lady Wicksfield has finally admitted that Reggie is not interested, she is determined to accept Almont. But he will make Harriet miserable. Reggie told me about his other family." She blushed.

"Then why not pass that information to Lady Wicksfield?"

"I have—several times—but she doesn't care. All she wants is a suitor who has the power and fortune to help Lord Wicksfield out of his current morass. Wethersby lacks both."

He frowned. "You had best start at the beginning, Joanna."

"I suppose so." She sighed. "A few months ago, Wicksfield lost most of his fortune in a bad investment. He needs money to modernize Wicksfield Manor if he is to recoup. He could sell the town house, but pride prevents him from admitting his poor judgment to society."

"Not an uncommon failing," he said dryly.

"True. He preferred to seek a husband for Harriet who could either convince a bank to grant him a loan— they have already turned him down—or who would make the loan himself. He hired me to chaperon her, believing that I would keep his affairs secret."

"Which you have," he murmured when her face twisted with guilt.

She shuddered, but continued. "He also needed someone to look after his family. Harriet is young, and Lady Wicksfield is too irresponsible to watch her. He even put me in charge of their funds to prevent Lady Wicksfield from running up further debts. And he ordered me to find a husband Harriet could be happy with—he has no wish to sacrifice his daughter, you understand."

"So he hoped that she would find a wealthy lord who would also suit her. Why did he not come to town himself?"

"He could not spare the time. He has thrown himself into agricultural reform. But his steward needs constant supervision to carry out some of the more controversial changes."

"He must think highly of your sense."

"I would not go that far. We had never met before."

"What?"

"You cannot believe he would have hired me had he understood my penchant for walking into trouble—a problem familiar to everyone who has ever seen me." Their eyes met in humorous communion that recalled their earliest meetings and relaxed them both. "He is Mama's cousin. They grew up together, and he always admired her sense, so he believed her claim that I might suit his needs. I had just accepted a position as a governess, but he convinced my employer to hold the post until July on grounds that my visit to London would prove invaluable to his daughters."

"How did he expect you to screen suitors without any contacts in society?"

"He didn't say. Fortunately, Reggie has proved most helpful, investigating everyone in Harriet's court. I would have been lost without his help."

"So why didn't he help you this time?" He was holding his breath.

"I didn't ask. He lacks your credit."

"For what? Forcing Wicksfield to accept Wethersby? I thought you said he wanted Lady Harriet's happiness."

"It is not that simple." She sighed. "Lady Wicksfield is now chaperoning Harriet. I doubt she informed Wicksfield of my departure, despite her vow to ruin me." She bit her lip. "With everything that has happened, I forgot to do so myself."

"Understandable. And easily rectified. He can find a new chaperon easily enough."

"There isn't time."

"What happened?"

Joanna stared into the fire. "Lady Wicksfield never approved of a protracted recovery. She was willing to pay lip-service to the idea because she assumed that Harriet would choose a husband based on money and prestige—or at least follow her guidance. She expected Harriet's beauty to garner enough interest that she could play suitors against one another until one offered to give Wicksfield the money he needs. Her determination increased once we reached town. She is enjoying society too much to willingly spend future Seasons in the country. But that would require even more money."

"So she wants to sell the girl." His icy tone made her flinch.

But she was shaking her head. "Worse. Selling only works with dishonorable gentlemen who can gain a wife no other way or with cits desperate to gain access to society's fringes. But neither would provide what she wants." She bit her lip. "She is determined to find the richest husband she can, hoping to dip into his purse whenever she exceeds her allowance. When we arrived home from Lady Warburton's, she demanded that I arrange a compromise between Harriet and Reggie. I refused."

He stared, but she was looking at her lap.

"That is another reason why I cannot ask Reggie to help. Lady Wicksfield would love to force him into offering."

"Dear Lord."

She met his eyes, her own filled with pain. "Exactly. Harriet won't cooperate with such a scheme, but she may wind up the victim. Lady Wicksfield is plotting something underhanded, probably to trap Almont now that Reggie no longer goes near them. Almont is willing enough—I've deflected an offer for days—but I cannot allow her to sacrifice Harriet. Yet I have no idea how to prevent it. Nor do I know how to convince Wicksfield to approve Wethersby. If only he would let go of his pride! He can recoup without a loan. He's already learned a valuable lesson, for that investment scheme was questionable from the start. But his pride could never survive becoming the butt of jokes. He usually attends Parliament, so hiding his misfortune would be impossible."

"Do not work yourself into a megrim," he advised, toying with a letter opener. He had himself under control again, helped by her aversion to scheming and her genuine affection for Harriet. "There are several approaches we can try."

"Then you will talk to Lady Wicksfield?"

"That would be pointless. She hates me for elevating you, and I doubt she can influence her husband. But as soon as I confirm your assessment of Wethersby, I will speak to Wicksfield. What can you tell me about the lad? I know him only by sight."

Her eyes warmed to the color of rich chocolate, creating the same face that had laughed with Reggie. "He is a younger son who owns a small estate in Yorkshire. His income will comfortably support a wife as long as they rarely visit London—Harriet prefers the country, by the way. Reggie may know more. With everything that happened at Lady Warburton's, he never gave me his final report."

"It sounds ideal, as long as Wethersby does not believe Harriet is an heiress."

She frowned. "I doubt he expects a huge dowry, though there have been a few who did—most people still believe Wicksfield is wealthy. He never realized that hiding his problems might expose Harriet to fortune hunters. I've had to discourage more than one."

"Surely she has some dowry!"

"Of course. Five thousand guineas, which was placed in trust for her at birth. He is not trying to sell her, you understand, merely obtain the loan that will hide his poor judgment."

He nodded. "Set the problem aside," he advised, helping her rise. "I will deal with it. I have always despised parents who manipulated their children into unsuitable unions."

She raised her brows.

"Another time. You look exhausted, and no wonder. Get some rest. Lady Wicksfield will not force Harriet onto Almont."

Squeezing her hand, he accompanied her upstairs, then collected hat, gloves, and walking stick, and called for his carriage. If anyone questioned his presence in the clubs, he could claim he'd left his wife asleep.

Her meeting with Reggie had been to discuss Harriet's

suitors? He was not convinced he had the entire story, but it raised a glimmer of hope. Perhaps her affections were less engaged than he'd feared.

*Don't jump to conclusions.*

He wouldn't, but the future looked less grim. Gratitude alone warmed her face into genuine beauty, and she was as devoted to duty and honor as he was.

Almont was still at White's. It was no trick to pull him aside for private conversation.

"I heard a disturbing tale this evening," Sedge said once they completed the preliminary social sparring. "Lady Wicksfield seems determined to force you into offering for her daughter despite knowing that the girl is in love with another. She hopes to benefit from your fortune."

"What?" Almont's brows snapped together.

"I agreed to meddle in your affairs because my wife desires Lady Harriet's happiness," he said with a sigh. "I could hardly ignore so pretty a plea." He might as well further the image of his love match. "We both know that you need only ensure your succession. What would you do with Lady Harriet then?"

"Mother will keep her company."

"Turn her into a drudge, more likely. Is that a fitting end for an angel?"

"Mother wouldn't—"

"Lady Harriet comes with many drawbacks," he said over the protest. "A demanding mother, starry-eyed innocence, a *tendre* for another man—" He winced, for the words recalled his own situation. "—and the expectation that her husband will cherish her. Surely there are girls more suited to your needs."

"Were you about to suggest Lady Constance? She would expect no affection."

"But she *would* expect attention. She is the clinging sort, just like her mother, and would demand constant escort, falling into megrims and hysterics at any hint of neglect. You don't think Wadebrook hovers over his wife from choice, do you?"

"Good God! I had not considered that. Perhaps Miss Willowby would serve."

"Perhaps. She is independent enough and has the confidence to stand up to your mother, but she would cost a fortune in upkeep. She demands the best of everything— again like her mother. What about Lady Edith Harwood? You have paid her some attention, making an offer believable. Granted, she is not beautiful, but she is old enough to understand the rules, can run your household and keep your mother in line, cares for no one but herself, and would gladly accept your name and neglect. Plus, she is honorable enough to provide an heir before she looks elsewhere for companionship. An innocent like Lady Harriet would bring you nothing but grief."

He nodded. "A most pragmatic man. You surprise me, Lord Sedgewick. I had not thought you caring."

"I would rather keep it that way."

Almont smiled. "We all live behind masks. I was captivated by Harriet's angelic voice, but you are correct. I would rarely be in a position to hear it. And this explains why Miss Patterson has seemed so distant of late."

Sedge departed, satisfied that Almont would not be available for long. Lady Edith's betrothal would be on everyone's lips by the fashionable hour, or he was no judge.

His luck remained in force. Wethersby was watching a faro table at Brook's. Again, he had no trouble drawing him aside for a private conversation.

"Lady Sedgewick claims that you wish to offer for Lady Harriet," he began, skipping the preliminaries this time.

"Why should that concern you?" demanded Wethersby.

"My wife cares for Lady Harriet's happiness. Are her impressions correct?"

Wethersby frowned, but nodded. "Not that I have any chance of success," he added bitterly. "Lady Wicksfield considers my station unacceptably low. She has ordered me to keep my distance. I am not even to stand near the periphery of Harriet's court. I doubt the earl considers me in a better light."

"You do not know his thoughts. Nor does his wife. Can you afford marriage?"

"Harriet knows my circumstances," he said stiffly. "They are agreeable to her. I have not spoken with Miss—Lady Sedgewick on the subject, but I had thought her opposition was softening."

"You thought correctly. She believes you will suit, but I wanted to hear your side before speaking with Wicksfield. I will leave for the Manor in the morning. Would you care to accompany me?"

Wethersby's eyes nearly popped from his head. "Thank you."

"Thank my wife. Without her prompting, I would have considered meddling to be beneath my dignity. My carriage will collect you at seven." When he left, Wethersby's jaw was hanging open.

Ordering his valet to awaken him at dawn, he crawled into bed and slept soundly for three full hours.

Joanna blinked at the tray Morton placed beside the bed. Next to her morning chocolate sat a pile of letters. She recognized Sedgewick's hand on the top sheet.

*Almont will not offer for Harriet,* it read. *I will return in a few days. Reggie can escort you until then.*

The others were invitations to three balls and several routs. He must be ordering her attendance, for he had jotted notes on each one—blue silk, sarcenet ball gown, and so on.

A stab of anger at his curtness quickly faded. This was no more autocratic than his other orders. And his instructions were helping her more than she'd realized. They allowed her to issue orders to Morton, leaving the impression that she was a competent lady who made her own decisions.

It seemed that he had already dealt with Almont. His efficiency took her breath away. As did his willingness to tackle the problem. He could hardly care about Harriet's fate, but he must have gone to Wicksfield Manor.

Warmth filled her breast. The future was looking better. Had she misjudged him? If he disliked her, he would not have responded to her plea for help. So perhaps his dislike was for the unequal union. Once he calmed down, they might reach a modicum of comfort.

In the meantime, she could only await his return. Hopefully he had told Reggie to escort her. She had no idea how to get in touch with him, for he kept rooms elsewhere. Asking Lady Glendale for information was impossible. The woman clearly despised her—and *that* hatred was personal.

With luck, she could avoid her. And since Sedgewick had said nothing about afternoon calls, she could please herself. Lady Hartford was at home today.

# Chapter Fourteen

~

Harriet sought out Joanna at that night's ball. "Have you seen Jonathan—Mr. Wethersby?" she corrected herself when Joanna frowned.

"Not this evening."

Harriet blinked back tears. "He said he would be here. In fact, he asked me to save a waltz for him—Mama grows easier to distract every day. So where is he?" The girl had moved a long way from the clinging, fearful child who had arrived in London only a month ago.

"Some crisis probably arose. You can hardly expect him to send you a note. That would be most improper. But if anything is seriously amiss, he will contrive to let you know. At least you need no longer fear Almont. He has offered for Lady Edith."

"I heard." She giggled. "Mama nearly fell into hysterics in Lady Debenham's drawing room. We skipped the rest of our calls lest she embarrass herself. She has been ranting ever since."

Joanna glanced at Lady Wicksfield, who was clearly out of sorts despite the frigid smile pasted on her face. "You are in no danger at the moment. I would not fret unduly over Mr. Wethersby's absence. Are you still planning that outing to Richmond?"

"We must. The invitations have already been issued. Mama is not happy about it, but there is little she can do. Almont has already declined, as has Mr. Stoverson—he disapproves of anything as frivolous as a picnic."

"Is your mother considering him?"

Harriet frowned.

"Keep smiling," she warned.

"Of course. She has said nothing yet, but he is the most attentive of my remaining suitors. Mr. Parkington has shifted his allegiance to Miss Mason."

"He was never serious. The man is not ready to wed."

"What can I do about Mr. Stoverson?"

"A little care will deflect any scheming."

"How?"

Joanna lowered her voice. "Mention that Mr. Stoverson is too steeped in frugality to consider helping your father."

"That will merely turn her attention to Lord Penleigh."

"Not for a day or two. She will need that long to recover from losing Almont and to accept that Ellisham will not even speak with her let alone put himself in a position to be compromised. Is Penleigh accompanying you to Richmond?"

"Yes. As are Lord Braxton and Mr. Reynolds."

"Braxton is a fortune hunter, so don't ever see him alone. She might consider either of the others, but not before Tuesday. Let me know of any new plans. I am working on a way to convince your father to accept Mr. Wethersby."

"What—"

"I can say nothing more at the moment, for I do not wish to raise your hopes without cause." Sedgewick had to have gone to Wicksfield Manor. His intention when they had parted had been to speak with Wethersby, then with Wicksfield. Surely he would have informed her if his plans had changed. At the very least, he would have left word with Lady Glendale. Suppressing a niggling voice that questioned whether the marchioness would have shared any information, she turned the conversation to the day's *on-dits*.

News of Almont's betrothal had shocked those gathered at Lady Hartford's, though most of the surprise revolved around his astute choice of bride. Few believed Almont capable of such cleverness.

She had remained silent, unsure of where the boundary lay between family loyalty and acceptable gossip. Sedgewick must have named a suitable bride and ordered Almont to settle the matter. It gave her another glimpse of the real man.

*Society has seen fit to set me on a pedestal, so why should I not exercise that power?* Which he did. To help others.

Warmth filled her breast.

But other gossip had revived her older fears. Brumford had left town. Despite his stated destination of Cornwall, most people believed he was bent on recovering Miss Lutterworth. His obsession had driven him to the brink of insanity.

Could she protect Harriet from a similar fate? Lady Wicksfield was allowing Braxton to dance attendance on the girl, apparently uncaring of his financial woes—she was determined to keep Harriet's court as large as possible. Joanna had no proof that he was obsessed, but the gleam in his eye bothered her. She could only hope that Wethersby would claim Harriet's hand before anything happened.

But when two more days passed with no sign of Wethersby, she began to wonder. He seemed to have disappeared off the face of the earth. She hoped he was with Sedgewick, but the fact that he had told no one that he was leaving made it unlikely. He could have met with an accident or become a victim of foul play. Or he could have gone home to Yorkshire. Had he been toying with Harriet's affections?

The question was far from idle. Every day brought new proof that she did not understand the polite world. A gentleman she had considered hopelessly toplofty stopped to assist an injured street urchin. A lady of impeccable manners burst into a tirade worthy of a Billingsgate fishwife because her new riding hat was missing one feather. A lord who strongly supported educating tenants gave the cut direct to a dowager for urging him to establish schools for the lower classes.

People were far more complex than she had thought. They could not be neatly labeled.

The admission increased her impatience for Sedgewick's return. He was a mass of contradictions. In public, an empty-headed fribble pursuing a useless life of fashion and gossip. In private, a well-educated gentleman capable of dealing with any emergency. He offered subtle guidance to young people and a willing ear to crusty older folk. Yet after forcing her into an unwanted marriage, he was helping Harriet escape another, claiming he hated such unions.

No such contradictions applied to Lady Glendale. She had demanded Joanna's attendance in her sitting room the previous afternoon. Under the guise of becoming acquainted, she had laid bare every shortcoming, including several Joanna had never considered.

"You are familiar with your new duties, of course," she had said without preamble.

"I believe so." The statement was rash, but she had hoped to prevent any questions. She might resent Sedgewick's tutelage, but his assumptions were easier to bear than the malicious gleam in Lady Glendale's eyes.

"I doubt it. Why have you made no attempt to instruct the staff?"

"It is your home, madam," she'd said without thought.

"You had been here two days before my return. Are you even familiar with the duties of the servants? I hate to think of the errors you might introduce into the household accounts." She had let out a long-suffering sigh. "But at least I need not fear you will disrupt Glendale Close. Reggie will wed soon, so your ignorance and incompetence will not overturn centuries of tradition. Mismanaging Meadowbanks will be bad enough."

By the time the woman finished quizzing her on every nuance of running an estate, Joanna was tongue-tied and stammering. But when Lady Glendale exposed her ignorance of how to organize a ball and entertain royalty, embarrassment gave way to fury.

"I doubt I will face such a challenge in the immediate future, my lady. Nor do I believe Sedgewick would leave arrangements entirely to me. He is too particular to allow even you to plan his gatherings."

"You are so naïve." Lady Glendale shook her head, the sorrowful expression on her face belied by the fury blazing in her eyes. "Gentlemen never dirty their hands with such low occupations. They go their own way, expecting their wives to deal with any crises."

"Lord Glendale may have done so," said Joanna recklessly. "But a perfectionist like Sedgewick never relinquishes control."

"He interferes only when incompetence threatens his credit. I am surprised he has not already hustled you out of sight to protect the family from scandal."

Joanna refused to cringe from the barrage of barbs, though every shaft stabbed her heart. Coming to terms with Sedgewick's mother seemed impossible. The woman would never accept her. And she had a point. Joanna had not been trained as a society hostess, which boded ill for a future tied to society's leader. Perhaps she had been mistaken when she thought Sedgewick might be softening.

To make matters worse, his absence from town had been duly noted. New rumors claimed he had fled, unable to tolerate his wife a moment longer. Others suggested that he was searching out a remote site so he could banish her. Still others swore that she had blatantly seduced him, then rushed him into marriage in the name of honor. But he was pursuing an annulment.

The calumny was eroding his image even further. Several cubs had already switched their allegiance to Kingsford, claiming his sense of style surpassed Sedgewick's. Others had reverted to more flamboyant dress. How would he react to his diminished standing? She was ultimately to blame.

Sedge headed for Joanna's sitting room. He was exhausted—not from the long trip, though Wethersby's company had worn thin long before they returned, but from the distaste of prying into another man's affairs. At least Joanna need no longer fret over Harriet.

He had to approve her sense of duty. Few ladies would care about a former employer once fate had catapulted them into luxury. Fewer would risk themselves to rescue a child described by many as a limb of Satan, or teach a legless soldier to read and write so he could find work, or pester a landowner until he opened a school for tenant children. Yes, this trip had taught him much about his wife.

Reggie had not exaggerated her breeding. In fact, she was connected to more great houses than he had expected, which would ease her entrance into his world. He had not realized that her mother had literally grown up at Wicksfield Manor, sharing the nursery with the current earl, who was only one year her junior. When Wicksfield had devised his scheme, he had consulted the cousin who was closer than his sisters. She had suggested Joanna. It had been an admirable choice.

Joanna had been correct that Wicksfield was not venal, nor was he completely destitute. The man was entitled to a modicum of pride under the circumstances. If he had not faced the imminent launching of three daughters, he could have retrenched with no one the wiser.

Wicksfield had been shocked to find two London gentlemen on his doorstep. But that reaction had rapidly changed to fury. . . .

Sedge let out a long sigh before rapping on the sitting-room door.

"You're back." The words were prosaic, but Joanna's smile made him feel almost welcome.

"I trust you adequately entertained yourself in my absence."

The smile disappeared. "Of course. Reggie has been most attentive. Did your business go well?"

He nearly flinched. First he'd put her back up by implying that she could never manage on her own. Then he'd raised the reminder of her devotion to Reggie. How could he have been so stupid? A watcher would think he'd never set foot in the polite world. "Lady Harriet should be receiving an offer from Wethersby within the hour."

"Wonderful!" Her smile flared, imparting the glow that brought out her beauty. "How did you manage that? If you feel up to talking about it," she added. "You must be exhausted."

The sincere concern raised warmth in his chest,

though the rapid emotional swings left him reeling. She was right about the exhaustion. But he joined her on the settee.

"I took Wethersby with me to Wicksfield Manor," he began.

"Thank goodness. Harriet has been frantic over his disappearance. No one knew anything, so she naturally assumed the worst. Last night she was convinced he'd abandoned her. The evening before she was stammering about footpads and a body dragged from the Thames."

"Wethersby must be the world's greatest gudgeon! Didn't he leave word when we left?"

"Not that I know of."

He shook his head. "I knew he had limited sense by the time we reached the Bath Road, but I never suspected such shocking manners. Perhaps I should not have promoted this match. How will he manage to keep her?"

"According to Reggie, he has a very able steward and is smart enough to hire a good man of business. He is well suited to Harriet, for her own understanding is not the best."

"I suppose there is merit in that."

"But how did you convince Wicksfield to agree? You must have done so."

"You were correct about his finances. He had hoped that Harriet would succeed, but he is unwilling to sacrifice her merely to salvage his pride. Once Wethersby earned his consent, Wicksfield wrote to his wife. I suspect he chided her for allowing her greed to overlook Harriet's interests and for failing to apprise him of our marriage. In fact, he was so angry over that last that I feared he might suffer an apoplexy. But my appearance on Harriet's behalf confirmed his trust in you."

"Thank you, my lord. Words cannot express my gratitude."

"Do you not wish to hear the rest?"

"There is more?" Her eyes widened.

He grinned. "Having bestirred myself to travel all the way to Oxfordshire, I was not about to leave the problem half-solved. Lady Harriet has two young sisters who will also need husbands." He sighed affectedly.

"So what additional sacrifice did you make?" Her grin removed any sting from the words. It was the first time she had teased him.

"Wicksfield's losses arose from heeding an incompetent man of business. I offered him the loan he needs, on condition that he replace the man with my cousin, whose acumen has already been demonstrated."

"Why would such a paragon be available to take this new position?"

"His previous employer died. Geoffrey never got along with the heir, so settling him solves one of my own problems—or Reggie's, actually; Father dislikes that branch of the family, so they've learned to bring their troubles to Reggie. But Wicksfield's finances should be better than ever within five years, particularly if he leases out Wicksfield House for the next Season or two."

"Keeping his free-spending wife close to home."

"Exactly. I also recommended a prospective governess for Sir Brendan. Wicksfield will make the arrangements, having just learned of your marriage."

"Heavens! I had forgotten all about that. How can I thank you, my lord?" Tears glistened in her eyes.

"You can start by calling me Sedge." The request was not spontaneous. He had taken a hard look at his marriage during his days away. His regrets were making the situation worse than it need be. Hiding anger and bitterness while producing the affection he wished to show the world had required all his energy. The strain had taken its toll, contributing to the cold fury that surfaced in private. But such an attitude was unworthy of a gentleman.

Marriages of convenience had been the standard for centuries. Half of his ancestors had met their brides for the first time at the altar. Most of the unions had worked well enough, and some had spawned close friendship and even love. But whatever the future held, Joanna did not deserve his anger. He must refrain from now on.

Time away from public scrutiny had mitigated his ire. Now he must set aside regret. The die was cast. He could only look forward and try to build rapport with his wife. This meeting was a new beginning for both of them.

Reggie remained a problem, but reflection had convinced him that Joanna's face lacked the depth of feeling that Reggie's showed. Since he doubted she could exert that much control, she must merely be infatuated. Thus they could eventually come to an accommodation. The first step was to cultivate her friendship.

She was as much a victim as he. More so, in some respects, for the past few days could not have been pleasant. His sudden departure must have worsened the rumors, exposing her to suspicion and outright antagonism. He could only imagine what interpretation Lady Wicksfield had placed on his absence.

Then there was his mother. He should have considered her hostility before leaving town. With luck, she had not vented her spleen on Joanna, but it was not a question he could ask. Admitting aloud that his mother deplored this match would hurt her.

But this was no time for deep thinking. "Shall we drive out for the fashionable hour?"

"That would be delightful, m—Sedge," she said, rising. "Be sure to tell Reggie he need no longer escort me. He cringes every time he calls—your mother pounced on him two days ago when he arrived early. He will be thankful to find your orders rescinded."

"That is an odd way of phrasing it."

"Why? There are a thousand things he would rather be doing than keeping the harridans polite. Cutting them merely turns a private skirmish into public scandal, but he lacks your skill with a quizzing glass so must resort to malevolent glowers. Not at all the thing."

"Who is being unpleasant?" He could not hide his anger.

She snorted. "You know these people far better than I do. And you know exactly how they feel about having me thrust into their world. But no one has dared cut me. Your power remains."

She almost sounded mocking. He must be more tired than he had thought. Or perhaps she was trying to tease him. He would accept her words in that light. And he would interpret any future situations in her favor as well.

He rose. "I must change if we are to drive out."

Joanna watched him enter his bedroom, her head swirling with more emotions than she could define.

He had provided far more help than she had requested. Not only had he settled Harriet, but he had bailed Wicksfield out of debt and completed her own unfinished business. She doubted that finding a job for Geoffrey had entered into it. A good man of business would have his choice of employers.

So she had been right to seek his help.

His actions supported her growing suspicion that his facade hid a sensitive nature—the sort of sensibility that made him susceptible to deep pain and would have left him helpless against his parents. Only by hiding it had he survived his father's demands for perfection and his mother's cutting disapproval.

Her own confrontation with Lady Glendale had been torture, but it had raised disturbing images of Sedge's childhood. Granted, Lady Glendale hated her low breeding and inadequate training. But the antagonism had run deeper, reminding her of an old neighbor. Both women abhorred anyone who dared to cross class boundaries. But buried beneath that automatic reaction was a powerful need to control—not just behavior and events, but people's very thoughts. Lady Glendale would despise anyone who failed to follow her lead.

Faced with a mother who demanded absolute obedience, Reggie had turned stubborn and Sedge had buried his soft heart under a facade of frivolous excess. Had he also sought society's admiration to offset the constant criticism he received at home? Perhaps that acclaim validated his worth—at least in his own mind.

It wasn't the same, of course. Public accolades could never replace a parent's love, especially when offered by a fickle society. But maybe she could help. He had seemed inordinately pleased at her reaction just now. Genuine gratitude had to mean more than the pompous posturings of youthful puppies or the fatuous fawning of witless matrons.

So perhaps their marriage would eventually work. She could not hope for anything beyond a comfortable friendship, but achieving that would be enough.

Or would it? She shivered to recall his firmly muscled body and his willingness to rescue a stranger from harm. His fury when she bumped Mrs. Stanhope into the street had cut more deeply than it should have. Their conversations had always been exhilarating. Even the confrontation at the masquerade—

She had remained groggy upon awakening to find him hovering over her. But that had not lessened his impact. He was very handsome. His eyes had been blue and filled with concern—at least until Mrs. Drummond-Burrell arrived. His dark hair had been disheveled where he had run his fingers through it. And his first words had drawn her attention to his mouth, to the sensuous lips she had wanted to touch . . .

*Surely I can't be that stupid!*

But the memories paraded inexorably through her mind. His overpowering virility at the altar that had forced her eyes to Reggie in search of relief—or to hide her reaction. Her pain when he declined to consummate their marriage. Her joy when he responded to her plea for help.

She had fallen in love with him.

*Stupid fool!* Though it had been inevitable. From the moment she had realized that he was more than a posturing fribble, she had been doomed. But this would add untold complications to her life.

Tears returned, stronger than ever. She could never admit her love, for despite today's softening, his eyes remained gray. He still resented her. Once he heard the latest tales, that would get worse. He would interpret any claim of love as a new form of manipulation, rejecting it out of hand, for it would seem to validate the stories.

Neither of them could ignore the difference in their stations. He might force his friends to accept her, but even he lacked the power to make society admit her.

His position was already slipping. In time, her presence would erode his consequence until no one followed his lead. If he truly was using society's regard to validate his worth, he would be devastated.

And he would come to resent her shortcomings. Lady Glendale's criticisms might have sounded cruel, but they were realistic. Time would reveal one problem after another until even Sedge would throw his hands up in despair. Eventually her clumsiness would mortify him in public, or nervousness would cause her to utter some gauche comment to a powerful society figure, or stuttering would make her a laughingstock.

She grimaced. Love raised the stakes of every encounter. His frustration would cut more deeply. His indifference would chafe. She would feel every diminution of his reputation, for it would be entirely her fault.

Yet Reggie's vow to remain unwed posed a worse problem. Sedge would have to father the next marquess. How would he feel about injecting her bloodlines into the family? Sooner or later he was bound to demand his rights—unless he had already considered the question and was avoiding her for that very reason.

She shivered. Could she hide her love if he claimed that ultimate intimacy?

# Chapter Fifteen

〜

"What the devil?" Sedge bit back further curses. He had already made Joanna jump.

The fashionable hour had been a pleasant diversion. He hadn't known what to expect after Joanna's inferences, but either she was overreacting to people's inevitable coolness as they evaluated a newcomer, or his credit drove animosity into hiding.

Everyone had been bursting with curiosity over his absence and eager to tell him the latest gossip, most of which he had heard from Joanna before reaching the park. A few more sprigs had transferred their allegiance to Kingsford, but he was happy enough to see them go. It was time to find a more substantive way to occupy his days.

His concern that Joanna might stutter had rapidly disappeared. Her poise had grown during his absence, becoming natural. In fact she now exuded a composure that he found very relaxing, and a calm that could provide an anchor for his life.

So his homecoming had seemed successful—until he entered Grosvenor Square. His father's traveling carriage sat before the house, footmen still unstrapping trunks.

"Is something wrong?" Joanna asked hesitantly.

"Perhaps. Father hasn't been to town in ten years— on orders from his doctor. I hope he has not suffered another spell. Did you know he was coming?"

"Of course not! How can you think I would have said nothing?"

"Forgive me. Such a stupid question reveals how weary I've grown." More than she knew. Hard travel aside, he'd slept little in recent days, and rarely soundly. "I expect he is here to consult a new doctor."

"I doubt it. He has the power to demand that a doctor attend him at home. He probably came to meet the upstart you thrust into the family." Bitterness had crept into her voice.

"You are no upstart, Joanna," he protested. "And we will be at the Close in less than a month, so he cannot have come for that. It must be his health—which bothers me," he admitted in distraction. "He hates leaving the steward in charge and once left thirty pages of detailed instructions for a three-day absence."

"Then why did he hire the man?"

"Always speak your mind to me, Joanna," he begged as she flinched. Her blush indicated that she was regretting the hasty words. "We must be honest with each other if we are to make this work." He pulled up behind the carriage. "The steward is better than most, for he not only knows his own job, he understands that Father needs to feel in control."

"So one must humor him?"

He shrugged. "I suppose that is true, though I've never really considered it in those terms. His demands have increased since his health began to decline. Every new restriction on his activity makes him less tolerant of opposition to his orders. I hope I never grow so autocratic."

She tilted her head, examining him from head to toe. "I doubt that is possible, Sedge. How could we increase your power short of handing you the throne? People already scramble to fulfill your every desire."

He laughed, squeezing her hand in delight. "How right you are. I can be insufferably arrogant, as Randolph reminds me all too often."

"Randolph?"

"My closest friend. We grew up together. But I doubt you know him. He left town the day we met. I was returning from his wedding when you jumped in front

of that carriage." He lifted her down from the phaeton,
tucking her arm through his own.

"Ah, Lord Symington."

"You do know him?"

She shook her head. "Lady Wicksfield mourned his
nuptials, for she coveted his wealth."

"You will meet him once the Season ends. His estate
adjoins mine."

"Where is your estate?" She again tilted her head. "I
actually know very little about you."

"A problem we must correct," he agreed. "Meadowbanks is in Kent, about fifty miles from London." He
described it as he escorted her into the house, using the
words to ease his trepidation over his father's arrival.
Whatever Glendale's reasons for coming to town, this
visit boded ill. His chest tightened.

Glendale was in the library, his glower making the
room seem colder than usual. Sedge set his face in an
expressionless mask, wishing that he had sent Joanna
upstairs. Only now did he recognize that she had been
on the right track. The man was here to read the riot
act for wedding without his permission.

The marquess sat in the position of power behind the
desk, as erect as a military officer despite his obvious
illness. His face contained no trace of warmth, the eyes
a hard, flat gray.

Sedge drew Joanna closer to his side, aware that she
was trembling. "What a surprise, Father." He kept the
tone carefully neutral, barely able to suppress his own
tremors. "This is Joanna."

"My lord." She curtsied to the precise depth required
for a marquess.

Glendale remained silent, only his eyes moving as he
examined her from head to toe.

Joanna tried not to lean on Sedge, though she was
grateful for the warmth of his arm. She hoped none of
her thoughts showed on her face. His neutral tone
masked more than surprise. It seemed to hide fear. Reggie had been called home shortly after befriending her.
Then Lady Glendale. Had Sedge refused a similar sum-

mons? He must know Glendale was appalled at his choice of wife.

She had no doubt why Glendale was here. Lady Glendale must have summoned him the moment Sedge had left. Considering the theme of the marchioness's lecture, they had probably planned to dispose of her before he returned. She should have expected this. Glendale was a perfectionist. Lady Glendale needed control. Both would do whatever was necessary to keep her out of the family.

Now she regretted not telling Sedge about his mother's antagonism. She had thought to spare his feelings, but ignorance would put him at a disadvantage in this confrontation.

Or would it?

The marquess had yet to speak a word, but his eyes clashed with Sedge's now that his harsh gaze had stopped stripping her bare. She glanced from one to the other and shivered. Even at his angriest, Sedge had never displayed his father's heartless fury. She suddenly knew that older quarrels already divided them. At least Sedge would not be caught by surprise. Without moving a muscle, they gave the impression of dogs warily circling.

The marquess finally spoke. "Miss Patterson may change for dinner." *If she knows how.* The unspoken criticism hung in the air.

"Lady Sedgewick." Sedge's correction was even colder. He turned her toward the hall—they had progressed barely two steps beyond the doorway.

"Sedgewick, you will remain here." The order was colder yet.

"My apologies, sir, but we are promised to the Caristokes this evening. We will wait on you in the morning. Together." He whisked her out of the library before Glendale could respond.

"Wasn't that rather rude?" she asked hesitantly.

"Perhaps." He let out a long sigh. "Forgive him, Joanna. He is never amiable after a journey. Had I known he was coming, I would have contrived to be away."

She frowned. He could not have missed Glendale's

antipathy. But there was no time for discussion. She would have to hurry if they were to make dinner. Caristoke would forgive them, but she would rather not cast a pall over the evening by mentioning Glendale's obvious fury.

"Don't look so anxious," he begged, covering her hand when they reached her door. "All will be well." Having uttered what at best was an exaggeration, he squeezed her fingers, then continued down the hall to his dressing room.

After dinner, Sedge returned to Caristoke's drawing room. Only his closest friends had gathered here this evening. They would all leave for the Rufton ball shortly. Joanna seemed at ease. Wormsley had her doubled over in laughter.

"Have you heard from Glendale yet?" asked Hartford.

"He showed up this afternoon."

Hartford nearly choked on his wine. "Good God! Did he vent his spleen on your wife?" But he was already shaking his head. "Can't have. She's too relaxed."

Joanna was now chattering with the other wives. "He had no time. I rushed her up to change and refused to speak with him myself—which will only make him worse."

"He'll come around once he admits what a gem you found."

Sedge skirted that topic, though Thomas's words confirmed that the reformed rake had lost neither his eye for an enticing woman nor his ability to look beyond the surface. He had to agree with the assessment. Joanna was indeed a gem—or would be once she abandoned her infatuation with Reggie and honed her confidence. "I doubt he will ever approve. He is the most exacting man I know. Nothing less than a duke's daughter would satisfy him."

"My mother is equally stiff-rumped. She made no effort to accept my marriage until she got to know Caroline. Then she couldn't help herself." He grinned. "By the time Robin was born, you would have thought she'd arranged the match herself.''

"Glendale would never be swayed by a child, not even by a charmer like Robin—he'll lead you a merry dance one day."

"He already does. That boy can get into more mischief than any four ordinary lads. Even more than the four of us at our wildest." He smiled to recall the days when Sedge, Caristoke, and Rufton had been his schoolmates.

Caristoke joined them, launching a convoluted tale about a squabble over a newly arrived actress. Sedge injected comments at appropriate intervals, but most of his attention was on Joanna.

She sparkled this evening. As in the park, she was more poised than he remembered. Yet she should not be. The rumors had grown while he'd been at Wicksfield, many of them casting aspersions on her background. She ought to be a stammering, clumsy idiot by now.

Unless she was responding to his own changed demeanor. In fact, that was the only explanation. His father's antagonism would have started her stuttering only a few days ago. But he was calmer now. They had laughed together, teasing each other into relaxation and sharing the amusement he always felt over people's behavior. Her interpretation of society's recent antics had been identical to his.

And that was good. So far, the day had gone well. He would see that she enjoyed the ball. With luck, a frank discussion once they returned home would lay her infatuation to rest, so he could consummate their union. Erotic dreams had plagued him for days.

Harriet pounced the moment they arrived at the ball, her smile a mile wide, exuberance broadening every gesture.

"Thank you, Joanna. And you, my lord," she added to Sedge. "Words cannot convey my gratitude for what you have done for us."

"I take it your mother accepted Mr. Wethersby," said

Joanna after reminding her former charge to control her excitement in public.

"With reluctance, but Papa's letter left her no choice. We will return to the Manor next week. Jonathan will escort his family there at the end of the month, with the wedding scheduled a fortnight later. Will you attend?"

"Of course," said Sedge before Joanna could respond. "And may I offer my best wishes?"

"Thank you."

Noting that Harriet was again ready to erupt into paroxysms of joy, Sedge smiled at Joanna and left them alone.

She led Harriet to the retiring room. "Jump up and down and scream if you must," she said with a laugh. "Just do it here lest you make a cake of yourself in public."

Harriet grabbed her in a suffocating hug, then did indeed jump up and down. "How can I ever thank you? I was so miserable, terrified that Mama would do something awful."

"She may well have."

"And how could I have been so wrong about Lord Sedgewick?" Harriet hadn't heard her. "I thought him hopelessly arrogant, yet look at the trouble he took to convince Papa to accept Jonathan. He is the most wonderful man. You must be the luckiest girl alive—after me, of course. I can hardly wait for the wedding. Tell me what to expect."

"Another time," she begged. "You have more pressing concerns. Everyone will speak with you tonight, and you must show them what an elegant lady you are. Someone who is about to marry cannot act the giddy girl."

It took a quarter hour to blunt Harriet's exuberance. Sedge was waiting for her near the stairs.

"Has she recovered?"

"I hope so. She is so very young. One forgets how energetic girls are at that age."

"I doubt most girls are that bad."

"True. I have a sister a year younger. She wouldn't dream of making such a scene."

"Will you honor me with this set?" he asked as the beginnings of a waltz filled the room.

"Of course."

They did not speak much as they danced, for which she was grateful. Love weakened her knees. She was aware of each finger of the hand that rested on her waist, of the occasional brush of a thigh as they wove around other couples, of the virility radiating from him in waves. His eyes were blue again, the first prolonged blue she had seen in days. This duty dance no longer filled him with fury. Hiding her reaction required all her concentration.

"You've an excellent touch with girls," he said once the waltz concluded, nodding toward Harriet.

"I just hope it lasts. She might be under control at the moment, but anything could set her off again."

They separated, his trust increasing her confidence. He claimed a second waltz after supper, then sighed.

"Do you mind if we leave early?"

"Of course not. You must have been up at dawn to have arrived when you did."

"Exactly. I must plead weariness, though you will never reveal that fact. No gentleman of distinction would consider retiring at midnight."

"Nor are you. It is at least half past." Her attempt at a joke drew his smile.

"Bless you. Father will expect us in the library by nine. Whatever his reasons for coming to town, he will not neglect quizzing us."

She was again left with the feeling that something was seriously wrong between Sedge and his father, but they were not yet close enough that she could ask for details. Perhaps Reggie could explain.

Only then did she realize that Reggie was absent. And Sedge's plea of exhaustion did not entirely ring true. Had he realized that his position was in jeopardy? But that did not seem right, either. Wethersby's report of their journey to Wicksfield had swung the doubters back toward Sedge. Fewer people were whispering that he would lock her away in the country.

They arrived home to find a frowning Husby in the

hall. "I was about to send a footman, my lord. Glendale has taken ill. The doctor is on his way."

"Stomach pains?" asked Sedge.

"And faintness."

"I will attend him shortly."

Joanna felt him relax as he accompanied her upstairs, though something was clearly irritating him. "This is quite common," he swore once they reached their sitting room. "Father is supposed to avoid strenuous activity. Even this trip—which I can make in about ten hours— probably took him two days. And he has a long history of overeating. Huge meals combined with overexertion invariably cause trouble. Last time he was abed a full week."

"I thought you said he avoided town."

"He avoids London, but he exerts himself in other ways, riding neck or nothing over the estate, indulging in drunken card parties with neighbors, ringing peals over the heads of the steward, the groundskeeper, and anyone else who annoys him."

"So I was right. He came here to condemn me and attack you for wedding me."

He sighed. "We don't know that, Joanna. But no matter what his reasons, you are not responsible for his illness. He might well have made the trip anyway. He has been trying to force me into marriage for years. His insistence this spring surpassed everything that came before. If I were still unattached, he would have done something to make me follow orders."

"Very well. Should I await the doctor's diagnosis?" She doubted Lady Glendale would care for her company, but going to bed made her feel even more of an outsider.

"Get some sleep, if you can. I will need you to be rested tomorrow. If there is anything you can do earlier, I will send for you. Mama is with Father. Who knows where Reggie is, but I expect he will arrive shortly. This is not the first time we have gone through this. Nor will it likely be the last. Sometimes I think Father enjoys the attention these spells bring."

"Another comment I will not repeat. You are tired indeed. You need rest far more than I do."

"I will try. Sleep well, Joanna." Drawing her into a warm embrace, he kissed her gently on the forehead before heading for the other wing.

She lay awake long into the night, trying to make sense of the day's contradictions. But it was the thought of his warm lips that finally sent her to sleep. The memory invaded her dreams, leaving a longing ache behind.

Yet in the morning, she cursed her obedience. Glendale remained unconscious from an apoplectic seizure suffered during the night. Sedge was gaunt-eyed from lack of sleep.

# Chapter Sixteen

❧

Sedge escaped to the drawing room, unable to bear his mother's reproachful looks another minute. She blamed him for the attack, though even the doctor agreed that it wasn't his fault.

Yet yesterday's refusal to face the inevitable confrontation haunted him. It was the first time he had defied a demand to talk, and it had probably contributed to this attack.

Damn the old bastard all to hell! What had he hoped to accomplish by coming to town? It was too late to prevent their marriage. Divorce was out of the question, for the scandal would destroy him. Even the canny marquess could not know that an annulment was still possible.

Or could he?

Servants knew everything, so they must be aware that he had yet to visit his wife's bed. His mother would have interrogated them when she returned to town. She might even have summoned Glendale. Had they hoped to drive Joanna away before he returned?

"Never," he vowed, pacing the room. Renewed fury drove exhaustion into hiding. His parents had interfered in his life many times, but this was the last straw.

Now that he considered it, his mother had undoubtedly contributed to the rumors while he had been away. Lady Wicksfield's credit was too weak for anyone to believe her. And the woman hadn't the intelligence to concoct some of the stories. Leaving Reggie to escort Joanna should have deflected any suspicions over his absence. Only another family member could have caused the brouhaha he had found last night.

Thomas had warned him, so he had been able to laugh at the questions. And once Wethersby confirmed his quest, most people had applauded his actions. But it still hurt that society had turned on him the moment he was out of sight, ignoring ten years of exemplary behavior on the word of someone he had been publicly at odds with for nearly that long.

*Deliberately seduced him . . . Left town to escape her scheming . . . Arranging to incarcerate her . . . Will certainly annul . . .*

He could hear his mother's voice uttering every charge. If they had managed to drive Joanna away, society would believe that he had locked her up. No denials would have erased that impression.

"Is there any change?" asked Joanna, appearing in the doorway.

He tamped down his anger. Without proof, it served no purpose. Only after verifying his suspicions could he decide how to proceed. "He remains in a coma."

Tears glistened in her eyes. She had been angry that he'd let her sleep through the initial attack, but she could have done nothing. The doctor had already been there. Reggie had been in shock. His mother would have insulted her.

But his decision had fed her guilt. How could he convince her that she was being foolish without revealing that he had been trying to protect her from his mother's venom? And from his own jealousy, he admitted. He remained unsure which brother she might have comforted.

"Father is the most stubborn man alive," he said, then flinched at his choice of words. "He has refused to follow his doctor's orders for years. It was inevitable that it would catch up with him."

"But it would not have happened now if we had not wed."

Again he flinched. "Fustian!

"Not fustian. You know he only came here to rebuke us."

"So blame me. I'm the one who insisted on marriage.

I'm the one who scheduled the wedding before he had even learned of our betrothal. And I'm the one who refused to meet with him yesterday."

"I won't tolerate you shouldering my guilt. If I had stopped to think, I would not have pounced on Mary that night. I would have realized her occupation and known she would lash out to prevent exposure. Then you wouldn't be trapped."

His face heated. So much else had happened that he'd nearly forgotten that confrontation. Thus he hadn't considered that Joanna might know Jenny's duties. Former duties. She was now under Lord Peter Barnhard's protection. But this was no time to discuss it.

Resting his hands on her shoulders, he gazed into her eyes. "You are blameless, Joanna. As am I. Father's poor judgment brought on this attack. Did your own father teach you nothing about God's will?"

"God's will does not require a man to martyr himself on the altar of public opinion. But it *does* admonish children to obey their parents."

*Ouch.*

"The doctor has returned, my lord," said Husby from the doorway.

Sedge sighed. Somehow he must convince Joanna that he did not regret wedding her—not an easy task, considering that it had initially been true, and one that must wait until later. "I am coming," he told Husby, then turned back to his wife. "This is not the time to argue blame or guilt or anything else. Once this unpleasantness is behind us, we will discuss everything openly and honestly. In the meantime, ask Cook to set out a cold collation in the breakfast room. I doubt any of us will be sitting down to regular meals. And send regrets to Lady Delwyn and the Heberts. We will not be going out tonight."

Releasing her, he followed the doctor to his father's bedchamber.

Joanna stared at the empty doorway. Here was more proof that she would never be part of this family. He would not have spoken to his secretary so sharply.

Of course, he was exhausted and probably terrified. No matter what disagreements existed between them, losing a parent was difficult. And he probably felt as guilty as she did.

So her reaction was unfair, she admitted as she headed downstairs to find the cook. Sedge must recognize his mother's antagonism. Introducing his wife into the sickroom would increase Lady Glendale's distress. And if Glendale awakened to find her there, he might suffer another attack.

Nor should she have mentioned Mary. Aristocratic wives ignored their husbands' liaisons. She could hardly demand that Sedge give up his mistress for a wife he hadn't wanted. That was no way to foster closer rapport.

But whatever Sedge's motives for isolating her, she had no excuse for brooding about it. A single week of marriage was hardly long enough to recover from the shock, let alone adjust to the reality they both faced. Yet they were slowly making progress. Perhaps he wanted to make this union work. It might be the realization of how little they knew each other that had led to his vow of an open, honest discussion once his father recovered.

"There you are, Doctor," exclaimed Lady Glendale when they arrived in the sickroom. "Glendale's eyes just blinked."

Sedge raised his brows at Reggie, wondering if she was imagining a change.

"It's true," he said. "His hand also twitched."

Relief weakened his knees. Perhaps this would relieve Joanna's guilt. This attack might be the most serious yet, but it was far from the first. Nor would it be the last. Eventually one of them would kill him.

"If you will leave the room, I can examine his lordship," said the doctor.

Reggie helped Lady Glendale rise, then followed Sedge across the hall. He left the door open so they could hear any summons.

"He will be all right now," said Lady Glendale.

"Perhaps." Sedge was unwilling to predict the future. Though there had been no lasting effects from earlier attacks, none had produced so prolonged a coma. "But he must follow the doctor's orders from now on."

"He won't." Her response confirmed what they all knew. Glendale's anger when his activities were curtailed was as dangerous as overexertion.

Conversation lagged. Reggie joined him in pacing the floor. The waiting was intolerable. Even his mother was restless. Her hands twisted, shredding a handkerchief.

He paused at the window, noting that straw had been laid down in front of the house to deaden the noise of hooves on cobblestones. The custom was meant to ease the suffering of the dying, but he doubted whether Glendale could hear sounds from the square even if he regained his faculties. His bedchamber faced the garden behind the house. The only real purpose the straw served was to advertise the severity of Glendale's illness.

He resumed his pacing.

The doctor was taking forever, raising his apprehension. Had the marquess suffered yet another attack? He was on the verge of checking when the man finally appeared.

"Lord Glendale has emerged from his coma," he announced as he joined Lady Glendale on the settee.

"Thank God!" She sagged against the back. "How long until he can rise."

The doctor cleared his throat. "I cannot say, my lady."

Reggie stared as Lady Glendale gasped.

"Out with it," growled Sedge. "Suspense is inappropriate under the circumstances."

"The seizure caused considerable damage. Though he is conscious and understands simple requests, he is unable to speak. Nor can he move his right arm or leg at the moment." He patted Lady Glendale's hand in an ineffectual gesture of comfort.

"Is the condition permanent?" asked Reggie.

"It is too early to tell. While many patients remain paralyzed, others improve with time. This may be a temporary annoyance while his body works on making a full recovery. Or some form of impairment might remain for the rest of his days."

"How often does a man in his state actually recover?" demanded Sedge, irritated at the doctor's dithering.

"I have seen it happen," he insisted, again patting Lady Glendale's hand. "Each case is different, so no purpose is served by comparing one to another. It is important that Lord Glendale remain calm. He is understandably frustrated over his current state. Further irritation will lessen his chances of recovery. Anger can trigger another fit, which might kill him. Do nothing to annoy him."

Leaving them stunned, he retired to the marquess's bedchamber.

Reggie was the first to react, reaching for his mother's hand.

She recoiled. "How dare you pretend sympathy after causing this trouble!"

"Enough, Mother," commanded Sedge. "We are all in shock, but that does not excuse saying something you will regret."

"Regret?" Her voice rose to a scream as her temper shattered. "How can one regret the truth?" She glared at Reggie. "You are killing him. Your spiteful stubbornness has caused most of his spells. Last night was the final straw. How could you refuse to do your duty? It is a small price to pay for the wealth and power you will soon enjoy." Her voice cracked, but she swept on. "You know that marriage need not curtail your other activities, yet you swore to his face that you would abandon the marquessate rather than wed. Don't deny it," she added as he opened his mouth. "I overheard every word. He ordered you to wed. You refused. And your language! We will become laughingstocks. Everyone heard you. You were shouting so loudly, passers-by in the square must have heard you. He would not be lying in that bed if you showed the least loyalty to your family. You heard the doctor. Only calm will allow him to recover. So give him that calm. Choose a bride so he can be at peace."

"You are absurd, madam." Reggie was hanging on to his own temper with difficulty.

"If anyone is absurd, it is you. Why do we have such ungrateful sons? And I do mean ungrateful," she contin-

ued, turning her glare toward Sedge. "You are just as
guilty. How dare you marry a nobody without even
looks to recommend her? You have made a mockery of
everything this family represents."

"Lie down, Mother," he said. "Your nerves have overset you."

"Overset me!" She surged to her feet, slapping his
face. "You have overset me! You are deliberately ignoring your heritage. Don't you dare trot out that ridiculous
claim that you had no choice," she added as he stared
at her in shock. "Her breeding is so base that anyone
of sensibility must consider her a trollop. She is fit for
nothing beyond whoring in the streets."

"Enough, madam!"

"You must accept the truth, Sedgewick. That girl is
a disgrace."

"I said enough, madam!" Anger boiled in his chest.

"You are so stupid," she snapped. "Why did you not
wield your vaunted credit? You know very well that you
could have escaped her greedy clutches. No one would
have dared criticize your judgment. If you had exposed
her as a grasping fortune hunter, society would have
applauded. Instead, you let her besmirch your good
name. Half of society already ridicules your judgment,
and the other half questions your taste. The young men
are abandoning you in droves. Your reputation is in
shambles. You will be driven from town in a fortnight."

"You exaggerate—"

"Never! And you actually had the gall to install her
in my house! How can you expect me to be civil to
her?" She wrung her hands. "Why did you return so
soon? If only you had stayed away, Glendale could have
convinced the archbishop to annul this abomination. But
it can still be done. File the application, Sedgewick. Ease
your father's suffering. Restore his faith in you."

"What the—"

She ignored his shock. "If it is too late for an annulment, at least have the decency to hide her away in the
country so people can forget the stain you have placed
on our name. The arrangements are already in place.
And Reginald must wed immediately. We cannot allow

her baseborn blood to taint the marquessate." She turned to her oldest son. "Lady Dorothy will arrive in two days. I already have the special license. We will expect an heir within the year."

"Absolutely not!" Reggie fisted his hands. "You have gone too far this time, madam. Way too far. Despite my repeated vows to have nothing to do with that brainless wench, you persist in pursuing an alliance. Do not deny it," he charged over her protest. "Do you think I am stupid? Your vow that I would wed her has already done her untold harm. Her father turned down Sir Henry's offer barely a month ago. Now you have ruined her beyond redemption, for I will not take her. Ever. I would see the marquessate revert to the crown first. And I will send her father a letter describing your unconscionable lies. You will have to live with the dishonor for the rest of your life."

Sedge fought past the red mist that had obscured his eyes at the lengths his parents had been willing to go. If he had returned even a day later, Joanna would have been gone without a trace. "Your arrogance surpasses anything I've ever seen," he growled, pushing her back on the settee and looming over her. "I will excuse your rudeness because I know you are concerned for Father's health, but you will never utter such rot again. Your efforts to discredit Joanna have failed. She is accepted by all but your bosom bows, most of whom are reevaluating their position at this very moment, for your lies have now been exposed as the calumny they are. My credit is as firm as ever. You need a new source of gossip, by the way," he continued, dredging up a hint of his public facade. "The only truth you have ever spoken about Joanna is that her father is a vicar. There is nothing wrong with her breeding, nor with her looks. And her virtue was never in doubt. The only thing havy-cavy about her mother's marriage was her uncle's hope that she would wed the older brother, but when she chose the younger, he agreed. And believing Lady Wicksfield makes you look ridiculous. The woman is a brainless schemer pursuing a personal quarrel. She has long blamed Joanna's mother for Wicksfield's decision to keep her in the country—a decision based solely on her own reckless spending. And she was furious when Wicksfield placed Joanna in charge of the household."

"She has bewitched you."

"Never." His voice hardened. "I learned that fact from Wicksfield himself. As for your other absurdities, Joanna's brother occasionally does odd jobs for the blacksmith, sending the proceeds to his brother at Oxford. Her father's parishioners mourn her departure, for she was considered a saint in the community. You will either welcome her into the family or I will see that you are ostracized from society. Is that clear?"

"How dare you speak—"

"Enough, Mother," snapped Reggie, joining his brother to glare into her face. "You are completely out of line. Father's illness is his own fault—or yours for summoning him to town against his doctor's orders."

"He had no choice if he was to protect the title."

Sedge snorted. "He tried to protect the title by doing something he knew would kill him? How stupid can you get?"

Reggie overrode her response. "No, Mother. This has nothing to with the title. It has to do with your determination to retain your own power after he dies. You've a tongue like an adder, and you employ it freely. Do not think that I am ignorant of the lies you told to Father. I have seen the letters you wrote after I befriended her. You manipulated a dying man for your own ends. Your selfishness surpasses anything I have ever witnessed. But you lose. The day Father dies, you are moving out of the Close. To the dower house if you learn to keep your tongue between your teeth. To the Scottish property under guard if you don't. Sedge is right about Joanna's background, and all of society knows it. Your puny lies have only made you a laughingstock. Open your eyes for once. Those two are perfect for each other. As for me, I would wed an opera dancer before accepting one of your protégées."

Lady Glendale collapsed into hysterics, but Sedge let Reggie deal with her. His head swirled with guilt and shame.

What had he done?

Only now did he admit that his image of Joanna had been tainted from the beginning by his mother's criticisms. Not the ones about her looks, which he had always found desirable; now that she had a decent wardrobe, she was stunning. But he had questioned her motives and flinched at her breeding more than once. Yet he had welcomed girls with even worse backgrounds into society, and considered some of them friends. Caristoke's wife was a case in point. Why had he parroted his mother's judgments instead of thinking for himself? From her first tirade over Reggie's infatuation, he had accepted her word as gospel. If only he had listened to Reggie, but he had been so furious over being compared to Crossbridge that he had rejected any hint that he might also be jumping to erroneous conclusions.

His antagonism had not helped Joanna. She knew he hated being forced. And leaving her to his mother's mercy while he visited Wicksfield could not have been pleasant.

Reggie was making little headway.

"Leave me alone!" his mother shouted. "What did I ever do to deserve such wretched sons? If Glendale dies, I will never forgive you!" Slapping Reggie's hand aside, she stormed out of the room.

Glendale's door slammed behind her.

Sedge flinched. Temper had bested them all, prompting words none of them would easily forget.


Joanna finished the last note and handed them to a footman. The job was necessary, but she could not shake off the conviction that Sedge had used it to keep her away from the sickroom.

It was time she took her place in this family. Allowing Lady Glendale to exclude her set a precedent that would make the future impossible. She would not stay in the marquess's room, but at least she would look in to see how he was faring.

She was approaching his suite when angry voices halted her in her tracks. *How dare you marry a nobody*

*without even looks to recommend her . . . breeding is so
base . . . whoring in the streets . . .*

Dear God! She sagged against the wall. It was worse
than she had feared. No wonder Sedge had been furious.
She had never understood the extent of his sacrifice.

*Society already ridicules your judgment . . . cannot
allow her baseborn blood to taint the marquessate.*

Nausea choked her throat. Placing her hands over her
ears, she escaped to her room.

Sedge's immediate friends had welcomed her, but matrons like Lady Glendale would ultimately decide her
fate. Without their support, she could never become part
of his world, making his sacrifice useless. Even his
friends would balk when facing a choice between diminished credit and her company. She would hurt them and
would ultimately hurt Sedge. If he used society's esteem
to balance his parents' criticism, then losing it would
hurt twice over.

Or worse.

Already, their marriage was widening the rift with his
parents. And she had been right. Concern over this mésalliance was worsening Glendale's condition. Sedge's resentment would fester, hardening into real hatred.
London's premier dandy was a proud man. He had suppressed that pride long enough to wed her, but it would
not remain dormant for long. Their unequal union would
chafe, destroying every spark of congeniality.

She could not tolerate such misery. Nor could she
allow the rift between him and his family to broaden
into a permanent breach. Blood ties were important. She
loved him too much to ruin his life.

Dabbing at her tears, she turned to her dressing room.
Marriage had been a mistake, as she had known all
along. Why had she not listened to the voice warning
her that it could only bring disaster?

Dumping the hat from a bandbox, she filled the box
with her old clothing, then wrote a brief farewell before
slipping from the house.

# Chapter Seventeen

Sedge stared from the doorway to his brother as the sound of that abrupt departure reverberated through the room. Reggie was white-faced.

"She didn't mean it," Sedge said softly. "We are all too tired to know what we're saying."

Reggie sank into a chair, dropping his head in his hands. "She meant it. Every word." His shoulders shook with sobs. "Dear God, I can't take any more."

Appalled, Sedge shut and locked the door. A decanter of brandy remained from last night's vigil. Downing a glass, he poured one for Reggie, then returned to the window to stare into the square.

Not until he heard glass clink against the table did he turn back to the room. "How can you take her tirade seriously? You know it arose from fear of the changes she faces."

"This is not the first time she has uttered those charges. Or the tenth. Or even the twentieth. Nor will it be the last." He poured another drink, then stared into the fireplace. "Father is dying. I doubt the doctor has ever seen a man recover from this level of impairment. All that pap about keeping him calm was merely to give Mother hope, but the situation is hopeless. He won't last a month."

"Agreed."

"You will have to deal with it, Sedge. I won't be here."

"What—"

Reggie looked like he was facing an executioner. The

lines in his face had deepened, making him look fifty. "Sit down, Sedge. The title will be mine within the month. I can escape Mother's pressure by sending her to Scotland, but she is not the only one. Aunt Barkley is just as bad. Half of society already condemns me for reaching the advanced age of four-and-thirty without doing my duty. The rest will soon follow. I can't take it any longer. My valet is already packing. We will be out of the country within the week."

"My God! Why?" He stared as the awful suspicion formed. "Surely this is not about Joanna!"

Reggie actually smiled. "Dear Joanna. You still do not realize what a jewel you have, do you?"

He slammed his glass onto the table.

"Relax, Sedge. I have no designs on your wife, though I will admit this once that I love her. Deeply. But she has never returned my feelings, thank God. I am merely a friend and brother."

"You are not making sense."

"I suppose not." He bit his lip, swallowed more brandy, then released a long sigh before finally meeting Sedge's gaze. "You have never believed my vow to avoid marriage."

"Who can predict the future? You might meet someone who can return your love one day."

"God, I hope not!" He swallowed hard. "You've no idea how thankful I've been that Joanna doesn't care. Any hint of infatuation would have meant cutting all contact. Treat her well, Sedge. She will bear the next marquess."

"How can you—"

"Please!" interrupted Reggie. "Don't make this more difficult than it already is." His eyes glistened in the afternoon sunlight. "I've always vowed I *would* never wed, but it would be more honest to say I *can* never wed."

"Do you have a secret wife tucked away?" Preposterous, but better than any other possibility.

"No." Pain filled his voice. "I should have told you years ago, but it never—" He swallowed. "You deserve the truth before I leave. I cannot function as a husband should."

"Oh, my God." His knees buckled. Reggie was right. He should have sat down. "What are you saying?" he whispered hoarsely.

"It doesn't work."

"Doesn't wo— You feel nothing?"

"I wish it were that simple. Unfortunately, the desire is there, but I can do nothing about it."

"You have nev— But what about your mistresses?"

Reggie shrugged. "They have been aging courtesans, abused by previous protectors, who needed a safe place to recover and a friendly ear to listen to their problems. Most of them chose to retire to country cottages. I may take Pru with me—she has no family left and is fascinated by talk of foreign places." He shook his head. "But that is irrelevant."

"Are you sure the condition is permanent?" Fatigue and shock made their conversation seem unreal.

"Yes. It has never worked. I consulted the best doctors in Scotland some years ago—anonymously. They've no idea why, but all agreed the problem is unlikely to disappear."

"Yet you said nothing."

"How could I?" His eyes revealed unimaginable torment. "Have you any idea how hard it is to confess I'm only half a man?"

"I don't consider you so."

"I do." His raised hand halted further protest. "Living with deceit is no longer possible. I cannot remain in England, for life will become intolerable once Father dies. Since I am not cut out to be a hermit, my only chance for a comfortable existence is to adopt a new name and build a life in another country—probably America."

"You sound so calm. I can barely think."

"I have been planning it long enough. This day was bound to come."

"At least remain until Father's death." Tears stung his eyes.

"No." His voice hardened. "You do not understand,

Sedge. Father and I have fought for years. Bitterly. Last night's argument was the last straw. I no longer care whether he lives or dies. Nor do I care what Mother wants or what society thinks. I would leave tomorrow if there were not loose ends I must tie up. My solicitor is drawing up papers that will give you control of my affairs, including everything to do with the marquessate. I would give you the title if I could. The fortune I already control should be sufficient to cover my needs, so everything else will be yours. And I must say good-bye to Joanna."

"I see. There does not seem to be anything else to say. But please stay in touch." This time, his tears spilled over.

"Don't," begged Reggie.

"I can't help it."

"You must. I cannot afford to collapse yet. In fact, Mother's latest start means I must leave sooner than I'd planned. Lady Dorothy's reputation might be salvaged if I am gone before she arrives. Meet me at my solicitor's at ten in the morning."

"Very well. But I expect to hear from you."

He sighed. "If you insist. I will travel for a year or two before settling down to become an eccentric. But I will write."

Downing the last of his wine, Reggie straightened his shoulders and left.

Sedge poured himself another drink. Back-to-back confrontations had left him feeling limp.

*Cannot function as a husband.*

Poor Reggie. He could not imagine a worse hell than feeling desire he could not satisfy. No wonder Reggie refused to wed. How could he put any woman through that? A lady's primary duty was to provide an heir. Failure was always laid at her feet. And Reggie risked becoming an object of ridicule if society learned the truth.

But dwelling on Reggie's problems served no purpose. His own pressed heavily on his shoulders. His life was changing in ways he had never expected. He must make peace with Joanna and build a real marriage with her, inform his parents that Reggie would not return, take up the burden of the marquessate . . .

He shuddered.

He knew little of the Glendale affairs, for he had never expected to deal with them. Nor did Reggie, for that matter. Their father had been loath to involve his heir in estate matters, lest doing so reduce his own power.

Reggie was right about their mother. Unless he moved her out of the Close the moment she became a widow, she would cling to her position, refusing to believe that Reggie was gone forever. Whether he moved into the Close himself would depend on where she lived. He would not subject Joanna to her spite.

But that was for the future. He needed to talk to Joanna. If Reggie was right—and he prayed his impressions were correct—then he had wronged her yet again. She did not love Reggie. In any case, she must know the truth, for Reggie's departure would affect both of them.

Dear God, he hoped Reggie was right. He needed her. She was the only rock left in his turbulent world.

But he could not find her. When he reached her room, he spotted a letter on her dressing table. A letter addressed to him.

*I cannot cause a breach between you and your family,* she had written in a hand that visibly shook. *Nor can I inflict further damage to your reputation. Marriage was a mistake, as you must know. I regret allowing you to press me, for I knew that you did not want so low a connection. Even your vast credit cannot force the dowagers to accept me. Persisting can only hurt you. My training did not prepare me for entering your world, as events have proved. There should be no problem getting an annulment. Perhaps one day you will find someone you can care for.*

His glass shattered on the floor as the realization hit him. She had heard part of his mother's tirade, though she must have fled before his own response—not that she would have believed it. His mother's insinuations threaded every word of this note.

This third shock left him teetering on the brink of total collapse. How much could a man take in one day?

Shaking his head, he read the note a second time. Why should he be surprised at her regret? He had made little effort to hide his anger before leaving town. He had left her to his mother's vicious tongue. And they had had no chance to talk since his return.

He groaned. He had treated her badly. Even his anger was not her fault. In retrospect, he had been using her love for Reggie as an excuse to vent fury over his own carelessness.

She had been blameless.

The admission hurt. He had ignored her objections to marriage, believing they were an attempt to present a demure image. But she had been serious. She did not want him.

Yet he did want her, he admitted as he left her room. She was intelligent, caring, and altogether delightful. In fact, she possessed nearly every virtue of that ideal wife he had envisioned finding. But he had been too stubborn to admit it. What an ass he was. Something about her had attracted him from the first, though his conceit had balked at the idea. Perhaps his carelessness had been less inadvertent than he'd thought.

He had to find her. They needed to talk with no misconceptions to cloud their thinking. Where might she have gone?

A moment's thought dismissed Wicksfield House. No matter how grateful Harriet was feeling, Lady Wicksfield would not welcome her. Would she seek Lady Hartford's help?

He frowned. They had formed a fast friendship in recent days, though he doubted she would risk seeking out one of his friends.

But he suddenly knew where she was. While protesting against marriage, she had mentioned her mother's burdens. She had gone home to the vicarage.

Damn! He did not know where her father lived. Wasting no time on summoning a servant, he headed for the stables.

"I need help," he admitted when he reached Reggie's rooms.

He glared. "Is this some misguided attempt to keep me here?"

"Devil take it!" He inhaled to curb his temper. "No. Joanna overheard Mother's tirade and bolted." He handed over the letter. "I think she's headed home."

Reggie's eyes blazed by the time he finished reading. "What the devil did you do to her?"

"Dumped my fury and resentment on her innocent shoulders, then left her to Mother's vicious tongue," he admitted. "You can curse me some other time. Right now, I need to find her. Where is her father's living?"

Reggie stared a long moment. "Gloucestershire."

"Could you be more specific?" He drew in a deep breath. "I admit I never asked a word about her family. But you are right," he added. "She is a jewel."

Reggie examined his face, then smiled. "Her father lives near Cavuscul Hill. But she is probably taking the mail, which doesn't leave until six." He pulled out a pocket watch. "If you hurry, you can catch her at the Swan With Two Necks. We can postpone our own meeting until two." His smile broadened into a grin.

Joanna fought her impatience as men loaded luggage onto the mail coach. The marquess's illness had disrupted the household so much that Sedge might not know she was gone. Yet she would not relax until she was away from London. He would feel honor-bound to stop her, but with luck, he would not follow her until Glendale's health improved. She would remain at home for only a single night. Once he admitted that she was serious, he would annul their marriage and get on with his life.

She sighed. It might be better to disappear directly, but she had to explain to her parents. Papa might be shocked, but he would understand. And he might even know where she could go.

The call finally came to board. Pulling her cloak tighter, she headed across the stable yard. The inside seats had been claimed before her arrival, so she must endure an outside perch. At least it wasn't raining.

"Joanna!"

Her heart leaped as she spied the figure jumping down from a familiar phaeton, but she immediately quelled its pleasure. "Go home, Sedge. Honor has led you too far astray already."

He flinched. "Joanna, we must talk. Please? I will never hold you against your will. If we cannot come to an understanding, I will provide transportation to wherever you wish to go. But at least hear me out."

He was more tense than ever, but the quality had changed almost to fear, though that seem absurd. Unless his father was worse.

"How is Glendale?"

"Awake. Incapable of speech or much movement. Dying."

"You should not have left him."

He glared. "You are far more important than he is. Even if we return to find him dead, I will not regret following you."

"Can't you let go of your pride long enough to admit the truth?" she demanded.

"What the devil is that supposed to mean?"

"Marrying me was less a matter of honor than of your overweening conceit. London's premier dandy would never tarnish even the lowliest female. Never mind that we were strangers who had no interest in marriage. Never mind that you disliked me even before that night. You care for nothing beyond appearances. Why else are you here?"

He clenched his teeth. A coach clattered into the yard, splashing him with a sloppy mixture of manure and horse urine. "I never disliked you, Joanna. Distrusted you, perhaps, though that did not survive the masquerade. I was angry even before you arrived that night, and I was furious at my own stupidity, but none of it was aimed at you."

"So you admit that marriage was a stupid idea."

"Never. It was right then, and it is right now. The stupidity was placing you in a compromising position and thus drawing society's censure onto your head. Please forgive me for not making that clear earlier. I wronged you in many ways, Joanna, not least of which was using you as a target for my irritation over other things. But I want to make a fresh start. Perhaps something good can come out of this day. God knows everything else is collapsing."

"Give 'im a chance, miss!" shouted a groom.

" 'E's jes tryin' to turn ye up sweet," warned a maid. "All the fancy coves lie. Don't let no purty words turn yer 'ead."

Joanna flinched, but Sedge seemed oblivious to their growing audience. His eyes were anxious, but blue. He radiated tension, but not antagonism. She shrugged. "Very well. We will talk."

Two grooms broke into a cheer as the guard tossed down her bandbox. Sedge lifted her across a mudhole, holding her so tightly that she could scarcely breathe. His cheek brushed her forehead in what might have been a caress. By the time he placed her in his phaeton, the mail coach was gone.

Gathering up the ribbons, he headed for Mayfair.

She stared at his profile, trying to decide what he really wanted and why. Huge circles rimmed his eyes, reminding her that he had been up since dawn yesterday. Lines around his mouth added a grimness to his countenance that she had never seen. But his first words caught her by surprise.

"You overheard Mother, didn't you?" He stared at her, ignoring a flurry of curses when his team nearly ran down a sailor.

"Not deliberately. I despise eavesdroppers."

"Too bad. If you had remained longer, you would have discovered that neither Reggie nor I agreed with her tirade."

"I know you both well enough to expect that."

"Then why did you flee?"

"I cannot be responsible for creating a breach with your family—as I explained in my note."

"You are not responsible." He glared. "There has been a rift since Reggie and I were in short coats. Father demands absolute adherence to his orders—which neither of us can give—and Mother is the most unyielding, intolerant woman of my acquaintance. She disapproves nearly everything, up to and including my position in society, which is more influential than her own."

"Not anymore," she muttered.

"You are wrong. Everyone knows she was behind the worst rumors, just as they now accept that she lied. Despite her efforts to destroy us both, she failed. You were at the Ruftons last night. Did anyone cut you?" His eyes bored into hers.

"N-no."

"You are stuttering." His voice sounded weary. He negotiated a corner before continuing. "I am not angry with you, Joanna. Surely you know I would never hurt you."

"Yes, I know that, Sedge." At the moment, her biggest fear was that he would see into her heart, but that wasn't something she could explain. She was still reeling from the fact that he had abandoned a dying father to come after her. "But my presence will hurt you. You must have noticed how many of your admirers have turned elsewhere in the past week."

"They would have done so soon enough, anyway," he countered. "I am getting too old to hold their allegiance. Marriage merely accelerated the inevitable defection. I knew it would happen, and I welcome it."

"You are putting a pretty face on the situation, but you must admit that my low origins are hurting your position."

Somebody shouted.

"Look out!" she cried.

"Damn!" Jerking his eyes back to the street, he hauled up on the ribbons, pulling the horses to one side and barely missing Cathcart's curricle. Two bystanders hooted with laughter.

She recognized both as society dandies.

"We'd best finish this at home," he said wryly.

"Of course. I would hate to cause you more harm. At this rate, you will be the butt of countless jokes by morning."

"It doesn't matter, but I would rather not injure some-one out of inattention."

A treacherous glow started in her chest. Had Sedge been so engrossed in their conversation that he had for-gotten everything else? Or was it merely multiple shocks atop lack of sleep?

By the time they reached Grosvenor Square, she was more confused than ever. Impressions. Words. Deeds. Nothing matched. Every time she thought she under-stood him, he changed.

"Any news, Husby?" Sedge asked as he escorted her inside.

"None, my lord."

"We will be in our rooms. Do not disturb us for any-thing short of death."

He escorted her upstairs, closing the door firmly be-hind them.

"You were explaining your mother's tirade," she prompted when it became apparent that he was not going to start talking.

"Yes." He paused. "We might as well get the worst subject out of the way. Mother not only disapproves of my interests, she is very unhappy with Reggie, though I did not realize how deeply that argument ran until today."

"What happened?"

"You have always known that he refuses to wed, haven't you?"

"Of course. He mentioned it at our first meeting. Oth-ers have made similar statements, but there was some-thing in his eyes that proved he spoke truly. He is not a man who puts on airs."

"You must be the only person in town who believed him. The situation has grown so desperate that he is leaving."

"Poor Reggie. I take it he is leaving the country, not merely London." He had threatened to take a Grand Tour if people did not stop pressing him.

"Forgive me. I am not making much sense. Yes, he is leaving the country. Permanently. We are meeting tomorrow to make me legally responsible for all his present and future affairs."

"You really had no idea of his intentions?"

"None." He paced to the fireplace and back. "I am still in shock. The announcement was bad enough on its own, but it followed hard on the heels of Mother's tirade and my realization that she and Father had hoped to get rid of you before I returned."

"To say nothing of a sleepless night and a dying father."

He raised his brows.

"I already suspected your parents' intentions. They probably planned to lock me away somewhere until an annulment went through."

"I still cannot believe they would go to such lengths to force their will on us. Poor Reggie, indeed. I would argue if I thought he was wrong, but he stands no chance of happiness here."

"So you fetched me back to settle the succession. Fool. Society will be even harsher about this mésalliance once they realize Reggie is gone."

"Will you stop it! There is nothing wrong with your breeding! Nor is there anything wrong with your manners, your looks, your training, or anything else your fertile mind can conjure up. Mother lied. Accept it. Don't believe a word she told you."

"I doubt society will approve my unladylike education."

He swore. "Very well. A few matrons despise learning—probably because their own minds are so lacking that they would lose a battle of wits with a tree—but they feel the same about every educated lady, up to and including the Duchess of Norwood, whose breeding is better than mine. Last night I was inundated with friends eager to tell me how fortunate I was to win your hand, and by a couple who accused Reggie of hiding you away until it was too late for them to court you. So quit this maudlin prattling about being unworthy. It makes you sound as if you were inviting compliments."

She sighed, looking out at the square. Pigeons settled into the trees as the sun dipped toward the horizon. "Your mother hates me."

"Probably. Reggie already threatened to banish her to a remote Scottish property the moment Father dies. I think it an admirable idea." His words spun her back to face the room. "But surely you realize why she hates you. She wants to run the Close after Father's death. Thus she will approve only the most weak-willed, insipid girl in society. You are not such a miss, thank God."

"True." She bit her lip. "Let us leave off society for the moment. You claimed you never disliked me, yet I could see it clearly in your face. So why should I believe you?"

"How? No one else noticed anything amiss."

"You have very expressive eyes, Sedge. Color. Intensity. Brilliance. All respond to your mood. Last night was the first time since the masquerade that they stayed blue."

"Interesting. And a little frightening. I had not realized that I inherited Father's eyes."

"If no one told you, that is hardly surprising. I doubt you stop to examine your face when in the grip of strong emotion. But if you know the phenomenon, then you can hardly protest my impressions."

"Yes, I've been upset, but it was not your fault, Joanna." He resumed his pacing. "Three months ago a schemer nearly trapped me into marriage. I was still reeling from my escape when we met, so Mother's claim that you were plotting to attach Reggie revived that earlier fury. Inadvertently compromising you made it worse, even though I knew you were nothing like Lady Cecilia. The situation also forced me to relinquish my hopes of finding a wife I truly cared for."

She managed to stifle her instinctive flinch, but cold pooled in her stomach. "You can still pursue that goal, Sedge. An annulment will leave you free."

"It did not occur to me that fate had served me well," he continued as if she had not spoken. "The anger finally passed while I was at Wicksfield Manor. I had hoped to make a fresh start, for I realized—much too late—that I had been wrong to ignore your own feelings. I should not have treated you so badly."

"Not badly, but as an ignorant child who might mortify you at any moment."

"Good God! I have been beastly, haven't I? I did not truly think you incompetent, but I needed to hold you at a distance because—" He broke off.

"Because why?" She waited, but he did not answer. "You said only yesterday that we must be honest with each other."

He sighed. "I thought you were in love with Reggie."

"What?"

"You seemed so close."

"We are friends, Sedge. Nothing more."

So she remained unaware of Reggie's feelings. "I know that now. But I couldn't—" Again he paused.

She met his eyes. "That explains it." She turned back to the window, unsure whether to feel insulted or pleased at the reason behind his failure to visit her bed.

"Give me a chance, Joanna. I've made a mull of things so far, but I want to stay."

The arrogant Lord Sedgewick Wylie begging? It didn't seem possible. "What are you trying to say?"

"You embody every trait I had hoped to find in a wife—and much more."

"Don't exaggerate."

"I'm not. All you lack is confidence, but that is already growing. Yesterday was the most enjoyable day of my life, despite Father's arrival. After Reggie announced his departure, I looked for you, needing your calm to restore my own. When I found you gone, I nearly died. I love you, my dear. Can you please give me a chance? If we start over, maybe we can get it right."

She hesitated, afraid that he was manipulating her again. But a glance over her shoulder revealed a Sedge she had never thought to see. His face was open, without a mask. She could read honesty there. And uncertainty. The great arbiter of fashion, who dictated to high and low alike, was terrified of her answer.

"I hope you know what you're doing," she managed. "I love you, Sedge."

"Joanna." He pulled her into his arms, crushing her close as he caught her mouth in a passionate kiss. "It's true. You really do care," he murmured when he paused to catch his breath.

"So do you." Her hand traced the line of his jaw, reveling in its rough texture. He had not shaved since yesterday morning—another indication of truth. He had chased her halfway across town in an open carriage, wearing a crumpled cravat and day-old beard. He hadn't even flinched when his fellow dandies had spotted him in mud-spattered clothes making a cake of himself with an exhibition of cow-handed driving. "What would your imitators think if they could see you now?"

"Who cares?" He scooped her up and carried her into his bedroom. "Let Kingsford look after them. I need you, love. After a day of losses, I need to celebrate what I have found."

"And what is that?" Her fingers untied his cravat.

"You. A woman of substance. Someone who can stand at my side, through joy and sorrow, victory and defeat. With your support, I can face anything." Her gown landed on the floor. "And thank God for that. Between Father's imminent death and Reggie's departure, life will be complicated for a good long time."

"But we can handle it."

"I know." He kissed her again, then tugged off his shirt, abandoning the last trace of languid boredom. "Dear God, Joanna. I've wanted you since that day on Mount Street."

"Really?" She saw the truth in his eyes and laughed. "Once you grabbed Maximillian and left, the first thing I did was thank God I hadn't blurted out something stupid about your broad shoulders or incredible strength. That's another of my failings when I'm embarrassed."

"Then I'd better embarrass you right now," he said, grinning as he twirled her around and set her on the bed. "I love you, Joanna. I should have realized it on Bond Street. Why else would your words have the power to destroy my control?"

Another kiss prevented any response, but she didn't care. Her last fears vanished, lost in the glow of his love.